Living All Day

In a world of wide-spread brain enhancements and everyday nanotech, one tiny breakdown means everyone is in danger.

PI Aidra Scott has one job: prove that Jean Claude Gascoigne killed a man. It should be easy. Gascoigne committed the murder in front of thousands of witnesses. But he claims that the nanotech enhancements in his brain made him do it. Now Aidra has to prove a man guilty by proving a technology innocent.

Aidra, like millions of others, has been using that same nanotech to sleep less and work more, keeping her business afloat and her son in college. She has to find the truth behind the technology, and she has to do it quickly.

Because if Gascoigne is innocent, no one is safe.

LIVING ALL DAY

Copyright 2016 by Alex Kourvo and Harry R. Campion

Ion Productions

All rights reserved under international copyright conventions

This is a work of fiction. All the characters and events portrayed are either products of the authors' imagination or are used fictitiously

Cover design by Amanda C. Davis

Interior design by QA Productions

Other Books by M.H. Mead

Good Fences
Zoners
The Caline Conspiracy
Fate's Mirror
Taking the Highway

As ever,
for Elizabeth

Living All Day

M.H. Mead

A Detroit Next Novel

CHAPTER ONE

"Homicide detectives never expect to see a murder."

Aidra Scott took a step back. She'd never heard that one before. She'd been a PI for twelve years and had met a lot of cops. She thought she knew all their superstitions. Always make the rookie drive the car. Never sit with your back to the door. Watch out for the full moon. And utter the words "too quiet" at your own peril.

But not expecting to see a murder? This one was new.

Before she could ask about it, Detective Sergeant Sofia Gao continued. "You get called in hours after it happens—days if the victim's been dumped. We got there in twenty minutes once when a murder went down a few blocks from the station. But this . . ." She gestured to the main stage of the Castle, three stories below.

The Castle was packed, overrun with families and tourists and the press and everyone who wanted to make a buck off them. The shopping and event center comfortably held thousands, but the careful arrangement of the levels, the walls and the holos meant that no one could see more than a few hundred people at a time.

Aidra walked to the edge of the balcony in front of her and looked down at the open atrium overlooking the stage. Dragons as big as Gulfstreams hovered and danced in the huge space amid a riot of neon signs advertising brands and store logos. She shook off a sudden feeling of vertigo. It was impossible to fall, no matter how far she leaned over.

Sofia Gao's voice came from behind her. "We're the clean-up crew. The janitors of the police world. What are we supposed to do with this?"

This was starting. A dais was sliding out and rising. A series of magnifying holos around the edge made giants of those on the podium—some famous, some about to be.

Aidra looked down at the dais and the people assembled there, scanning for familiar faces. The mayor, of course, and the city manager, along with a few other local politicians whom Aidra didn't recognize. Next to them were the corporate titans, including the two most famous CEOs in the country. She knew who they were. Everyone did. The lesser honorees were placed on the far edge. *People who should have been in the center*, Aidra thought. But the firefighter of the year, the teacher of the year, and the police officer of the year stood on the fringes.

"Homicide detectives are supposed to show up later, to secure and document the physical evidence. We interview witnesses." Sofia sniffed. "Witnesses. My partners and I make fun of witnesses. Say they saw it all. Didn't see anything. They leave out crucial details and tell me they didn't think it was important." Sofia's image stood on the stage in front of Aidra, while her voice came from behind. Disconcerting, but Aidra was intent on the scene before her.

It was beautiful. The Castle darkened to the blue-blackness of infinite space. Saturn drifted past in ringed glory and the dais beneath the honorees and dignitaries became a flying saucer. Muted music, rich in brass and deep woodwinds, hushed conversation throughout the cavernous building.

The ship skipped past Jupiter, dodged asteroids, and skimmed Mars before approaching the blue sphere of Earth. And then they were traveling downward, through clouds, to the United States, to the mitten shape of Michigan, to Detroit. Bubbles rose through the surface, bursting through rocks, ice, and concrete to hover above the city. As the music swelled to a crescendo, the bubbles burst, revealing a gymnast, a swimmer, a runner, and a diver. Detroit was finally making a formal announcement of its worst-kept secret. The next Olympic games would be held in the Motor City.

At the Castle, two men were being honored for their role in making that dream a reality. Nobody had pushed harder to get the

Olympics than Mackenzie Fox, the CEO of Exersleep. Not to be outdone, Jean Claude Gascoigne, his former best friend and current rival, had thrown in his own support, and that of his company, Learning Systems.

Both men claimed it was because they'd started their companies here, had benefited from Detroit's tech corridor grants and tax deferments, and were eager to give back to the city that had given them so much. And while that might have been true, what was even more true was that neither Fox nor Gascoigne could be outdone by the other.

Fox had already broken ground on a new Olympic gym.

Gascoigne was funding the pool.

Aidra wondered what would become of those projects now.

"This kind of thing doesn't happen here," Sofia said.

But it *had* happened. Three days ago. And was happening again before their eyes.

Applause rose as the finale of the music faded away. This became a roar of approval as the figures on the podium raised their arms together in a gesture of triumph. Sofia, looking severe and beautiful in her dress uniform, hair pulled back, makeup subdued, had dutifully raised her arms with the others.

That was when Jean Claude Gascoigne, one of the most famous, most accomplished, most admired businessmen in the world, shot and killed Mackenzie Fox.

It happened fast. Everyone's arms were up for only a few moments, but a few moments was all it took. In a single motion, Jean Claude Gascoigne dropped his arms and reached for the sidearm on Sofia Gao's hip. He popped the strap on the holster, drew the gun, thumbed off the safety, and leveled it at Mackenzie Fox. The gun spoke twice in quick succession and Fox crumpled to the floor, vanishing into the holoprojection still swirling around their feet.

"Stop. Stop right there," Aidra said.

The scene before her froze. Aidra moved herself to a different vantage point, hoping to get a better perspective.

She considered the extreme irony. The Castle was a family-friendly play place, an escape from reality. Hundreds of overlapping holofields could create any scene, real or imagined. In fact, several witnesses had assumed the murder was part of the show. And while parents of young children tried to shield their offspring's eyes, Aidra had heard mutters of approval and even a "Hell, yeah!" from some teenagers in the audience. After all, at the Castle, anything was possible.

And now Aidra was standing in a recreation of the scene, watching it unfold. She wasn't really there, but everything she saw and heard—no matter how extraordinary—had actually happened.

She turned to Sofia. "Can I see that part again?"

Unlike her projected self of three days ago, the real Sofia Gao was makeup free, her long, black hair unbound, her eyes tired. It was four-thirty in the morning, and they stood under the harsh lights of the police projection room, which weren't flattering to anyone, at any time of day. There was no weapon hanging from Sofia's belt. The gun in Jean Claude Gascoigne's hand in the holoprojection was now in an evidence storage unit somewhere. Sofia still wore her badge, although the news spins had made it clear that she'd be in the limbo of leave-with-pay until the investigation was complete.

"How far back?" Sofia asked.

Aidra hesitated. The murder had been caught on security video, news spins, private recordings, and the overlapping holos of the Castle itself. She'd already seen it unfold dozens of times. And yet, she was confident that once she saw an official reenactment of the shooting, she would know exactly what had happened and how to prove it. This was what Fitz-Cahill insurance company had hired her for.

Fitz-Cahill had an entire team of PhDs looking over the scientific side of things. But Aidra's job was the human aspect. She was supposed to notice the details, see the connections, and intuit the motives. She'd assumed that having the murder caught on camera would make things easier. Instead, it was making things impossible.

"Back to the arm raising part?" Aidra asked. "Slower?"

Sofia commanded the system to go back two minutes and play at forty percent speed. The scene dissolved and reformed, crawling toward the lethal moment.

Aidra searched both men's faces for some hint, some sign of what was to come. As the slow motion cheer erupted again, Mackenzie Fox spent the last few seconds of his life lifting his arms in an obligatory gesture, heavy features set in a rueful grin. Jean Claude Gascoigne looked even more sheepish as he raised his hands, but in an instant, the animation drained out of his expression, leaving his narrow face as blank as a mannequin.

This time Aidra saw more—the brief widening of Fox's eyes as the muzzle of the gun caught his peripheral vision, the almost comical double-take of Sofia before she lunged forward, too late to stop Gascoigne from squeezing the trigger. The thudding ripples of the impacts. The awareness snuffing out of Mackenzie Fox's eyes.

They watched it all the way through. Sofia Gao seized the arm of the blank-faced Gascoigne, lifting and twisting and dumping him in a move that had sprained his wrist and split his lip. She peeled her gun from his grip and swept his hands behind him, kneeling between his shoulders to keep him down.

Through it all, the disarming, the securing, the cuffing with zip strips, Gascoigne's face remained immobile and unresponsive. Only when he was hauled to his feet with the assistance of half a dozen security and police did Gascoigne show any emotion.

The emotion was surprise. Amazement. Shock.

"Look at that," Aidra said, pointing. "Right there."

"Yeah?"

"Did you see Gascoigne's face?"

But Sofia wasn't looking at Gascoigne. Aidra followed her gaze. In the projection, Sofia had prized the gun from Gascoigne's grasp. It was now being taken again, this time by a suit-wearing cop who had *superior officer* written all over him. He had a small head on beefy shoulders, sandy hair cut into a bowl around his face, and skin that had never seen the sun. He was staring at Sofia's weapon as if it were a dirty diaper or a bag of puke.

"Cop of the year." Sofia said, regret dripping from her words.

"I take it the department is giving you a hard time about Gascoigne shooting someone with your gun?"

Sofia arched her eyebrow. "How many people do you think are talking about the Olympic bid this week? That's no longer the big story. This is."

"You're still the police officer of the year," Aidra said. "They can't take that away."

"Some of them would like to."

"Not the families you've helped. You'll always be the officer of the year to them."

Sofia had reunited six missing persons with their families. She'd found four teen runaways, a child who'd been kidnapped by his non-custodial father, and a grandma with Alzheimer's who'd somehow gotten across the river to Windsor, been put in a charity nursing facility there, and forgotten. The grandma was home now, being cared for by her children.

"I hear there's no one you can't find," Aidra said. "How did you clear so many cold cases so quickly?"

Sofia shrugged. "I just looked where no one else was looking."

Aidra couldn't tell from Sofia's tone if she was being sarcastic or modest. *Modest*, she decided. Sofia had transferred into the Cityheart division from Downriver last year, so they'd given her the lowest-priority cases. Most cops in her position would have tried for flashier ones, hoping to get the attention of the higher-ups. Instead Sofia had put herself to work where it would do the most good. It was nice to see that kind of quiet dedication acknowledged, and shitty that it had been snatched away.

Maybe I can help with that.

"Were you there for Gascoigne's interrogation and statement?"

"As a potential material witness—"

Aidra waved it down. Stupid question. "But you know he claims to have no memory whatsoever of the incident."

Sofia scoffed. "Everyone in jail is innocent. Just ask them."

Aidra tried to picture Gascoigne in jail. He wasn't in a country-club jail befitting his status. Gascoigne was awaiting arraignment in plain old Detroit lockup with the robbers and the domestic assaulters and the rapists. When everyone on the planet sees you kill a guy, you don't go to fancy jail.

"They did a blood screen on Gascoigne, didn't they?" she asked.

"A running set for the first day and a half." Sofia tapped at her interface. "Traces of nanotech, with the numbers falling as the little bugs degraded and died. Does that help Gascoigne or hurt him?"

"Don't know." Gascoigne's lawyers wanted to blame the murder on some kind of nanotech poisoning. Fitz-Cahill needed to prove it wasn't a factor before people started filing insurance claims and bleeding the company dry.

Gascoigne had n-tech in his system, but so what? He was a regular user of both Exersleep and Learning Systems. Of course he had nano-machines in him.

"Gascoigne helped develop this stuff," Sofia said. "He knows that this kind of n-tech can—and does—make you suggestible. It's not a big leap."

"That's what he's hoping for," Aidra said. "It's his best defense to a jury."

"And big trouble for your employer if people believe this nanotech makes you a killer." Sofia poked a toe into the holoprojection, then pulled it back to reality. "When you made the appointment, I thought you were wasting my time. Why would I want to talk to a PI attached to an insurance company?"

"So why did you?" Aidra asked. "Agree to talk to me, I mean."

"Might as well. We're looking for the same thing in the same place."

"Are we?" Aidra asked. "Once your perp is in jail, your job is done."

Sofia didn't answer for a long time. She stared at the holoprojection of her weapon. "Did he know he'd be standing next to a cop? Did he plan for that? Could it just as easily have ended another way?"

"Fitz-Cahill wants to protect Exersleep, and by extension, all n-tech. I doubt my investigation is going to answer . . . anyhow, that's up the DA to prove, not me."

"It's hard to know which way a grand jury would go with this. Public opinion is divided." Sofia's voice fell into a singsong cadence. "Half the world thinks Gascoigne hated Fox. Half the world thinks he's a victim of Exersleep. Another half thinks that Learning Systems is to blame. And another half thinks it's both of them at once."

Aidra knew the comedy routine and played along. "'That's a lotta halves!'"

"Better more halves, than have-nots." Sofia sobered. "And both of these guys are definitely 'haves.'"

"Does that make a difference?"

"People who can't afford Exersleep are jealous. People who can't afford Learning Systems are scared about being left behind."

"And the people who can afford both, the ones they call Supremiums . . ."

"People like Jean Claude Gascoigne and Mackenzie Fox?" Sofia gestured to the holorecording. "They're the ones people are really scared of. Soon this cop of the year will be competing for promotion against enhanced brains. Even now I have perps who don't need a residence to come back to. They're always on the move, never stop to sleep." Sofia snapped off the holo, making the scene disappear. They were alone in the room. "Can I ask what amounts to a personal question these days? Although looking at you, I probably don't have to ask."

Aidra had pushed her long sleeves above her elbows in the warm projection room. Now she self-consciously tugged them over her toned forearms. "Go ahead."

"I know Scott Investigations is doing pretty well after that mess over at GeCreations."

She tried not to shudder. "Yes."

"But I didn't know you were doing *that* well."

"Fitz-Cahill underwrites Exersleep Group, so I get a substantial discount as a job perk. I Exersleep to keep in shape." Aidra was proud that at forty years old, she could still turn heads, but a bit defensive about using the technology to literally buy more time. But wasn't that what time was for? She wasn't wasting it. She was working her ass off. The success of Scott Investigations had nothing to do with her reputation and everything to do with her increased productivity.

"I'm not judging," Sofia said. "I'm jealous as hell, but I'm not judging."

"Really? Because it sounded like—"

"What is going on here?" A tall man in a perfectly creased singlesuit stood in the doorway. Aidra recognized his pinched, disapproving face from the holo they'd just watched. Here was Sofia's boss in the flesh. "Gao? Explain yourself."

Aidra sensed Sofia taking a deep mental breath before speaking in a voice that could not be construed as disrespectful. She thought of it as a dealing-with-douchebags tone.

"Ms. Scott, may I introduce Deputy Chief Galen Browne." She placed an emphasis on the word *deputy*. "Deputy Chief, Aidra Scott is a—"

"I asked you a question, Detective *Sergeant*." Small muscles stood out like walnuts on either side of Browne's clenched jaw.

"I am attempting to comply with the directive of my commanding officer by—"

"Don't give me that," he snapped. "What are you even doing in the building? You are on suspension until—"

"Administrative leave."

He smiled a thin, two-second smile. "Call it what you will. My own imagination does not stray far enough to come up with a reason why you are here in the middle of the night, showing an official recording to unauthorized personnel."

Unauthorized? Now that wasn't fair. Aidra had gone through channels and set up this meeting in advance, taking care to make it all aboveboard. Just because Browne hadn't read the memo didn't mean she wasn't allowed to be here.

"Wait just a second," Sofia said. "She's—"

"I don't care who she is," Browne snapped. "I'm talking to you, Gao. You're sneaking in here in the pre-dawn hours, hoping against hope that no one will see you. I demand an explanation."

"Sir, I wasn't sneaking."

"I asked her to meet me here," Aidra added.

Browne glared at her and pointed to the door.

She considered it. She'd already seen what she'd come to see. A third viewing of the holorecording wouldn't give her any new information. She could leave and let the two of them sort it out. But Sofia deserved better.

"Perhaps this will explain." Aidra pulled what looked like a jet-black multi-card from her bag and handed it to Browne. He took it between finger and thumb and held it to the patch on his pad. A tone sounded and text scrolled across his display. His pale blue eyes widened in surprise.

He handed back the card quickly. "Of course. My office—that is—the department is—is only too happy to . . . What can I do for you?"

Aidra steered him toward the door. "I'm very sorry if we've taken you away from your own work. I'm sure you have important projects to oversee."

"Of course, of course. I never meant to interrupt. Please forgive me." Browne tried out the smile again. Now it looked like a wince. "I should be—that is to say . . . I'll leave you to your . . . good night. Er . . . good morning." He gave a polite nod and ducked out the door.

It sealed with a click and Sofia burst out laughing. "He positively scuttled! What is on that card?"

"Credentials. Of a sort. All inquiries lead to the Department of Justice, Special Operations and Investigative Division."

"You impersonated a federal officer?"

"I did no such thing. I handed him a card. He inferred the rest."

"Oh!" Sofia moved to the control panel on the wall, not bothering with voice commands this time. "This room doesn't just play back. It records. Passively. All the time."

"Shit. Can you erase it?"

"Yes. But not before I save a copy. There are people in this building who would pay cash money to see this."

"No! I don't want this shown around. Please."

"Oh, all right." Sofia moved her finger over the touch screen. "But I'm stashing a copy in my personal box. I'll watch it on special occasions. Or if I'm feeling down. Or if it's my birthday."

"Fair enough."

"You know Browne is going to run that ID as soon as he gets back to his secure line."

"It will hold. He might even get an official-looking reprimand for interfering in an ongoing investigation."

"Well, in that case, you've got about three minutes until Browne gets his revenge."

"Revenge? How?"

"The only way he can. Once the Feds muscle in, we like to sic the spinners on them." Sofia parked the computer and opened the door. "It's kind of a dick move, but sometimes dick moves are all we have."

"Okay-gotta-go-bye." She rushed out the door and into the corridor. Three minutes. Maybe less. She wondered if she'd make it to her car in time, and what would happen if she didn't. Her bogus credentials would stand up to any security check, but it wasn't her credentials the news spinners would be interested in. They could run a facial recognition program and link her image with Aidra

Scott, private investigator. And they would be happy to share that information with Deputy Director Galen Browne.

Why did she have to use those credentials? It wasn't necessary. She was a legitimate guest in the building for legitimate purposes. But she wanted to show off, put Browne in his place, and now it was going to bite her in the ass.

If the spinners figured out who she was, Browne would know she lied to him and he'd know Sofia helped. Humiliating for her, worse for Sofia. She needed to get out of the building before the spinners saw her.

Sofia hurried along beside her. They raced through the labyrinth of cubicles on the fourth floor, in and out of light and shadow. Detroit never slept and neither did its police department, but the tide ebbed and flowed. This early in the morning, few of the offices were occupied.

At the perimeter of the maze, a straight hallway led to the elevator. The indicator light showed a carriage on its way up. Aidra cursed and backed away, ready to dash off to find another exit.

Sofia blocked her path. "You don't know that it's going to stop on this floor."

"I don't know that it won't."

It did. The doors slid open enough for Aidra to see a young man wearing a headcam. She retreated into the nearest cubicle and waited until the spinners started walking toward Browne's office. "What else you got?" she asked.

"Stairs." Sofia led the way. "But they'll take you out the back. You'll still have to circle the building to get your car out of the ramp."

"I'll figure it out." They wove through twisty corridors to the stairs.

"I'll troubleshoot from up here. I'll talk to the spinners in the building, keep them busy. Here you go." Sofia pointed to the door.

"Sorry about Browne."

"He gets in my way a lot," Sofia said. "Maybe now he won't."

Aidra entered the stairwell and took a moment to pull a wide, black scarf out of her purse. It was made of thin microfiber and took up almost no space, but it had gotten her out of trouble more than once. She'd used it as a belt, a rope, a towel, and on one memorable occasion, a skimpy skirt.

She threw it over her head and smoothed it over her hair. She did some quick folds, crossing the scarf at her throat and tying it behind her neck. She tucked the ends under her collar. She wished she knew how to properly wear a hijab, but this would pass at a casual glance. A headscarf wasn't an invisibility cloak, but it was close. She stashed her jewelry in her purse and wiped the lipstick off her mouth, glad that she'd worn dark colors and long sleeves today.

She made it down three flights and was in sight of the exit door when it opened and a couple came through. Spinners. She didn't recognize them, although she recognized the look—heavy makeup, teased hair, running shoes. They carried lightweight video-audio pickup wands, and the woman carried a headcam, dangling by its straps. They were laughing about something as they started up the stairs.

Aidra thought about going back the way she'd come, but there was no subtle way to change direction mid-flight. She'd have to go past them, hoping the headscarf and averted eyes would be enough. She cursed herself for taking the stairs. She should have hopped on the elevator and waltzed right out the front door.

Then again, who knew how many spinners Browne had called? Someone in his position could summon as many as he wished— legit anchors as well as bottom feeders. She assumed there were already several in the building. As long as she escaped while they were tied up on the fourth floor, she should be fine.

She was almost level with the spinners now. The woman stepped aside to let her by, while the man kept going. She almost held her breath as she passed them. *Don't look, don't look.*

And she was past. She forced herself to keep a steady pace as she descended the last few steps. She put a hand on the exit door.

"Wait a minute, miss?"

She burst through the exit before they could start pointing their VAPs and headcams. She almost crashed into the police cruiser that was parked next to the door, but skidded around it and kept going. She was in a fenced-in lot, with room for about fifty cars, although it was half empty at the moment. Where was the gate? She cast her eyes left and right, looking for an escape route. Behind her, she could hear the spinners coming after her. She kept running.

She snugged her purse under her arm and wove through several more cars, trying to make out the perimeter of the lot in the dim overhead light. From the sounds behind her, the spinner couple were still together. They hadn't tried to split up and surround her. Now where was the gate?

There had to be a break somewhere. All she could do was head straight for the fence and then run parallel to it until it opened. She wished she had time to put on the oversized sunglasses that were bouncing around in her purse. But there was a slim chance they would fool the recognition programs and a certainty they would cut off her vision in the dark. Not worth it. She had to make sure the spinners didn't get a good look at her face.

They might have gait-trackers, but those were less reliable while someone was running. Just to be safe, she didn't run in a steady line or at a steady pace. She put her hand on the hood of a cruiser and vaulted over it, landing in a puddle on the other side. Water sloshed over the top of her low boots. She swore and kept going.

"Wait!" the spinner behind her shouted. "We just want to talk to you."

"That way, that way," the other said. They were splitting up and would cut her off soon. Where the hell was the gate?

She scrambled over the trunk of a cruiser, fell to one knee, rolled to standing, and dashed between two other cars. She reached a corner of the fence and made a right turn. She'd lost the spinners, but didn't look back. She had to keep moving.

There. Finally. Hidden behind a dumpster was an opening barely wide enough for cars but plenty wide for humans.

The female spinner stood in the center of it, headcam in place, waiting for her quarry to appear. Aidra thought about how many databases the spinner was connected to. Facial recognition programs worked fast.

The smart thing to do would be to back off, perhaps go into the building and find another way out, but Aidra could guess where the other spinner had stationed himself. Why chase someone through a closed area? Cover both exits and she'd be trapped. They could let her run herself ragged while they just waited.

She veered off, ducking behind a van before the spinner spotted her. She'd only get one shot at this. If she missed her chance, she'd be stuck here, and the disgrace of Aidra Scott would be today's top spin, thrilling Galen Browne and making Sofia miserable.

She peered over the cruiser's hood, waiting for her chance. The spinner was sweeping the area, turning her head left and right, getting a panoramic view of the lot. Aidra waited until she faced the other way.

In one movement, Aidra leapt to her feet and pulled the black scarf over her face. She ran blind—or nearly so. The fabric was sheer enough to make out big shapes. She zeroed in on the lump in front of her and tackled it.

The spinner went down with a satisfying "oof," tangling Aidra's legs in the process. Aidra rolled forward, kicking out and turning it into an almost-graceful somersault. She regained her feet, pulled the scarf away from her face, and took off.

She made it around the corner without being seen, and hid in the recessed door of a closed bail bonds office. She put her hands on her knees and gulped air until her breathing slowed to normal.

She peeked out of the doorway. No spinners. No pedestrians at all. Little traffic, either. She would wait.

Ten minutes later, she spotted an empty cab, hailed it, and told the driver to circle the block. He was unhappy about taking a fare such a short distance, but Aidra flashed some tempcash, promised him double the going rate, and got him going.

As they reached the municipal parking deck, she ducked down. "Do you see any spinners?" she asked the cabbie.

"Just one, in the back of my rig."

"I'm not a spinner."

"Right."

"Just tell me, do you see people?"

"All the time."

"Are there people standing around the parking area, waiting for someone?"

"No. Which means no customers for me. I should double your fee."

"You already did, remember?"

"I could double it again."

"I'll get out here, thanks." Aidra straightened up, put the tempcash back in her purse, and paid with her multicard.

This was definitely going on her expense report.

CHAPTER TWO

Aidra drove out of the municipal building garage and circled several blocks to make sure she wasn't being followed. No spinners had found her, so she decided to celebrate with some Blackstone's coffee. She got a cup to go and sipped it in her parked car while checking her datapad for messages.

The first was from Morris. Her sister Quinn and her friend Gilly had also left messages, but Morris always managed to prioritize his e-grams so they showed up at the top of her queue. She'd have to talk to him about that.

She tapped the message and Morris' true face filled the screen. He'd gotten a haircut since last time she'd spoken to him. He kept it government-issue short nowadays, not quite a buzz cut, but easing in that direction with every trim.

"Hey, how you doing?" He rubbed a hand over his jaw. "What am I saying? You're doing fine. I know you are, and if I was talking to you instead of leaving a message, you'd say that. And then you'd ask me how I am and I'd say I'm fine, too. It would take us forever to get around to the topic, so maybe this is better." His voice said that he found this anything but better.

"I'm in a boat," Morris said. "Isn't that what they say, when you're kind of in trouble, but not really? In a boat? On a boat? No, that's something else. But I know it's not a boatload of trouble, because that would be more than I have."

Aidra smiled. Morris didn't get out much. Until a few years ago, he didn't get out at all. He'd worked at home as a hacker—*viker*, she told herself—doing other jobs as a cover, one of which was working as her data man and assistant. At one point, she thought he might be more than her assistant. That is, until he got dragooned by the NSA, hauled off to Fort Meade, and started hacking for Uncle Sam. An eight hundred kilometer distance was asking quite a lot of a budding relationship. Yet neither of them were willing to let it die on the vine, so she got—and gave—a lot of awkward messages.

"Anyway," Morris continued. "You had to use those government credentials and I'm sure you had a reason. Just give me a few days to plug up some security holes before you use them again."

That was quick. She wondered what kind of trackers Morris had embedded on the card. Maybe she should have saved them for something more important than embarrassing a petty bureaucrat. But it was worth it. She thought of how happy she'd made Sofia Gao. *Totally worth it.*

There was another pause and Morris looked away from the camera and back again. "Well, that's all I wanted to say. I hope you're doing okay. What am I saying? Of course you're doing okay. Better than okay. So call me. Sometime. Also, that job we talked about? Are you still thinking about it? Call me. If you get the chance. But not in the middle of the night. Bye."

Aidra checked the time. Too early. She stowed her datapad in her bag and started her car. Listening to Morris' messages made her think about calling Noah Raintree. Her new data man wasn't as good as Morris, and he probably wasn't going to work out long-term. At least once a day, she thought about firing Noah and doing her own computer stuff, but always talked herself out of it. So what if Noah wasn't witty or charming or interesting? She didn't pay him for his personality. Actually, she didn't pay him much at all. He worked cheap, stayed available 24/7, and was discreet. She couldn't ask for more than that.

It was several more hours before she could contact Noah. She went home and leashed up Madeline, taking advantage of the pre-dawn light to go for a long walk. She liked to walk the caline at odd hours, passing Madeline off as an ordinary dog to anyone who might see them. The leash was part of the disguise. Madeline didn't need it, and Aidra apologized for it every time, but it felt safer to use it since a caline attracted a lot of attention.

Madeline was priceless and nearly unique, not to mention adorable, which made some people—kids and women especially—fuss and coo. But not all the attention was positive. Aidra had heard a muttered "freak" a few times too often. Most people didn't know much about genetically engineered pets, but some were against them on principle. No matter that poor Madeline never had a choice. She was what she was.

Home from the walk, she got Madeline fed and watered, then let her ride along for the next job—staking out a suspected insurance fraud. She pulled to the curb in full view of the subject's house. She hoped to find the construction worker with the "bad back" practicing karate in his front yard or building a tree house for his kids, or at least getting them ready for school and skipping along to the bus stop.

But more than that, she wanted him to see her, to notice that she'd been parked outside his house for three days in a row. The best way to force his hand was to let him know he was being watched.

She stroked Madeline's soft fur with one hand and opened up her datapad with the other. Paperwork was never-ending, although she wondered how much longer they could still call it "paperwork" when no paper was ever involved. Whatever you called it, the task was odious. Her supervisors at Fitz-Cahill insisted on detailed logs of her activities. She always gave them at least fifty hours a week, but she worked off-site, so the logs were the only way to keep track. She wondered if anyone ever read her reports. She suspected it was just for show, like the leash she used on Madeline.

Her boss probably wouldn't be thrilled about her doing this side-job, either, but her next appointment—a visit to Mackenzie Fox's widow—wasn't for another two hours, so why not?

She opened a line to Noah. She propped the datapad on the steering wheel so she could keep one eye on the construction worker's house while talking to her assistant. Multi-tasking. She was all about the multi-tasking. No one, not even Exersleepers, got more than twenty-four hours in a day, but she was going to make every one of them count.

The screen bloomed to life and Noah looked back at her. He always looked wide-awake, fully dressed, and ready to go. On the one hand, she admired his work ethic. On the other, she didn't trust that she was seeing the true Noah Raintree. Multiple algorithmic scanning co-processors were getting more and more common, allowing anyone to be whomever they wanted in the electronic universe. She was certain that Noah's face was hidden behind a MASC.

"Are you calling about that thing I sent you?" he asked eagerly.

"What thing?" Aidra split the screen and paged through old messages. "Right. No. We're not doing that."

"Why not?" Noah asked. "It will be interesting."

Aidra glanced at the message again and then out the window. Noah was constantly bringing her what he called "fun little side cases" and what she called "pains in the ass." This one, a mayoral candidate looking to discredit his rival, was the most inappropriate one yet. Taking it on would be time-consuming, possibly dangerous, and worst of all, newsworthy.

"This isn't really my style," Aidra told him.

"No, I suppose not." Noah slumped in his chair and rested his chin on his hand.

"I'm going to need your support with some Fitz-Cahill stuff. Did you see the notes I sent you this morning?"

"Looking at it right now," he said. "My research options aren't huge. It's not like these nanotech companies share information with all and sundry."

"Do what you can. A lot will come out in legal discovery once the court formally charges Jean Claude Gascoigne and the lawyers start building a case. In the meantime, there should be some government patent or regulatory agency stuff you can tap."

"For what?" Noah asked. "How are these things approved? Who has jurisdiction? At some point, someone decided it was safe to squirt tiny machines into our brains. How?"

"A branch of the FDA," Aidra said, irritated that she had to tell him. This was the kind of thing *he* should be telling *her*.

"Hmm."

Aidra glanced over the top of the datapad at the house across the street. Her quarry still sat reading near the window. She turned back to Noah. "They've been regulating n-tech since before the turn of the century."

"Okay."

"The nano-machines have to pass three tests." She held up one finger. "They have to be neutral. They can't do things they are not supposed to do." She added a second finger. "No Von Neumann machines allowed. These things can't reproduce." Third finger. "The brief life has to be specified. They do their job and then die a harmless death, never to be seen again." The actual law used the word *excretable* but Aidra didn't feel like saying that.

"Mmm. Hmm." Noah was no longer looking at her. He'd been humming the entire time she was talking. Not loudly, barely audible through the crappy speakers of her datapad, but just loud enough to be annoying. It sounded like someone stepping on bagpipes in a distant room. He did it whenever he was concentrating, and she could bet he wasn't concentrating on her.

"Nano-machines are delicious," she said. "I make them into curry and spread them on toast."

"Mmm. Hmm."

"And then I wash my socks in them and feed them to my goldfish."

More under-the-breath humming.

"They put me in a mood," Aidra said. "Like right now? I'm in the mood to take off all my clothes."

"Hmm." Noah startled and looked her way. "Wait, what?"

"Oh, so now you're listening."

"I heard every word you said."

"No, you didn't. You were humming."

"So?"

"You hum when you work. It's your tell."

Noah stared back, defiantly. "And where are you right now?"

Aidra glanced around her. "Well, I'm—"

"You're in your car," Noah said. "From what I can see past your giant head, you're in some kind of residential neighborhood and it isn't yours."

"Your point?"

"You also keep looking out the window and always to the same place. You're on a stakeout, yes? Probably that insurance thing from last week."

Aidra pointed at the screen. "Don't."

"Don't, what?"

"Don't call me out on my bullshit when I'm busy calling you out on yours."

"I'm just saying, I am also capable of doing more than one thing at a time."

Aidra blinked. *Busted*. "Fair enough. But right now, I need you to focus in. Do you think you can single-task for a minute?"

Noah smirked. "If you promise to keep your clothes on."

"Fine," Aidra said. "But you don't know what you're missing."

Noah raised his eyebrows, but let her get in the last word. He split the screen so they could both see the files she'd sent. "I might have known Jean Claude Gascoigne was a killer. I mean, didn't you just know the little rat was bad news?"

"He's one of the most admired businessmen on the planet."

"And a liar, and a thief, and now a killer."

"What are you talking about?" Aidra asked. "Where do you get *thief?*"

"Everyone knows it," Noah said. "When Gascoigne spun off his own company, he took a lot of intellectual property with him."

"That was never proven," Aidra said. "They settled out of court."

"Meaning somebody paid somebody. I can guess who."

Aidra raised an eyebrow. "You need to stay away from pop media and start reading the digests." No matter how it was spun, the facts behind the rift were well known. There had been two feature docu-dramas about the dispute that ended the partnership between Mackenzie Fox and Jean Claude Gascoigne, both detailing how their promising work with n-tech went in two directions after they split—Fox to found Exersleep and Gascoigne to found Learning Systems.

There had been lawsuits, and even though they'd settled them quickly and privately with sealed records, Mackenzie Fox was generally seen to be the winner in the n-tech turf war. His Exersleep company got off the ground faster, was more popular, and made more money. Not to mention that Mackenzie Fox married Hannah Wells, their top researcher. The whole thing seemed like a story made for Hollywood. No wonder Noah had already picked sides.

"So, the killer, *Jean Claude*." Noah emphasized the vowels in the name. "I like to say his name. It sounds French."

"When you say it like that, it doesn't sound French."

"What does it sound like?"

"Ridiculous."

"What's ridiculous is the way he always uses both his given names. *Jean Claude*." Noah made his fingers into a gun and pretended to shoot. "Jean Claude."

"Could you please not do that? I know that Jean Claude Gascoigne shot Mackenzie Fox. Our job is to find out why."

Noah circled some of the text on the screen. "Gascoigne's lawyers are claiming that the n-tech made him do it."

"Yeah, they think they can make that stick."

"What if Gascoigne got himself some black market n-tech? Or

he got a bad batch? I hear there's some crazy stuff coming out of Mexico."

"You don't really know how this stuff works, do you?" she asked.

"Do you?"

"I'm learning. Anyway, a bad batch of nano-machines would just be ineffective. It wouldn't be harmful."

Noah took her documents off the side of the screen, replacing them with a photo of Jean Claude Gascoigne. It was a publicity still, and looked recent. Gascoigne looked ready for work in a suit and tie. The light was from above, shining down on his bald head. "Do you think this man is guilty?"

"Everyone saw him shoot Mackenzie Fox."

"That's not what I asked. Do you think he's guilty?"

"Don't you?" Aidra asked. "You just said you thought he was a killer."

"That's the thing. It doesn't matter what you think or what I think. Rich white men get away with everything."

Aidra leaned forward in her seat, tilting her head and looking more closely at Noah. He resented the rich and white, meaning he didn't identify as either of those things.

His MASC had always presented himself as a young guy with pale skin. Just because that was the default option for anyone who worked in computing didn't mean that's who he really was. But did it matter? What mattered was that he didn't feel comfortable showing her the truth.

"Rich white men still have to follow the law," Aidra said.

Noah's expression remained skeptical, but he didn't respond.

"It would help if I could meet with Gascoigne face to face," she said. "I need to get inside the prison. I need to look him in the eye."

"Does he want to see you?" Noah asked.

"Probably not."

"Then you're out of luck."

"You're being very annoying," Aidra said. "We've been hired to do a job and you're not helping."

"Wow. That's the first time you've said that."

"Said what?" Aidra asked.

"*We've* been hired."

"Don't get used to it."

"Too late." Noah grinned through the screen. "Scott and Raintree Investigations. Or should that be Raintree and Scott?"

"No and no with extra no."

"So *now* you're listening."

"Oh," Aidra said, all sweetness. "Was I supposed to listen to you?"

"Only if you want the information I have."

"What information? I think we've established that I know a lot more about this than you do."

"This whole time we've been talking? I've had some engines scrying around the electronic universe digging into things."

"And?"

"The reason I was even searching is because I thought I heard something a couple years back, about a guy with n-tech on the brain who killed his family."

"Does this person have a name?"

"Not yet, but I'll find it."

"So you *thought* you heard something about someone who *might* have gone crazy because of n-tech? See, Noah? Right there. That's why I pay you the big bucks."

"That's why you pay me for shit," he mumbled.

"Get to work so I can pay you at all. If this person exists, a name would be nice. An e-dress even better. A location, best of all."

"Location? He killed his family. His *location* is probably jail."

"Then he's not going anywhere," Aidra said. "That should make him easy to find."

CHAPTER THREE

Aidra pulled off M-50 and down a private dirt road, heading toward the Fox residence in the rural area south of Detroit. Halfway between the small villages of Dundee and Tecumseh, the straight, flat roads cut through a mix of working farms and new developments with the kind of billion-dollar country homes no local could afford. She wondered what the towns were like. A feed store next to a yoga studio? A country church next to a gourmet soap emporium?

She was still three kilometers from the Fox family estate when she passed a knot of desperate spinners focusing on the house with long-range lenses. They stood on the public road, just on the edge of the property line, unable to legally move closer. A swarm of eye-dot drones hovered overhead, observing the perimeter.

The privacy laws were strict and clear, especially when it came to homesteads. A spinner setting foot on private property risked a career-ending jail sentence. So the Foxes had built their own personal buffer by buying up all the land around their house.

Must be nice, Aidra thought. Her own homestead was a two-bedroom condo in the city with shared walls and a common lawn. Although it was in a gated complex, spinners had been known to lurk in the parking garage and on the shared sidewalk without consequence. None of them would dare enter her building, but the moment she stepped onto public property, she *became* public property.

Aidra honked to clear the spinners from the road, igniting their interest, which was just fine with her. Unlike her encounter with spinners early this morning, this time, she was using her own face, her own credentials, and her own position. Her meeting with

Mackenzie Fox's widow would be spun for broadcast, which was exactly why her boss had set up this meeting.

With Gascoigne in jail, trying to blame his actions on nanotech of every kind, Hannah Wells-Fox was dealing with a double blow. Not only was her husband dead, his company was in danger, too. She would probably do anything to protect n-tech in general and Exersleep in particular, including meeting with their insurance company's representative. If all she did was meet Aidra and shake her hand, Hannah's objective would be met. The poor widow would appear properly forthcoming, Aidra would appear properly industrious, and the spinners would have another day of news.

Aidra was hoping for more. She needed to find a plausible motive for Jean Claude Gascoigne to kill his rival. Why would Gascoigne kill Fox after all these years? What set him off? Aidra hoped that Hannah Wells-Fox knew the answer, or at least could hint in that direction.

She drove through the scanning ribbon across the Fox's driveway and parked next to the house. She double-checked the map on the Octave's dashboard, not sure she was in the right place. She'd expected a mansion, something befitting a corporate titan married to a comboview star. But they lived in a classic Midwestern farm house. It was large—had obviously been expanded over the years—but sitting on two acres of manicured lawn in the bright morning sunshine made it look the perfect size. Aidra could bet the house was Hannah's choice. Its country-cute charm fit her image perfectly.

The front door opened before Aidra even stepped on the sensor mat. "You're the investigator." The words came from a six-year-old with pale skin and wide brown eyes. She wore a plaid jumper reminiscent of a school uniform, but with a neon yellow t-shirt underneath it and bright purple sneakers on her feet. "Mother told me to let you in."

Aidra stepped into the foyer, which held a small table with flowers and two framed photos. "Thank you. I'm Aidra Scott."

"Pleased to meet you." The girl held out her tiny hand for a confident shake. "I'm Juniper Fox."

Aidra didn't need an introduction. Everything about the girl, from her carefully chosen outfit to her intricate hairstyle, had been documented on *JJToday*. Hannah Wells-Fox's comboview was the fifth most popular combo in the e-verse, and number one among viewers ages 20-45. It was impossible to be a woman of childbearing age and not know about *JJToday*. The two Fox children, Juniper and Jovan, were at least as famous as their parents.

"You work for my father's company," Juniper said.

"Not quite. I work for the company that insures your father's company."

"Of course, insurance." Juniper said it as if she had to deal with corporate insurance every day. She had such poise, it was like talking to a miniature adult. The effect should have been surreal and disturbing, but Aidra found herself charmed.

"May I take your coat?" Juniper asked.

"Thank you," Aidra removed her light spring jacket.

Juniper hung it on a low hook in the hall closet, since she was too short to reach the hangers. She closed the closet door and leaned against it with a proud smile. "Mother is expecting you. I'll see if she can be interrupted. Would you care to wait here?" Juniper flounced off before Aidra could stop her, leaving her alone in the two-story foyer.

A staircase ran through the center of the space. To the right was a dining room and what looked like a study. These rooms were probably part of the original house, along with the formal front parlor to her left. It held a piano, a bookcase that acted as a room divider, and a small fireplace with a curiously large chimney.

The fireplace bothered her. The firebox was comically small in comparison to its massive mantle and chimney. The rest of the house and its furniture was all in perfect proportion, with every book lined up by size and every knickknack color coordinated.

Aidra couldn't imagine Hannah Wells-Fox tolerating something so imperfect. She stepped into the room for a closer look.

She told herself it was simple curiosity that made her ignore Juniper's wish that she wait in the hall. Would she be this rude if an adult had asked her? But who was she kidding? She was a PI. Snooping was second nature. She listened for footsteps or voices but heard nothing. One small look around. Nobody would ever know.

When she passed through the small parlor into the two-story great room, the fireplace suddenly made sense. It was open on two sides—no, three. They could enjoy a fire from the screened-in porch as well. On this side, the firebox was large enough for a child to stand up in, and the oversized chimney seemed just right. This had to be part of the new addition to the house. Comfortable chairs formed a conversation area around the hearth and Aidra pictured cozy winter evenings in the Fox household.

This great room, larger than her entire condo, was something you never saw on *JJ Today*. The front rooms were decorated in high-end casual, the kind of decor that cost a fortune to look like it was effortlessly put together. This room, however, felt like a true family room, where kids could play and adults could unwind. There were baby pictures on the walls and throw pillows askew and scuffs on the chair legs.

But even here, the modern world did not intrude, at least not directly. Aidra looked over her shoulder—still no sign of Hannah—and risked peeking inside a few of the box-shaped footstools. As she suspected, they held an assortment of electronic entertainment. She spotted the hidden holo-drop near the ceiling, explaining why the two massive sofas faced what looked like a blank wall.

Something else bothered her about the house, and it took her a minute to figure out what it was. It was the silence. Hannah was the oldest of three sisters. Where were the doting aunts? The neighbors offering comfort and company? Why wasn't the living room full of flowers and the kitchen counters laden with casseroles? Where was the staff? The gardeners and the maids and the other people who made this huge house sparkle?

If Hannah was one of those people who handled grief alone, she wouldn't want a PI there either, no matter how good it looked on the spins. Aidra would have to get the information she needed quickly, before she wore out her welcome. It was time to scoot back to the front door and wait like a proper guest before she was caught.

Too late. Juniper stood near the central staircase, her arms folded. She looked pointedly at the entryway and then back at Aidra, but did not comment. "Mother says you should join us in the basement. She's working with Jovan." Her voice dropped to a whisper. "He's being difficult. Again."

Aidra followed Juniper behind the central staircase to the broad carpeted treads leading down, wondering what *difficult* meant. She forgot to wonder in the next moment as she and Juniper descended the stairs into a different world. At last, here was the technology and the sleek look of modern life.

There was at least as much of the Fox house underground as there was above. Like the upstairs, the basement was large and open. From the landing, Aidra could see cameras, a holo-stage, recording equipment, imagers, a rendering deck, and their own computer server to store it all. The ceiling was a bank of lights with dimmers, gels, and softeners for any effect. This was a room fans of *JJToday* never saw. The Fox family captured the raw images upstairs, but down here was where the serious production work happened. Here, Hannah Wells-Fox and her children used every tool of a modern studio to create the illusion of old-fashioned family life.

Hannah had started *JJToday* during the techshun movement several years ago. And even though the mantra "keep it real" was already starting to sound like a cliché, Hannah Wells-Fox was still extremely popular, if not without her detractors. Moms and dads rolled their eyes at her, all the while copying her recipes for vanilla-scented play-dough and dressing their children in an imitation of Juniper and Jovan. Hannah had her own line of cookware, her own brand of Halloween costumes, a wide range of art supplies, and a set of carpentry tools in adult and kid sizes. Most importantly, she had a dedicated fan base who cooked her recipes, made her crafts, and planned their children's days according to her calendar.

Jovan Fox, age four, stood in the center of the holo-stage, whining. "Please, Mom, I want to do this whole thing."

"You don't have to," Hannah said. "We can finish this part later."

"No!" Jovan shouted. "I want to do it *now*."

"The fans can wait," Hannah said.

"I'm not doing it for *them*. I'm doing it for—" He caught sight of Aidra and stopped mid-sentence.

"Hello," Aidra said. "I didn't mean to interrupt."

"Oh, no. Quite all right. You must be Ms. Scott." Hannah Wells-Fox held out her hand. Her dark hair was arranged just as creatively, if less elaborately, than Juniper's. She wore little makeup and there were dark circles under her eyes. It had been a terrible few days and Aidra admired how well Hannah was keeping it together for the sake of her children.

Juniper was at her side. "Ms. Scott, may I present my mother, Hannah Wells-Fox, and my brother, Jovan. Mother, Jovan, this is Aidra Scott, she works for an insurance company but does not work directly for Exersleep."

"Thank you for that lovely introduction." She held out her hand to Hannah. "Please call me Aidra. I'm very sorry for your loss."

"I appreciate that," Hannah said. Her grasp was brief, but warm.

"You're pretty," Jovan said.

"Well, thank you, Jovan."

"She smells good, Mom." He put his hand in his mother's. "She smells like you."

"Must be because I'm a mom, too," Aidra said.

Hannah smiled. "How many?"

"One. He's in college."

"In college?" Hannah asked. "That is hard to believe. Since you're clearly just out of college yourself."

Aidra laughed. "I kind of had him instead of going."

"You did it the smart way." Hannah laughed with her. "Some days, I wish I'd started earlier, but these little ones were worth waiting for." She gave Aidra's forearm a brief squeeze.

She and Hannah were about the same age, but in opposite stages of motherhood. Not to mention that Aidra's experiences were so different, having started young and raised Jon alone. But mothering was a shared bond no matter the circumstances.

"I love your manicure," Aidra said. "So playful."

Hannah spread her fingers, showing off tiny panda bears painted on the tip of each one. "I should change it, but Juniper and I had such fun doing it."

"I remember the comboview," Aidra said. "It made me want to do mine the same way." She curled her fingers, hiding her ragged nails, wondering why she'd said something so awkward. She hadn't meant to say anything about the combos at all, intending to play it cool, but she found herself a bit starstruck. Hannah was so authentic and open on the combos, Aidra felt like she already knew her. She had to remind herself to keep things professional, that she was here as an investigator, not a fan.

Jovan ran his fingers over the sound board. "Can I finish now? Mom? Can I? I need Juniper for this part."

Hannah turned to Aidra. "Jovan is eager to finish composing. We're working on a tribute to Mackenzie."

"If this is a bad time . . ."

"No, of course not. If you're here to talk about—" she stopped herself and glanced at her children. "Give us a moment and I'll be right with you."

Aidra could imagine the sadness of the *JJ Today* fans, their sympathy for the grieving widow and the newly fatherless children. It would probably be one of their highest-rated combos ever, no matter when Jovan wrote his song.

Juniper volunteered to help her brother and Hannah lingered over them for several minutes, touching their shoulders and hair, murmuring approval for their musical talents. Aidra thought it more than a little odd that the children would want to get back to work so soon after their father's death, but kids—even special ones like the Foxes—thrived on routine. Hannah probably sensed that breaking them out of it would be worse. She nodded at her children and with one last pat on the back for each of them, invited Aidra upstairs for tea.

Aidra half-expected Hannah to pluck leaves off a tea bush she'd raised from a sapling and serve it in mugs the children had thrown on their own pottery wheels and painted by hand. But she heated water in an auto-kettle and plunked tea bags into plain white mugs. They sat at high stools around the island of the big farmhouse kitchen.

"Are you here alone?" Aidra asked. "Don't you have family nearby?"

"It's been a madhouse," Hannah said. "Police, lawyers, reporters. We needed quiet. So I dismissed the cleaning staff for the day and sent my sister to town with a shopping list. Juniper and Jovan need uninterrupted time to be creative."

"Your children are amazing," Aidra said. Juniper had won her over as soon as she opened the door, and Jovan's mix of focus and vulnerability made Aidra want to scoop him up in a protective embrace. "How are they holding up?" she asked.

"About as well as can be expected." Hannah lifted her mug.

"They're remarkably polite."

"Don't sound so surprised."

"I'm sorry, I didn't mean it like that." Aidra poked at her tea bag with a spoon. "It's just that you hear stories about children who start Learning Systems so young, that it can cause anti-social behavior, tantrums, things like that."

"Oh, those stories are true. There are reasons that Learning Systems isn't recommended for children under eight."

"But Jovan is only four."

"Yes, but I understand the technology, how best to use it. After all, research studies often draw their more alarming conclusions from exaggerated-use scenarios. I worry sometime that they'll do a research study on the overuse of water and discover drowning."

"But your children don't Exersleep, do they?"

"Oh, God, no. Not until they're fully grown." Hannah leaned in for a secret whisper between moms. "I need them to sleep."

They laughed together.

"People think it's odd," Hannah said. "That we'd use our rival's technology more than we use our own. But it's foolish to think of Exersleep and Learning Systems as being in competition when they are so clearly compatible. It's only with an application of both that a human can truly reach her full potential."

Hannah leaned back on her stool and swished her hand through the air. "Ah, listen to me. I sound like an advertisement. But I believe that we are just beginning to see what this technology can do."

"They've already done some amazing things." Aidra remembered an explosion, darkness, and a long road back to wholeness. N-tech had saved her life once. It had saved a lot of lives.

"We could be doing more." Hannah swallowed, looked away, then back. "Soon we'll be curing Parkinson's, treating Alzheimer's, or alleviating bipolar disorder. The medical applications are what interested me at first. But Exersleep is where the money is. I can do good with that money in other ways."

Aidra nodded. Hannah's charitable foundation focused on children in the disincorporated zone, getting them immunizations and other medical care.

"Is that why you left the company?" Aidra asked.

"I left the company for the greatest reason in the world. Once Juniper came along, and then Jovan, I never wanted to do anything but be their mother."

"And you're very good at it. There's a reason they call you America's Mom."

Hannah hid a smile behind her cup. "Besides," she said. "The important nanotech therapies will still be done. Exersleep is a means, not an end."

"Was that what Mackenzie was working on?" Aidra had glimpsed a lab in a corner of the basement with sterile sinks and what looked like a high-powered microscope. Rumor was that Mackenzie Fox kept current with all the research his company did, providing hands-on support and technical help.

"My husband was working on a variety of things," Hannah said. "Always something new. That's how you stay in business. A tech company is a constant race with no finish line."

"So how do you win?"

"The trick is not to lose. As long as you're innovating faster than your rivals are, you stay in the race."

"Sounds exhausting," Aidra said.

"Not if you're succeeding. It's being in second place that will wear on you." A shadow crossed Hannah's face.

They sipped their tea in unison, and Aidra wondered if Hannah was thinking of the fact that her husband was out of that race forever.

"When did they last see each other? Mackenzie and Jean Claude, I mean." Aidra winced internally at her poor choice of words. The day Jean Claude Gascoigne shot Mackenzie Fox was the last time they saw each other. Aidra hoped that Hannah would take her meaning.

"They run in the same social circles. Ran. They couldn't avoid one another. And it isn't as if they spent parties and fundraisers on opposite sides of the room, glaring at one another. They kept up appearances. They were always civil."

"Did that go for you, too?"

"Of course. As you know, I'm in the public eye. Appearances mean a great deal to me."

"So you and Jean Claude were close?"

"We had a history, yes. But that was a long time ago. It seems like another lifetime, another me." Hannah lifted her mug but did not drink. Her eyes focused on something far away. "I think I loved them both, in some ways."

"But you chose Mackenzie," Aidra said.

"He chose me. It was sudden and passionate and I suppose I was swept off my feet."

Aidra tried to picture Mackenzie and Hannah in a whirlwind romance. Hannah, yes. On her comboviews, she was always emotional and affectionate and intense. But Mackenzie Fox was more reserved. He'd seemed pleasant enough in the holos and documentaries she'd seen, but their marriage had always seemed like more of a smart business move than a grand love affair.

"Jean Claude didn't have a chance," Hannah said. "I always thought he . . ."

"What?" Aidra asked.

"Nothing." Hannah set her mug down and covered her eyes. "This is very confusing for me. I can't help thinking about the Jean Claude I know, the one who would never do something like this in a million years and another part of me thinks he's some kind of monster who killed my husband and should rot in jail forever."

"A lot of people want that," Aidra said. "It would help if I could find a reason for his behavior. Everyone saw what happened so the case should be open and shut, but his lawyers are building a case that says the n-tech made him do it.'

"Of course." Hannah's voice was flat. "It plays perfectly to people's emotions. To their fears. It seems like it could make sense, so that's what gets passed off as truth. And the hell of it is, he might very well get away with it."

Hannah gestured around the kitchen, pointing to the spider cameras hidden under the rim of the oak cabinets. She flourished her hand at a knife block shaped like a Stegosaurus, positioned next to an oiled cutting board. Then she opened a drawer to reveal a modern power chopper. Aidra guessed that the chopper stayed out of sight during Hannah's comboviews.

"People see what they want to see," Hannah said. "I know that better than anyone."

"So we need to direct their attention elsewhere," Aidra said. "Otherwise, everything your husband worked for is going to be lost. We need to find a motive that wasn't the n-tech."

"What do you want me to say? Jean Claude killed my husband in a fit of jealousy because he never got over me? That I didn't *let* him get over me? My God, what does that imply about my marriage? About my family?"

Hannah stood and poured the rest of her tea into the sink. "I don't want the technology blamed and I certainly don't want Jean Claude to get away with murder. But my husband is dead. I'm trying to put my life back together. I have children to raise. And I'll be damned if I drag my family through some cheap tabloid gossip just to play with a possible jury's emotions. Anything that Jean Claude and I had was in the past." Her voice had become shrill and she was nearly shouting now. "I've been happily married for ten years!"

Hannah turned her back and leaned over the sink. She ran water in her empty mug, but didn't move to wash it. She let it fill and overflow and fill again.

Aidra ran a finger over the edge of her tea mug. *Careful.* Grief could do funny things. Hannah seemed to be holding it together, but she was all alone at a time when someone really shouldn't be.

"I want to help you," Hannah said. "Truly, I do. But I need to keep my family—my children—out of it. Whatever happened had nothing to do with them. I need to protect them, and myself, from the spotlight."

Aidra bit her lip and tried to decide how to hold her face. Hannah was a combo star. She'd made her children household names.

"Yes, I know my children are famous," Hannah said to Aidra's unspoken question. "But their *fame* and their *lives* have nothing to do with one another. What I sell is fantasy. Our real lives belong to us alone. Please help me keep it that way."

Aidra toyed with the handle of her mug. She knew it wasn't

fair to ask Hannah to use her past, her family, and her fame to help Gascoigne look guilty. But part of her was disappointed that Hannah wouldn't take the easy road. Her entire public life was an illusion—she'd just said so herself—so what was one more thing?

Aidra stood and joined Hannah at the sink. She tipped her cup, chasing Hannah's tea down the drain with her own. She was better than this. She wouldn't ask Hannah to manufacture stories just to make her own job easier.

"Jean Claude won't get away with this," she said. "I'll do every—"

"Mom, Mom, you've got to listen to this!" Jovan came rushing up the stairs, Juniper on his heels.

"We finished." Juniper's face was flushed with excitement. "Wait until you hear our song, Mother. It's beautiful."

Hannah inhaled deeply and turned to her children, all smiles. "I can't wait to hear it, darling. Is it catchy?"

"So catchy," Juniper said.

"And delightful?" Hannah asked.

"As delightful as me!" Juniper and Jovan said at the same time. Jovan put his arms around his mother's waist and she patted his head. He turned to Aidra with a hopeful smile, inviting her into the joke. Aidra got it immediately. *Delightful* was the most common adjective used to describe the Fox children on all the fan sites. It had become a code word for one fan of *JJToday* to identify another. Aidra gave Jovan a thumbs-up.

Juniper turned to Aidra. "Would you care to hear our song, Ms. Scott?"

"Now, that wouldn't be fair, would it?" Hannah asked her daughter. "To give her exclusive access before anyone else got to hear it? Shouldn't we wait until we can share it with everyone?" Her tone was light, but Aidra got the message.

"Actually, I have to be going. But I look forward to hearing it on the combo. Juniper, Jovan, it was lovely to meet you." Aidra found that she meant it. She'd been worried that the children who were perfect on camera would turn out to be over-privileged little brats in real life. But the combos didn't lie.

    She wasn't sure about Hannah. Was the warm, intense, devoted mother on the combos the real Hannah? Or the prickly, wary widow in front of her? She'd doubted that Hannah herself was sure right now. Nor did she know if Hannah would ever be able to help her, but winning this one for Fitz-Cahill would at least be a help to Hannah.

CHAPTER FOUR

Two hours later, Aidra parked in the private ramp rented by Fitz-Cahill. She was less than half a block from the waterfront building, yet it took her ten minutes to get to the front door. First she had to cross the street and cut through an alley because the sidewalk and road were both blocked by construction equipment. Yet another hotel being built in anticipation of Olympic tourists.

Then she had to pass a knot of spinners and anchors camped outside Fitz-Cahill. Their recognition programs had her name matched to her face instantly, and she was hassled with questions about her relationship to Fitz-Cahill (salaried contractor), her feelings about Exersleep (positive) and her speculations on Jean Claude Gascoigne's motives for killing Mackenzie Fox (no comment).

Once safely inside the building, she flashed her multicard at security and was allowed access to the private elevator to the sixth floor. She passed through a hall that still smelled of fresh paint and noticed that the walls were now a sunny yellow, replacing the quiet blue that had been the color scheme the last time she was in the building. Fitz-Cahill was forever redecorating, and she wondered how much of the premiums they collected went into beautification. But she supposed it was part of the cost of business. It wasn't enough to *be* successful. A company had to *look* successful.

Even with the new decor, Fitz-Cahill felt like home. She'd been working for them off and on for years. They'd formalized their agreement six months ago, making Aidra a full-time employee. She'd negotiated hard before signing on, taking a lower hourly fee in exchange for a generous expense allowance and a subsidized gym membership.

Fitz-Cahill usually gave her small assignments that she could wrap up in a day or less, and on to the next. She didn't always love the work, but she loved the steady paycheck. She picked up freelance cases on the side, keeping her skills sharp and her independence intact. It was easy to do with Noah acting as her backup, especially since Exersleep let her live all day.

She'd fit the odd-shaped pieces of her life neatly into place. She had a system, with all the gears turning in a clockwork fashion. Noah didn't work for free and she still had to pay for half of her gym membership, but taking on extra cases more than made up the difference, allowing her to cover her own expenses and keep her son in college. Besides, what else was she supposed to do with the extra waking hours Exersleep had given her, take up stamp collecting?

But now she was wondering what would happen to her carefully managed routine. A high-profile case like this would take all the time she could give it. The hands of the clock never stopped turning, and if she dropped her freelance cases in favor of this one, they wouldn't be there when she wanted to pick them up. On the other hand, if she didn't give Fitz-Cahill full value for their dollar, freelance cases would be all she had left. She'd have to be careful to stay in that sweet spot between employee and businesswoman.

She usually went straight to Bryan Lynch's office whenever she was in the building. Bryan was in charge of the legal and investigations department and her direct supervisor. But today she was here to see someone named Pohl Erbie over in the technical division, and it took her a few wrong turns and backtracking to find his office.

Office turned out to be too generous a word. Pohl Erbie rated a beat-up folding table in one corner of a windowless conference room that he shared with two other young men. All three of them were hunched over a single datapad, one of them sliding his finger through the interface while the others gave cryptic suggestions. They reminded her of her son and his friends playing flatscreen games, although they didn't look serious enough for that, so she assumed it was work. The one with the datapad noticed her standing in the doorway. "You must be Aidra Scott."

"Pohl Erbie?" she asked. "Bryan Lynch said I should talk to you."

"Yeah, come in." He turned to his co-workers. "Guys? Can we have the room?"

"I don't want to kick anyone out," Aidra said.

"It's not a problem," one of the men said.

"Happens all the time," said the other. He gathered up a couple of datapads and they both left.

Aidra shook Pohl Erbie's hand across the table. He was in his mid-twenties, skinny, with rich brown skin and a round face. His hair was buzzed short on the sides, longer on top, emphasizing his jug ears.

"Mr. Lynch said you would be coming here, but I don't have any place . . . this office isn't the most private." He moved some electronic parts off a chair and gestured for her to sit, but she waved off the invitation.

He picked up a datapad and flicked through it. "Let's see, Ms. Scott . . . Ms. Scott."

"Aidra."

He smiled, a brief flash of white in his dark face. "Call me Pohl. Remind me again why you're here?"

"Learning Systems," she said.

"Don't do it."

"Do what?"

"Let them stick n-tech in your head."

Too late, Aidra thought. "I don't use Learning Systems."

"Of course you don't," Pohl crowed. "Who'd want to?"

"Lots of people." Of the two technologies, Learning Systems was the newer, edgier one. It made some people uncomfortable, much the same way genetic enhancements made people uncomfortable. Nobody liked to think about unfair advantages.

Exersleep, on the other hand, had been around long enough to have lost its stigma, if there ever was one in the first place. Some people called Exersleep "zombiecise," but most of them liked anything that would help fat Americans get off their lazy asses and work out. Learning Systems' popularity was growing, but it had a long way to go before it would be as easily accepted as Exersleep.

The door opened and one of Pohl's co-workers came back.

"Hey," Pohl objected. "You said I could have the room."

"Relax. I forgot my lunch." He retrieved a bento box from a small desk that was shoved into a corner and left again.

Pohl waited until the door closed. "You were saying?"

"No n-tech?" Aidra asked. "At all? You don't Exersleep either?"

"No."

"You get a company discount, you know."

"Not interested." Pohl fiddled with the flat files on the table. "I'm not squeamish or old-fashioned. I just don't see the need."

"That's what people tell themselves when they're squeamish," Aidra said. "Or old-fashioned."

The door opened again and Pohl's other co-worker popped in. "Excuse the interruption. I'll be gone in a second." He took three flat files off the desk. Pohl stopped him at the door and tapped the file at the top of the stack. "You know you can't take that, Dave. Not without signing it out."

"I'll be back in five minutes."

Pohl pointed to a pad attached to the door frame. "Sign."

Dave thumbprinted the ID box and scrawled the file number on the list. He left without looking back.

"Sorry about that," Pohl said.

"It's okay," Aidra said. "So, I know how Learning Systems works. If you could tell me—"

"Do you?" Pohl asked.

"Do I what?"

"Know how Learning Systems works? Because most people think they know, but they just echo what the company sells them.

The ads make it seem as if Learning Systems learns *for* you. Like you're implanting knowledge."

"I know it's not like that," she said. "It only gives you the capacity to learn better. It strengthens the neural connections in your brain. Making them . . . I guess stickier is the word."

"Stronger. Faster. Longer-lasting. But it's a trick. All they're doing is enhancing the connection between sense and memory." Pohl crossed to the tiny desk on the opposite wall and opened a drawer. He pulled out a pack of chewing gum and unwrapped a stick. He held it in front of Aidra's nose. "Smell this. If you didn't know it was gum, what would you think?"

She inhaled. "Mint. Candy canes. Christmas."

"See?" He popped the piece of gum into his mouth. "Your brain already does it for you. With Learning Systems, you do the same thing when you teach yourself new information. You learn it in an instant, retain it for a lifetime, and enjoy doing it."

Aidra thought of her son, poring over college textbooks. How much tuition could she save if Jon used Learning Systems? He'd still have to study, but he could probably finish school in a single year, not four. The thought simultaneously thrilled and terrified her. What if this became the norm? Would Jon graduate from college right when a bunch of enhanced super-learners flooded the job market?

What if Jon was one of them?

"Hard to see how this is a bad thing," Aidra said.

Pohl spit his wad of chewing gum into a wastebasket. "I won't use it. Nobody should. You know about the early experiments."

"I know it was originally meant for Alzheimer's or dementia, to repair failed neural connections. But it didn't work if things were too far gone. Then they decided to try it on healthy brains and—"

"No," Pohl said. "I mean the *early* experiments. When the Foxes and Gascoigne were still working together. The monkeys they turned into quivering drool machines. The human trials that didn't fare much better. Without a filter for bad experiences, you end up a paranoid basket case."

"But every tech fails before it succeeds," Aidra countered. By the time it came to market, Learning Systems was safer than having a glass of wine. Perhaps that's what bothered people the most. They weren't pissed because the n-tech was dangerous or risky. They were pissed because it *wasn't*.

Pohl tapped a finger on the table. "It's just not necessary. Nobody needs n-tech in their brains."

Aidra took a step closer to Pohl. She parted her hair above her right ear and turned her head, tracing with her forefinger the fine, nearly invisible scar that ran from her temple to the back of her head like a seam.

Pohl leaned over the table for a better look. "What happened?"

"Accident," Aidra said. "I was hit by a door. Knocked in the head."

That was enough of the story, and the only one she ever got to tell. She left out the classified part, about the artificial intelligence that had rigged her furnace to explode, and the way her front door blew her halfway across the lawn. She also had to leave out the part about Morris saving her life. Although to hear him tell it, it was his fault she'd almost been killed. It was complicated. Like everything between them.

"I had brain injuries," Aidra said. "With bleeding. Without n-tech, I'd be dead."

Pohl stared at the side of her head. "Hard to be objective about tech that saved your life."

She flattened her hair over the scar, hiding it. "Can I ask you something?"

"Of course."

"I'm just wondering. Why do you work here?"

"What? Oh, you mean . . ." His palms-up gesture took in the room. "I work for Fitz-Cahill. I don't work for Exersleep. I'm a consultant. I'm here to support scientific research."

As opposed to what? Emotional research? Aidra supposed that was her job.

The door opened again and they both turned to it. Dave was back. "Just need my keys," he said, walking to the corner desk and rummaging through a drawer.

"Hey, Dave?" Pohl said. "Hand me a marker."

"I don't think I . . ."

"Come on, I know you've got one in there."

Dave dug a little deeper and came up with a fat, black pen. He tossed it to Pohl who caught it and walked his friend to the door. Pohl wrote GO AWAY on the outside of the door before shutting it.

Aidra gestured to the pen in his hand. "You know that's permanent ink, right?"

"Don't care." Pohl crossed his arms and glared at the door as if daring it to open.

"I'm going to be quick before someone else comes in," Aidra said. "I need to know about the n-tech they found in Jean Claude Gascoigne at the scene. What if he overdosed on Learning Systems? Or Exersleep?"

"Impossible."

"What happens when people overdo it?"

"That's what I'm trying to tell you," Pohl said. "It's impossible to overdo it. More is not the same as better. There is a finite amount of building material in your head. No matter how much nanotech they squirt in there, you don't get any extra benefits from it, so who would waste their time and money?"

Aidra had thought as much, but it was nice to have confirmation. "So it's down to Gascoigne. I understand you've been looking at his psych evaluations."

Pohl crossed to the folding table and lifted a datapad, scrolling through pages that looked like legal forms. Aidra figured them to be part of the discovery process. Gascoigne had been arrested, the lawyers were at work preparing their cases, and the legal system required the sharing of certain information with the other side. Pohl found the data he was looking for and turned the screen to show her. It looked like a mass of colored blobs.

"There you have it," he said. "The most beautiful CAT scan in the world. No tumors or other physical abnormalities. His blood work shows no drugs and his psychological profile was normal. Jean Claude Gascoigne is as sane as anyone can be."

"Except he shot someone."

"Well, there's that." Pohl tapped the screen. "I'm sorry. I know you wanted me to show you a messed-up brain. Something that could explain what he did."

Aidra pointed at the pad. "You've eliminated some possibilities. It still doesn't mean the n-tech is at fault."

A knock at the door made Pohl growl.

"Go ahead and let him in," Aidra said. "I've got to talk to Bryan."

She caught his sleeve as he was reaching for the doorknob. "And Pohl? I like Fitz-Cahill. I like Exersleep. And I like nanotech. But that doesn't make me less objective, and it certainly doesn't make me forget my integrity. I'm looking for the truth. That's my whole agenda. If I find out that the n-tech is the least bit dangerous, I will tell the cops, the DA, and any regulatory agency I can find. I'd rather never Exersleep again than see even one person hurt."

"I never meant . . ." He was staring at her scar again. "I'm sorry if I sounded rude. I want the same thing you do."

"I'm glad to hear that. It was nice meeting you, Pohl. Thank you for your help." She walked past Pohl's co-worker and made her way to the other end of the building.

She almost turned into Bryan's old cubicle before she remembered that he'd been promoted and now had a corner office. She looked at the e-sec screen. It recognized her and told her that Mr. Lynch was currently handling two overseas calls but would finish them as soon as possible and be right with her.

A minute later, the e-sec told her to go in, but before she could knock, Bryan opened the door.

"I'm sorry, I—" he said, while Aidra said, "I need to talk to—"
They laughed and each gestured the other to go ahead.
"Come in," Bryan said.

Aidra's datapad chirped for attention as soon as she crossed the threshold. She glanced into her purse for a discreet peek at the caller. Morris.

"Do you need to get that?" Bryan asked.

"Not right now." Funny, Morris hadn't called when she arrived at Fitz-Cahill. He hadn't called when she was talking to Pohl Erbie. But the moment she stepped into Bryan's office, Morris needed to talk to her. She'd brush it off as mere coincidence if it didn't happen every single time.

Bryan's office wasn't large, but he made it look big by using minimal furniture. The window treatments were simple, framing the view of the Detroit River six stories below. Aidra wondered why his desk faced the door. If she had a view like that, she'd stare out the window all day. Maybe Bryan had put his back to the river to get any work done. Or maybe he liked looking at the rotating photo display on the opposite wall.

Aidra believed she could tell who someone really worked for by looking at their office walls. Diploma proudly displayed? Paying off student loans. Wedding photos? The bills for the expensive honeymoon were still rolling in. Aidra hadn't quite figured out the abstract painting or fish tank people, but her theory worked more often than not. She was just as transparent. Her companel's home screen was her son's senior portrait.

Bryan's wall was a rotating display of family photos featuring his mom and brother. So she hadn't been surprised to learn that his brother had severe cerebral palsy, still lived at home, and that Bryan sent his mom half his paycheck to help out.

He gestured her to the guest chair and leaned against his desk. He looked sharp in his ornate-style suit, the flowered lapels adding a dash of color to his plain jacket and white shirt. His dark hair was thinning on top, but only a little, and Aidra liked that he didn't try to hide it with a comb-over or excessive bangs.

"I enjoyed drinks the other night," he said. "I've been meaning to ask you again."

"I could just as easily ask you," she said.

"So, why don't you?"

"Want to get drinks after work?"

"I'd love to." Bryan tapped his fingers on the side of the desk. "But you're not here to ask me out."

"I just talked to Pohl Erbie."

"And you asked him out?"

"Not my type. But I learned some things."

"About your type?"

"About Jean Claude Gascoigne. Erbie doesn't think he's—"

"Exersleep is already getting lawsuits," Bryan interrupted. "Learning Systems, too."

"I heard about those." Aidra's newsreader had told her in the car. "Those claims aren't going to succeed."

"All it takes is one." Bryan held up a finger. "One case gets brought to trial, and we've set a precedent. People will claim 'mental anguish and hardship.' They'll quit their jobs and say the n-tech made them too afraid to function, hoping for a big payday from us. We have to be proactive. We don't just need to do something, we have to be *seen* doing something. That's why we need you."

"For my image?"

"No. I mean, well, yes. But that's not the only reason." Bryan waved a hand in front of him as if brushing off his own words. "Exersleep corporate offices has cops and lawyers marching in and out of their building all hours of the day. Even we've got national media attention, and we're just their insurance company. It's all over the e-verse, with every pundit and newscaster spewing half-formed nonsense. I need someone of your caliber, Aidra. I need someone whose credentials speak for themselves. You're good at what you do and you're good in front of a camera."

"I'd like to think that first one is more important."

"They're both important," Bryan said. "I set up an interview for you with Ugly Ben."

"That is a terrible idea."

"I thought you liked Ugly Ben. Do you want a different spinner?"

"I don't want any spinner at all."

"You need to give them the facts. Right now all they're doing is feeding public panic."

"Of course they are. They're spinners. Without public panic, they don't have a job." She turned up her palms. "Don't you have PR people for this?"

"I have *you* for this. You should be working inside the building. I've been trying to find you an office."

"Why?" She didn't quite say *ewww*, but she came close. If she had a desk of her own, she'd be expected to sit at it. And then how would she get anything done?

"Oh. I get it." Bryan said. "You want all the benefits of working for Fitz-Cahill, but none of the responsibilities. Can't blame you. It's a nice arrangement."

"You know I took a pay cut to work here, right?"

"Sure, we're not paying your freelance rates, but I authorized the benefits package, including Exersleep." He ran a hand along the back of his neck. "Now the finance office is starting to ask if that was the right decision."

Aidra gripped her handbag in her lap. "When have I not come through for you guys?"

"Well, there was the Liberty Finance thing last year, and Starwood a couple of months ago and—"

"Those were not my fault."

"We paid out thousands in claims. Hundreds of thousands in the Starwood case."

"As you should have." Aidra jabbed a finger at him. "You owed those people money. That's why they bought insurance."

She rubbed her temple. Bryan had it wrong. It was Fitz-Cahill that wanted the benefits of a full-time PI with none of the drawbacks. They liked it when she turned up evidence in their favor, but when it went the other way, not so much.

Bryan said nothing, just stared at the family photos on the wall.

"What is this really about?" Aidra asked. "Is my job on the line, here?"

Bryan let out a heavy breath. "I just need your cooperation on this."

"I am cooperating. I'm here, aren't I?"

"Then don't worry about it."

Bryan hadn't answered her question. Or maybe he had. "Bryan, it's me, Aidra. You're my boss, but we're also friends. You can tell me what's going on here."

"You've been hired to cast doubt."

"Doubt that the n-tech caused Jean Claude Gascoigne to kill Mackenzie Fox, yes."

"We need more than that. We need a slam dunk. Gascoigne's lawyers are the best."

"Yes, they are."

"Be better."

"I don't have to be better. The cops know he's guilty. The DA is going to charge him."

"We have to face the fact that Gascoigne might win. And what happens if he does."

"That sounds like an ultimatum."

Bryan cast his eyes around the room, and then gazed out the window. "You know how I got this office? Not because they promoted me, but because they fired the last guy who had it."

"That doesn't mean you're next."

"They're talking about outsourcing the entire investigative division. Good for you, bad for me. You can go back to charging freelance rates. I'll be out of a job."

Bad for both of us. Aidra put her purse on the floor, then picked it up again, then put it down and smoothed her hands over her knees.

Bryan thought she'd be happier without Fitz-Cahill. He was wrong about that.

Being her own boss meant constantly scrambling for work, never turning down an assignment for fear that new ones wouldn't come. Working for herself, there had been some easy days with big paychecks. There had also been days she'd been harassed, followed, shoved, and generally scared shitless. And she remembered a long, dark night, deep in the zone west of Detroit, when she'd held a gun on an innocent kid and threatened to shoot him with it. She never, ever wanted to do that again.

But the absolute worst was when she'd almost died at the hands of a madman. She'd been trapped in the GeCreations building, not knowing if she'd get out alive. Not knowing if her son would make it.

She tried to never think about that night. She sometimes managed to forget about it for two or three days in a row. Working at Fitz-Cahill helped. Her son was happier with the arrangement, too. When she picked up freelance assignments on the side, they were things with zero risk, like background checks or worker's comp frauds.

She didn't want to, but if she had to, she could go back to working for herself. Bryan didn't have that option. He wasn't an investigator. He was an administrator whose skills only made sense in a corporate context. He needed this job.

He straightened the pictures on his desk. "I didn't want to say anything. I mean, I know you'll come through for us. Your work is half done already. We all know Gascoigne did it. All you need to do is find out why. And please, dear God, don't let it be the n-tech."

Her datapad chirped. Morris again. She reached into her bag and shut the machine completely off, although she knew it wouldn't stop him. At least, not for long.

"The public killing of Mackenzie Fox hasn't made my job easier," Aidra said. "In a thousand ways, it's made it harder. Everyone's looking at Gascoigne, and everyone's looking at me, and everyone has already made up their minds. They've begun to form a story about what happened and why, and that's the story they'll tell me. It's the truth because people believe it. Finding Gascoigne's motive for killing Mackenzie Fox is going to be a bitch."

Bryan moved around the desk and leaned on it again. "We can't have things be inconclusive. Inconclusive equals lawsuits. Ideally, Fitz-Cahill would like no n-tech to be at fault at all, but at the end of the day, we'll settle for blaming Learning Systems."

"Do you want blame, or proof?"

"Either one is fine. Tell the cops what you find out. Tell the DA. And for God's sake, tell the spinners. Anything you can do to help Gascoigne get convicted."

"So that's my goal? That's what's going to make Fitz-Cahill happy?"

"When he's convicted, everyone will be happy. Even his own company wants to pave over him. They've got their own investigation team trying to prove the same thing we are."

"I'm aware."

"You're probably also aware that the stockholders are selling off, the corporate boards are in an uproar, and there is almost no leadership of either company. Fox and Gascoigne were both such hands-on managers, their companies are heading right down the toilets without them. We need to end this."

"So why bring in Pohl Erbie?" Aidra asked. "He's practically a techshun."

"No, he's not. He's one of the more savvy people we have."

"He's squeamish."

"Yes, he is. That's why he's the perfect person to work the tech angle. Does he think the nanotech is at fault here?"

"Well . . ." Aidra considered everything Pohl had told her. "No. Not necessarily."

"There you go," Bryan said. "If even an nanotech-hater like Erbie thinks Gascoigne acted on his own motives, then he probably did."

Pohl hadn't exactly said that, either.

"I spoke with Fox's widow yesterday," she told Bryan.

"I caught the spin. How is Hannah holding up?"

"I'm having a hard time getting a read on her. She's thrown herself into her work, her kids. Same thing, I guess. I don't think she's going to be much help."

"Give her time. Grief hits us all differently."

"I've got a few more things I can try. It would be a lot easier if I could meet with Gascoigne."

"Can you?" Bryan asked.

"I was hoping you could help me with that."

"Impossible."

Aidra stood to go. Of course Bryan couldn't get her in to see Jean Claude Gascoigne. She wondered if anyone could. She couldn't even bluff her way in since she'd burned through her only set of false credentials saving Sofia Gao's skin at the Cityheart police station, and Morris hadn't restored them yet.

As if she'd summoned him, Aidra's datapad repowered itself and chirped in a message from Morris. She grabbed it with two hands and yanked the battery.

"What about the love triangle thing?" Bryan asked.

"Everyone always brings up the love triangle thing." Aidra dropped the datapad into her purse and zipped it closed. "I can assure you, that's not what we're dealing with."

CHAPTER FIVE

"Most important meal of the day," Sullivan said, his heavy brows furrowing over the absurd reading glasses perched atop his shapeless nose. When the waitress appeared from somewhere behind Aidra, his face curved into a smile for her, making him look suddenly handsome. "Hello there, Mandy dear."

"Good morning, Sully. The usual?" The Pancake House still dressed its waitstaff in uniforms from the last century and Mandy had the legs to pull it off. She put down two mugs of coffee without being asked and turned to Aidra. "And for you?"

"I'll have a small oatmeal." Ordering breakfast was an easy way to forestall Sullivan's rant about the Exersleep lifestyle. Through trial and error, Aidra had found that her body liked eating four light meals evenly spaced throughout the day rather than three big ones. That usually meant eating alone and she rarely made it three days in a row. Today, she had no "fast" to break, but she'd make herself eat to be sociable. Besides, a little extra fiber might be a welcome surprise to her stomach. She could stay awake for twenty-three out of every twenty-four hours, but digestive enzymes worked on their own clock.

"So what do you think?" she asked Sullivan when Mandy left.

"I think you're too fucking skinny for a bowl of oatmeal to do any good."

"Your mother know you talk like that?"

"Where do you think I got my extensive vocabulary?"

"I'm not eating a stack of pancakes just to make you feel better about your beltline."

Sullivan leaned back and patted his belly. "Solid muscle, right here. Still stop a bullet."

"So will any off-the-shelf ballistics gel."

He pinned her with a look and she saw him deciding to let it go. "I've missed you, kiddo."

Aidra decided to let that go in turn. Sullivan would never stop calling her *kiddo* and it was useless to ask him to. She sipped her coffee, savoring its soothing warmth. She used to drink several cups a day, reaching for her first right after her morning run. But her coffee maker had been broken for the last month and she'd never got around to fixing it. Exersleep made her feel so good, she didn't need the caffeine, so why bother? Coffee had become a social drink for her, a pleasure to be savored with friends, not a daily dose pounded down in a morning rush.

And of course, Sullivan frequented the most hole-in-the-wall diner in the most obscure neighborhood with the best coffee she'd had in ages. She appreciated his taste. She also appreciated his knack for staying out of the spotlight. The last thing they needed was for spinners to see them together and get the wrong idea.

Sullivan was currently on the payroll of Westrock Financial Insurance Group, underwriters for Learning Systems. Westrock had made a casual inquiry about employing Aidra but she'd cited a conflict of interest and suggested they call Sullivan instead. She hadn't mentioned that fact to him. Wasn't sure how he'd take it.

She didn't mind working the opposite side of the fence from her former mentor. They were on the same mission—to find out the true facts. Why not pool their resources? She was about to ask him for their game plan but forgot her question when she saw his jaw go slack and his eyes become unfocused and confused. He was sliding into his favorite role, the one he called Poor-Old-Uncle-Sully. He put it on when he wanted people not to notice him, to look away in embarrassment. He suddenly seemed infirm, vulnerable. Maybe not-quite-there. She hated that look.

She hated it even more that she automatically took up her

corresponding role, the one she'd worn like a tight-fitting glove when she'd been his assistant. Aidra became "Holly," a well-educated and ambitious woman forced to care for and supervise her elderly Uncle Sully. She felt her lips thin in disapproval and barely disguised irritation. Glancing at him and then away, as if she wanted to look anywhere but at him, she used the opportunity to case the restaurant.

Sullivan raised his head to look through his glasses at the table as if he'd never seen one before. "Has she brought coffee, yet?" he demanded too loudly.

With a minimum eye-roll she leaned forward and maneuvered the half-full cup closer to him. "What are we doing?" she murmured.

He responded by looking at his watch and tapping the face. *On the clock. Working.*

Aidra sized-up the other customers. Several tables had recently been seated, most of them families, but a young couple sat two tables away. As she watched, the woman rose and trailed her fingers lightly over the man's hand. She swayed like a willow toward the ladies' room.

Sully drained his coffee cup and let it drop to the floor. The cup didn't break, but it rang the hardwood with a thump and splattering of dregs. With Holly's sigh of disgust, Aidra knelt to wipe up the coffee with her napkin.

"Watch the lunk," Sullivan murmured.

The man had risen from the table as well, leaving behind his coat. Admirably broad shoulders, enviably slim hips. He also took the route toward the restrooms.

"Oh, don't tell me."

Sullivan had dropped Poor-Old-Sully and was grinning. "You saw the ring?"

She had. A wedding ring on her finger, none on his. "So they are . . ."

"Every Tuesday for breakfast with a little exercise between ordering and eating."

She resumed her seat. "In the bathroom? Gross."

"The ladies' room. Which, I am told, is marginally better than the gent's."

"Still. Gross."

Sullivan produced a small box from his pocket with the casual air of a magician and thumbed it open. Three spiders gleamed there. "I need you, kid."

"No. No way."

"We have a very limited window." Calm. Matter-of-fact. Sullivan at his most reasonable. "This handbasket has been hanging over my head for a month now. I've planted spiders, but she runs a sweep before he comes in. I can't go in there and it has to be while they are *flagrantly delicate*."

"Delectable," she said, automatically filling in her half of the inside joke.

He chuckled. "Flippin' delicious."

That, Aidra decided afterwards, nursing her ankle and wringing out her sock, was when the ingrained habit of helping Sullivan overrode her common sense. The shorthand jokes, the easy sense of shared camaraderie, the way he made her feel clever, to push her buttons and get her moving.

She'd pushed open the door to the ladies' room with no special care. The couple had to know that other people would come in, do their business and leave. She moved to the sink, washed her hands thoroughly, and walked back to the door. She opened it, released it, and heard it sigh smoothly shut on its pneumatic hinges. She waited, listening to the bathroom.

There was a slight stir of movement from the corner stall, an exhalation much quieter than the door. Then a series of regular breaths, quiet panting.

Private detectives got a lot of proof-of-cheating work. Sullivan always referred to these as *handbaskets*, as in "going-to-hell-in." And he needed them to be caught in the act—*in flagrante delicto* in legal parlance. This was awfully *flagrante*. Aidra thought they must both have an exhibitionist streak a kilometer wide to make this a regular thing.

She crept forward, glad she'd worn the shoes with the quiet, non-skid soles. The happy couple was happily coupling in the handicapped stall. The door of the stall beside them hung open, a perfect avenue of approach.

She fixed her gaze on the top of the partition. She adjusted the surveillance spider's legs and oriented it so that it would train its wide-angle optics down onto the scene. She wanted to place it quickly and leave. She bit her lip and grimaced at the set-up. The partition was high and the toilet seat in front of her was up. She didn't dare lower it for fear of the noise. Why did some women raise the damn seat? Why, why, why?

She put one foot on the narrow curve of the bowl and froze when she heard the tiny squeak from the rubber sole of her shoe. But the couple next door didn't react. Their breathing was now more audible, ragged and hoarse, the slick slap of skin on skin unmistakable. If the handbasket was closing in on hell, she might have only a few more moments to document. That was another of Sullivan's favorite verbs—*document*. As if they were war correspondents or highbrow filmmakers instead of sleazy peepers, paid to mind other people's business.

Aidra stood with one foot on the toilet rim, wondering if she should even be doing this. She didn't have to pull herself up onto a public toilet seat. This wasn't her case. She wasn't working for Sullivan. Not anymore. How had she fallen so easily into doing his dirty work? Just because he was playing Uncle Sully didn't mean she had to become Holly.

She was already here, already halfway done, might as well shut up and finish the job. But this would be the last time. No matter what, this was the last.

Up she went, her fingers poised delicately around the spider, reaching for the wall. Aidra peered over the partition to see if she'd gotten it right.

The woman was bending over the toilet seat—*in fragrance disgusting*—and holding the metal pipes connecting the toilet bowl to the wall. The man was behind her, his tanned fingers digging into her waist just above her hipbones. Her skirt and his pants were hung neatly on the doorhook behind them.

"You!" The man must have caught her shadow with his peripheral vision, and the woman turned her head to look. Both of them stared up at Aidra with mingled surprise and anger.

Her foot slipped.

With a splash, Aidra's right leg plunged into the bowl. Water gouted up like an obscene fountain, and the ball of her foot wedged into the drain hole. Even ten minutes ago, she would have bet a hundred dollars that her sneaker was too wide to jam into the drain hole of a toilet bowl, yet here she was.

She tried to pull it out, and yelped when her left foot slid on the wet floor, throwing her sideways against the wall and twisting her trapped ankle. She flailed upward and shot both arms out, bracing them on either side of the stall's partition walls. She used all the strength in her arms to hold herself in place while trying to free her shoe from the trap.

"You spying bitch."

Fire flared in her scalp and she lost her hold on the wall as she was pulled backward.

"Planting spiders isn't good enough for you?"

Aidra's foot, leaving her sneaker behind, came free with another splash that wet her to the knee. She went tumbling out of the stall and onto the tiled floor.

She grabbed the hand that had twined itself in her hair,

preventing it from pulling further. She wrenched herself free, using elbows and forearms to knock the person off her. Moving on instinct, Aidra rolled and tumbled as bare legs lashed out at her. It was the man's voice she'd heard, but she wasn't sure which one had tried to tear her hair out. She registered that both of them were kicking at her as she scrambled backward and into a yet-unvisited stall. Getting herself up against the wall behind the toilet, she regarded the owners of the handbasket, both of whom were now shiny-eyed with loathing.

"Well, well," Aidra said with a lightness she didn't feel. Her ankle hurt like fury. "Which one of y'all is coming in here to get me? That way there'll be one left to call an ambulance."

"Did you smash the camera?" the woman asked softly. The man nodded. "Good. Get the pepper spray out of your pocket."

A bubble of laughter escaped before Aidra could stop it. "I'm pretty sure boy-toy left his coat at the table, honey. Unless you've got pepper spray jammed up your narrow ass, I'm betting you need a new plan." She looked the man up and down. "You've got nice taste, though, sweetheart. I'll give you that."

As if only now aware of their nakedness, the two reddened and backed away, scurrying into the corner stall for their clothes. Aidra waited while they dressed, muttered, and left. Apparently it had not occurred to them that the spider might have been a transmitter instead of just a recorder. Aidra hoped they would not consider the possibility until later.

Shitfire. What if they actually came back with the pepper spray? Aidra limped around to the second stall, reached into the cold water, and yanked her shoe free. With the need for witnesses beating on her brain, she pulled the door open a crack and peered out.

"Kiddo? You okay?" Sullivan was there, his face watchful and concerned.

"Give me a second." She used nearly every towel in the dispenser to dry her shoe and foot as best she could, then washed her hands up to the elbow in very hot water and plenty of soap.

She limped back to their table, noticing that the couple had departed, leaving behind cups of coffee that were sure to grow cold, unpaid.

Sullivan was checking his datapad and smiling at the recording. "Not much of it, but what's there says winner."

"How about I kick your ass for you? Would that still say winner? Or should I just bill you for a new pair of shoes? Because I'm never wearing these again."

He looked down. "And did you learn anything today? Pair of shoes is a cheap price for a lifelong lesson."

"Stop it. I'm not an intern so quit treating me like one. Why are you picking up handbaskets anyway? You said you were done with that."

He shrugged. "Times are tough. It pays the bills."

"I thought Westrock was paying your bills these days."

"Not looking to cut me out and trade up, are you?"

"I *got* you that job. They called me first." The words were out before her brain caught up with her temper.

He ducked his head and half-closed his eyes, giving her a flash of poor Uncle Sully. "Helping out an old man, eh?"

His act cranked her temper another notch and she took a moment for a calming breath. She'd love to get up and leave, stick him with the check, maybe even step on his foot with her soggy sneaker on her way out, but he had something she needed. Something she couldn't get for herself—a way in to see Gascoigne.

She had just put him in debt to her. And she could get instantly repaid if she played this right. "Let's call it professional courtesy. I help you, you help me. We're working two sides of the same job. We might as well combine forces."

"Like old times," Sullivan said.

"More like a sharing of equals."

"That's what I said, didn't I?"

"Sure." *Old times* meant her doing all the work and Sullivan taking all the credit.

Their food arrived—pancakes, bacon, eggs, and hashbrowns for Sullivan. What looked like a kiddie pool full of oatmeal for her, accompanied by a rack of condiments including brown sugar, three kinds of fruit compote, and nuts.

Aidra stared at the bowl. If this was a small oatmeal, what did the large look like? It reminded her too much of the toilet she'd splashed into. She pushed it aside and put both elbows on the table. "How do you want to play this one? Have you talked to Gascoigne yet?"

He chuckled long and low in his dry voice, although Aidra didn't see what was funny. He held up his cup for more coffee as Mandy passed by with the pot. After she left, he shook his head and said, "This is a hell of a business we're in, huh kid?"

She waited with a half-smile.

"Don't you think it's funny? We're in a people business, the most people business there is, yet we've been hired to prove the innocence of a technology by proving the guilt of a person." He popped a huge forkful of pancake into his mouth and murmured around it, "That's a week-old, greasy, crap sandwich. That's what that is."

"Maybe we're the champions of progress and the future. What have you done so far?"

"There's nothing to do on this except collect a paycheck."

She figured he was stalling, waiting for her to share first. "I've already interviewed—"

He waved his hand. "Of course, of course. You talk to folks, you take notes. I'll talk to folks, I'll take notes. Maybe a few spinners see us doing our talking and taking. That would be useful. You still on Ugly Ben's good side?"

"Have you seen him? That man doesn't have a good side."

"Lighten up, kiddo. We're just pretty faces for public consumption." He shoveled in a mouthful of hashbrowns, chewed, swallowed. "It doesn't really matter whether it was Gascoigne using Learning Systems that did it or his being an Exersleeper or some kind of psychotic episode that has fuckall to do with either one. We get our payday no matter how this whole thing pans out."

Aidra sipped her coffee. The last thing she needed was for Sullivan to know how close to the line she was at Fitz-Cahill. He wouldn't even need to gloat out loud. His sympathy would be an acid bath for her soul. She could hear him in her head: *Trust me, kiddo, you'll be happier off the corporate tit, making an honest living with the rest of us working stiffs.*

She decided to try another angle. "Public opinion hasn't decided what they think yet and Gascoigne's legal team—"

"The *public*." Sullivan made a rude noise. "The public can't decide whether wiping your ass after taking a dump is a good idea. And the publicity won't hurt Exersleep or Learning Systems in the long run. Hell, making it sound dangerous makes some people want to do it more." He chewed his way thoughtfully through half a pig's worth of bacon. He gave the Pancake House the look-over again, observing her from the corners of his eyes. "I'm a little surprised you haven't gone for Learning Systems yourself."

"Maybe I'm smart enough the way I am."

"It won't make you smarter. That's just the line they use to sell the stuff."

"I know. It only increases your capacity for learning. Same thing, right?"

Sullivan poured a sweet waterfall of syrup over what remained of his pancakes. "If you layer in some ambition, sure. You've got that. And you already screw up your mind for the sake of your body."

"Why, Patrick Sullivan. Is that a compliment?" She ran a hand down her side and across her hip.

"You know what I mean. Why Exersleep, but not this? Why are you afraid of one, but not the other? They're both icky."

"I cannot believe you just used the word 'icky.'"

He picked up his fork, jabbed it at her then attacked the haystack of hashbrowns.

"Seriously, Sullivan, you're a constant source of mystery and surprise."

"No I'm not. And you didn't answer my question."

"Okay, then. The only reason I can afford to Exersleep is my status at Fitz-Cahill. I couldn't afford Learning Systems even if I gave up my condo and my car."

"And that," he said, "brings me around to my point." He divided an egg into quarters, speared the pieces onto his fork and paused with them halfway to his mouth. "All this Supremium bullshit is just another way for the haves to get more and the have-nots to go without. It would be a lot better for everyone if this just went away."

"I swear to God, if you say 'back in my day' I'm pouring this entire cup of coffee on you."

"Waste of good coffee." Sullivan frowned. "Why are they called Supremiums, anyway? Who came up with that?"

"Does it matter?" Aidra asked. "That's what they call themselves."

Sullivan scratched his big ear. "You call someone who Exersleeps an Exersleeper. Where's the cute term for someone who uses Learning Systems? A Learner? A Systemer? You see? It doesn't flow."

"The name isn't the issue here. We don't even know how many people use both technologies. Does anyone even know the exact number? The most reliable data I have says five thousand Supremiums, but that was from last year. More are starting all the time."

"And here I was hoping it was just a fad."

"Of course, there are hundreds of thousands of plain Exersleepers, too, like me. We should get our companies talking with each other, compile their databases."

Sullivan snorted. "Yeah, that will work. With Exersleep and LS both pointing the finger at each other—and giving each other the finger with the other hand—they aren't going to go for a compilation of databases so the media can go on a witch hunt." He shoveled in a forkful of pancake. "It would be easier if every learner . . .

systemer . . . every Learning Systems client had to go to a dedicated facility like you do for Exersleep. But with models getting smaller, some people have opted for chairs you can use at home. Hey, maybe that's what you can call them."

"What?"

"The Learning Systems users. You could call them chairs."

"I don't think that will catch on."

"Pity," Sullivan said. "I could get a royalty. But I don't know why it has to be a chair at all. Those things are as big as a recliner. Why can't it be a helmet, or just a hypospray?"

"People will pay more if they think it's more complex." Aidra watched Sullivan eat, trying to keep her queasiness under control. "Maybe Gascoigne can give me some insight into that. Have you talked to him yet?"

"No."

"Good. You can take me with you when you go."

"Can't," Sullivan said. He swilled coffee. "No point in trying."

"Of course there's a point."

"You think you can get him to just throw up his hands and say, 'You have found me out. I hated that feckless prick and I needed only one small reason to blow him away.'" His gift for mimicry was as sharp as ever, with the precise pronunciation she'd seen from Gascoigne in interviews. Sullivan dropped the pose. "You're dreaming, kiddo. Dreaming."

"But he *is* guilty. And I'm going to prove it."

"Yeah? How?"

"I'll find out why he did it. I'll crawl inside his life and discover his true motive. I'll cast doubt. Come on, Sullivan. This is what we *do*."

Sullivan pushed away his empty plate and picked up his cup in two hands. "I know you don't like to be wrong."

"I'm not wrong."

"This isn't just about the job. You need these buggers to be safe, otherwise your world doesn't make sense."

"If n-tech isn't safe, nobody's world makes sense. You might as well repeal the law of gravity or have your compass point south. Do you know how long this technology took to get to market? How much it was tested?"

"And then, one day, Jean Claude Gascoigne—"

"You don't stop driving just because some idiot got behind the wheel drunk. You don't stop using your computer just because someone might plant a virus. The stupidity of *humans* doesn't make the *technology* less safe."

"You saw him, Aidra. Gascoigne looked like a zombiecizer when he killed Fox."

"And you looked like that five minutes ago, *Uncle Sully*."

"Try to see Gascoigne if you want, babycakes, but you're not gonna get your peace of mind back from him."

Aidra stood and slung her purse over her shoulder. "Okay. Nice talking to you."

Sullivan laid a hand on her arm. "You haven't touched your breakfast."

"I'm not hungry and I'm not going to pretend I am. In fact, I've got an appointment at my gym."

"That's cute."

"What is?"

"That you still call your little napping room a gym."

"I call things what they are." Aidra touched her multicard to the credit point on the table, paying for both herself and Sullivan. She grabbed his collar and planted a fierce kiss atop his balding head. "Bye, Sullivan. Good luck with your *work*. If you still call it that."

CHAPTER SIX

Aidra had been moving her living room furniture when her friend Gilly called. She'd only meant to stop at home to pick up her workout gear, but once there, she was bothered by the furniture arrangement and decided to change it for the fifth time since buying a new couch. She'd liked the couch well enough in the store, but once she got it home, she realized that its size was awkward and it didn't go with her favorite chair. But she wasn't ready to upgrade the rest of her furniture, so she kept moving it around.

Her living room wasn't large. The front door was at one end of it and the half wall separating the kitchen from the rest of the space was at the other end. Still, she knew she could shoehorn the couch, the chair, and the shelves into the room if she could just find the perfect arrangement.

She plopped down on the couch she'd just put next to the window and answered Gilly's call, intending to show her the living room and ask for help. Gilly was a building contractor. Maybe some of that spilled over into interior design. But one look at Gilly's red, puffy eyes made Aidra put that thought aside.

"Oh, no. What's wrong?"

The woman looking out of the comscreen did her best to look surprised by the question, but in the years Aidra had known Gilly Tanizake, she'd never seen her neighbor look anything but stunningly composed. Her dark skin wouldn't show the blotchiness that went with prolonged crying, but the trembling at the corners of her over-bright eyes, the redness of her nose . . . either she'd been cutting onions or—

Nope. Gilly dissolved into a storm of weeping. She reached offscreen for tissues and clutched a wad of them to her face. Aidra waited, wearing her most professional expression. Experience with upset clients had taught her that it was best to stay silent. Gilly would talk when she was ready.

At last, Gilly got herself under control and let out a shuddering sigh. "Sorry. Sorry. I promised myself I wasn't going to do that—that I would just call and ask you again to please come to book club . . ."

But . . .

"But you saw right through and . . . Aidra. Aidra, I don't know what to do." She seemed on the verge of another meltdown.

"Calm. Calmly. Tell me what happened."

"I'm being blackmailed."

All thoughts of furniture arrangements left her head. "Hang on a second." Aidra muted out and switched screens to tell Exersleep to put her slot on hold. She didn't know if they could get her in later or not, but she broke her appointment anyway. She got right back to Gilly. "Tell me what happened."

Gilly swallowed and Aidra watched her sorting thoughts.

"And don't just tell me what you think I ought to hear. I have to know how bad it is, or I can't help."

Gilly sputtered out the story in fits and starts, but Aidra got the gist. Gilly Tanizake and her husband were general contractors, weaving together the services of several dozen construction companies. Two months ago, Gilly had entered her office to find a man sitting behind her desk.

"He scared the hell out of me, but when I started to call the police, he said—said—" Gilly's voice broke, but she swallowed and went on. "He said that he was a private investigator. He said—said one of our vendors had hired him." Tears spilled out of her eyes. "We bid for jobs, city projects and private ones, too. Usually whoever comes in lowest lands the contract. This PI said he had proof that we had traded overbids with other contracting firms."

Aidra got it. Gilly's firm would overbid, throwing the business to another company. They, in turn, overbid on the next project and let Tanizake Construction bid higher than they otherwise would have and still get the job. "And did you?"

"No! Never!" Gilly shook her head in denial. "Of course, we talk to many of our competitors, everybody in our business knows each other. But there were a few situations where we came in high to Ulrigh and Mann right after we had dinner with Raymond Ulrigh." She sniffed. "It would look *terrible*. Building contractors live and die by reputation. Even to have it suggested would poison the market for us for years. We might never get it back. Especially now when we're bidding for Olympic construction projects. This is the worst possible time to be in this position."

"Let me guess. This PI wanted to offer you a deal."

"He said that instead of handing over the evidence to his client, he would start a little bidding process of his own and see if I could come in on the high side. He said I'd be good at that. He laughed about it." Gilly sniffled. "Laughed and laughed like he'd worked that joke out ahead of time and couldn't wait to use it."

Aidra tightened her fists under the desk where Gilly couldn't see. There were bad apples in any profession, but sleazy PIs were her pet peeve. There was no governing organization she could appeal to, no board of ethics. It was up to the community to police their own. And in this case, it was something she'd gladly do.

"Why did you pay him?" Aidra asked. "You didn't do anything wrong."

"He could ruin me, Aidra! My company. I thought if I paid him, he would go away."

"Guys like that never go away. Did he tell you his name?"

"He said to call him Jay. He wouldn't tell me anything else."

"Describe him."

"Blond. He wore dark glasses so I couldn't see his eyes. Big. Looked like the kind of guy who plays football in high school then drinks beer in college until he flunks out of his scholarship. He was in a nice suit, but on his way out I got a look at his shoes. Old, worn out."

"And after you paid him, he decided to make this arrangement an ongoing thing?"

Aidra tried to keep the flatness out of her voice. This wasn't Gilly's fault and damned if she'd make her feel like it was. "If it's any comfort, this happens all the time."

Gilly pressed the tissues to her face and wailed.

"Gilly, sweetie, take a breath. I doubt any of your vendors hired him. This may not be what it looks like."

Gilly lowered the tissues. "You don't know what it looks like."

Aidra thought about that. There seemed to be more to this story than Gilly was willing to tell. Still, she had to work with what she was given. "Listen, if he had a client willing to pony up for the info, he'd be a lot safer just getting paid than indulging in extortion. I think this was Jay's own idea. What kind of proof did he have?"

Gilly still seemed distracted. "Um. He didn't show me anything, but he quoted from several conversations. He recited times, dates, places. He knew . . . well, he knew some details. Things he shouldn't know."

"He probably doesn't have anything more incriminating than circumstantial evidence, but he's getting that evidence from somewhere." Aidra doubted Tanizake Construction's computer systems had much in the way of countermeasures. They were what Morris liked to call spongy—soft and full of holes.

"But if no one hired him—"

"That still doesn't get you off the hook. He probably has some kind of spike into your system. If you call his bluff, he can send anything he's got to your whole database. How much has he gotten out of you?"

"A . . . quite a lot. Mitsu is going to notice. And now he wants more." Gilly was looking down now. "He's hinting that—that—"

Aidra could imagine what he wanted. Gilly was a lovely woman. Loathing for the blond man tightened her stomach muscles.

"He's only dealt with you? He hasn't approached Mitsu about this?"

She looked terrified. "I—I thought I could handle him. Mitsu is so busy. And saving face is so important to him. To have his reputation tarnished would kill him."

Aidra had her doubts. She knew Gilly's husband. If they were truly innocent, he'd get indignant and air everything publicly. There was probably something they were trying to hide. She didn't for a minute think that Gilly was doing anything illegal. But unethical? Perhaps.

But nothing compared to the PI who called himself Jay. She didn't need to know the whole story in order to take action. "How does the PI get in touch?" she asked. "How do you pay him?"

"The calls come in voice-only. A different ID each time. I tried calling back one time and it was already disconnected."

Temp phones. Not impossible to trace, but beyond the resources of the average victim. "And the money?"

"He tells me to go to Re-Buy and bid big amounts on ridiculous items. Bottle caps. Single socks. An empty tube of toothpaste. He even sends the actual items to me after I 'buy' them."

How wonderfully deniable. The auction site was virtually untraceable unless you were selling something illegal, but maybe his sense of humor would do him in. She'd have to get Noah on that angle. The first step was to find out who this guy was.

"Can you help me, Aidra? Will you help me?"

"Of course." Bad PIs made business bad for everyone and she welcomed the chance to clean one of them up.

Aidra raced through town, hoping she could still get to the gym before her appointment window closed. She called Noah along the way and explained Gilly's situation.

"It will take some time," Noah said. "The security on Re-Buy is pretty tight. They pride themselves on it."

"How about you take pride in your own work? I thought hackers appreciated a challenge."

"I do," Noah assured her. "In fact, we could have some fun with this. How long is Gilly willing to string this PI along?"

"Oh, no, you don't. This is my friend. This is her life. This isn't entertainment."

"But you know what they say. If you do something you love, you'll never work a day in your life."

"You'll never work for me again if you don't settle down and get started."

"Can't we at least—"

"No."

"You didn't even listen to my idea."

"Because I know I'm not going to like it. We need to find this PI and stop him, and we need to do it soon. We're here to help my friend. We're not here to play."

"Yeah, yeah. We need to be serious. We're serious people who do serious things." Noah sighed. "Did you see that I cleaned up all your billing?"

"Yes. I noticed your invoice, too, which was paid along with all my other bills."

"Just being efficient. Since you got that chunk of change from Allied Mutual, I thought I'd help you spend it. Whatever happened with that fraud case?"

"The guy who was too injured to lift a shovel dropped his claim. He's going back to work tomorrow."

"So he doesn't have a bad back?"

"He's fine."

"How did you get him to drop the claim?"

"I took a chance. I let him see me. People with genuine injuries like it when a PI is called in. They feel like they're being taken seriously."

"But this guy . . ."

"Got spooked." She loved cases like this, when following her instincts paid off. She showed up, did her job, and got paid, but she didn't have to decide someone else's fate. She was more like the hand that was guiding him where he was always meant to go.

Too bad all cases didn't resolve themselves this easily.

CHAPTER SEVEN

Aidra steered her Octave toward the Detroit Athletic Club. She had just turned down Woodward Avenue when she had to slam on the brakes to avoid hitting a young woman crossing in the middle of the street. The woman was hurrying to catch up to a group on the other side, all of them gathering in a loose knot around the gym's front door. They stood under the wide awning, unwilling to stand in the spring mist that was blowing through.

Aidra crept along the street, straining to keep an eye on the road while stealing glances at the small group. They looked like new-age techshuns. The women all had flowing, undyed hair to match their flowing, undyed clothing. The men favored simple pants and coats with no glowstrips or power packs or color reflectors. Some of them held up homemade signs painted on cardboard. Aidra couldn't read them and drive at the same time, but the most legible one said something about "robbing people of their dreams."

That was their beef with Exersleep? Aidra thought about the nightmares she'd had before she started Exersleeping. Doing away with those was a benefit, as far as she was concerned. But techshuns clung to any little thing to justify their hatred of modern life.

Exersleep had always had protestors. It didn't seem to matter that Exersleep was the safest form of exercise anyone could do, with absolutely no side effects. Pop some n-tech into your brain, have a nice nap, and come out the other side both well-exercised and well-rested. They had exercise routines designed for anyone—old, young, pregnant, disabled. No wonder Exersleep caught on so quickly. Every week, her gym added dozens of new members.

Once past the misguided youth at the front door, she turned into the alley that led to the underground parking ramp. If the technots had done even a little bit of research, they'd realize that hardly anyone used the Detroit Athletic Club's front door. Those arriving by car used the ramp entrance in the back. So who was their little protest for? Themselves? Each other? She could bet they were filming it and would try to sell it as news to one of the local spins.

Aidra stowed her car in a numbered slot, grabbed her gym bag, and headed toward the elevator that would take her directly to the Athletic Club, eager to suit up and plug in.

She barely glanced at the holo ads displayed on the elevator wall. "You don't live longer, you live fuller," said the smiling model as the doors closed. Aidra turned her back. "Finally, you can buy time," said the other wall.

"I'm already a member, shut it off," Aidra mumbled. But the ads played to their captive audience, looping themselves to start again when she disembarked.

She covered a yawn, looking forward to the session. Coming awake from real sleep left her groggy and fumbling for coffee. After Exersleep, she felt instantly bright and alive. Was it any wonder she hadn't slept at home in ages?

She was spending less and less time at home, period. Why should she? Jon was away at college and her work kept her too busy for domestic chores. If it weren't for Madeline, she could probably give up her condo and live the carefree life of the no-fixed-address crowd. But you couldn't be NFA with a pet. *Or a son*, she reminded herself. Jon wasn't gone forever, just for the school year. He'd be home in a few weeks and things could get back to normal.

The elevator doors parted and she walked through the high-ceilinged lobby, past the smoothie stand and a cluster of fake palm trees, walking lightly and swinging her bag. She stopped by the front desk to see if they could squeeze her in, since she'd canceled her original appointment.

She waited behind the customer already there, trying to catch the receptionist's eye, but Kit had her hands full.

"I assure you, sir, you won't remember Exersleeping," Kit told the man in front of her.

"Why is that?" he asked. "Are you messing with the memory centers of the brain?"

"Not at all," Kit said. "It's because of the encoding."

"Encoding? What's that?"

Aidra glared at the man's back. A newbie. This could take ages.

"Do you remember falling asleep?" Kit asked. "No, of course not. But did you ever wonder why that is? It's because the cholines in your brain haven't finished encoding the last few minutes of your experience before you nod off. It never gets into long-term memory. Many Exersleepers don't even remember changing into their workout clothing."

Aidra tried to remember yesterday's session when she'd pulled on her snugsuit and slipped into her soft shoes. She'd done it hundreds of times and the memories blurred together. What did it matter if she didn't recall the exact sequence of events every time she changed her stupid clothes?

"Cholines," the newbie said. "I told you it alters brains."

"Exersleep is a natural process," Kit said. "No brain chemicals are added or taken away. We simply use the n-tech to control the balance of cholines and amines already present in the healthy brain."

"Yes, yes, I know about those," the man said in a singsong voice. "When you're asleep, your brain is full of cholines with just a few amines to allow you to dream. When you're awake, your brain is full of amines with just a little bit of cholines for memory. But there has to be more to it. There has to be. What aren't you telling me? Does it hurt? Will I feel the nano-probes going in?"

Aidra shifted from foot to foot. Hadn't this guy read any of the brochures or listened to the sign-up briefing? He knew just enough to be terrified of the whole process. But Kit handled it like a pro, explaining that the nano-machines were so unimaginably tiny, that they were so much smaller than nerve endings, they could not be felt. She went on to tell him how brain chemistry worked and how easy it was to manipulate. Add some n-tech to get the flow started, make sure the brain was flooded with amines, and the subject was essentially really, really awake. Awake, but without enough acetylcholine to process memory.

Of course, this also left the Exersleeper unable to make any kind of conscious decisions without help, which was one of the many reasons Exersleep was so expensive. It wasn't just the exercise equipment that provided a full-body workout. It was also the attendants. They were all highly trained, bonded, and insured. Every session was recorded. Aidra trusted them with her life.

At least, she'd like to trust them, if she could ever get in there.

She leaned around the newbie and tried to catch Kit's eye. How long would she have to wait? She was a regular. This guy was just a tryer. It wouldn't take Kit but a moment to change her appointment. Aidra made a show of wrapping two bills of tempcash around her membership card and held it where Kit could see.

"And this monthly fee?" the newbie asked. "That's a fixed amount? With all the bad publicity you guys are getting, I'd expect you to be slashing your prices."

Aidra rolled her eyes for Kit's benefit. So that was the game. He wasn't afraid of the process any more than any other newcomer. He was just looking for a bargain.

"What bad publicity?" Kit asked, all innocence. "If you're uncomfortable with the process, then perhaps you shouldn't try it today." She peered around the man and beckoned to Aidra. "Can I help who's next?"

The tryer whirled around to glare at Aidra before moving to block her line of sight, determined to keep Kit's attention. "I was just asking—"

Aidra moved past him and slid her card and the tempcash into Kit's hand. The cash went into the receptionist's pocket, the card into the reader, and a locker key was presented to Aidra, all without Kit turning her gaze away from the newbie.

As Aidra walked toward the locker room, Kit was explaining the brief life of a nano-machine, telling the newcomer how it died off once it exhausted its power supply, then was flushed from the body several hours later.

Aidra changed into her snugsuit slowly and deliberately, determined to remember every movement. She tested her twisted ankle, making sure it would go through the full range of motion. It felt fine. She emerged from the locker room and headed to the women's side of the gym.

She was greeted by an attendant named Veronica, a young woman with a thick Spanish accent and hair so long she could sit on it. Aidra kept her eyes on Veronica so she wouldn't have to look at the other women in the room. She didn't need to see their blank stares and robotic movements.

The n-tech delivery system wasn't complex, but it required a fair amount of hardware. The Exersleepers wore headgear that wrapped around the back of the head and up to their temples and over their foreheads. The women stood in cage-like machines with a series of pullies and counterweights to make for an efficient full-body workout. Each attendant took care of three customers, murmuring instructions and correcting posture as needed, the Exersleeper oblivious to it all.

"Full cycle today?"

"I always do a full cycle, Veronica."

"You sure? Your card says you've been here fourteen days in a row. Might be time to take a break."

"I've got a lot on my schedule."

Veronica shook her head, making her meter-long ponytail dance. "If you want. Full cycle for you."

Aidra relaxed, already anticipating how good she'd feel when it was over. Not only would she be flooded with endorphins, but her brain would feel like she'd had a full night's sleep. She closed her eyes as Veronica fitted the headgear around her neck and up to her temples. As always, she waited to feel something from the nano-probe, some indication that tiny, unseen robots were being injected at the base of her skull. But, of course, there was nothing.

"See you in an hour."

She opened her eyes and gave a little bark of surprise. "Get away from me!" In that one eyeblink, Veronica had been replaced by the hideous mug of Ugly Ben, the most popular news spinner in Detroit. Aidra pushed him away and sat up. She could tell by her sweaty body and loose muscles that her Exersleep session was over. She wondered how long Ugly Ben had been standing there, watching her move in the machines. And what had the creep done with Veronica?

"What the hell are you doing here?" Aidra demanded.

"Waiting to talk to you. Didn't Mr. Lynch tell you we set up an interview?"

"But not here!" Aidra gestured at the gawking attendants and oblivious Exersleepers. "Are you crazy? You can't just ambush a person at her gym."

"I believe I've proven that I most certainly can." Ugly Ben raised his eyebrows and ran a hand over his hairless scalp. He seemed to have gotten some new tattoos since Aidra had seen him last, but it was hard to tell. His bald head was almost completely covered in day-glow designs. He wore a white track suit stretched over his ample frame and white sneakers. It made him look like a demented nurse from a horror show.

Aidra stood and marched toward the door. Ugly Ben followed her into the lobby. "If you would simply see—"

"I'm not talking to you," Aidra said. "Not here."

"This is the ideal place to talk. After all, we both need to be seen. Why not be seen in a place that shows you still trust those little bugs in your head?"

Aidra stood in the shadow of the palm trees and glared at him. She could feel the endorphins from her workout fading fast. She was hot and sweaty and she had a hundred better things to do than to talk to a spinner right now. But Ugly Ben wouldn't quit. Next time, he'd catch her someplace worse.

"Come on," he said, seeing her waver. He was carrying a black, plastic case, which he switched to his other hand so he could draw out his wallet. "I'll buy you a smoothie."

"Fine," she said. "A small one." The smoothie stand was almost empty. Maybe this wouldn't be so bad. They could be done talking before more than a handful of people saw them together. Aidra captured the round table in the farthest corner and perched on the edge of a chair while Ugly Ben ordered.

A moment later, he placed two of the recovery smoothies on the table and took the seat opposite her. He placed his plastic case on the floor.

Aidra pointed to his cup. "And what are you recovering from?"

"Exercising my right to free speech."

"Clever."

"You think so?"

"Not really." She took a sip of the recovery fluid. Yuck. Ugly Ben had ordered the cheapest smoothie on the menu. It had none of the bee pollen and kiwi and pineapple she liked and all of the wheatgrass and alfalfa she didn't. She set it aside.

"How's your dog?" Ugly Ben asked.

Aidra bristled. "I don't have a dog."

"Of course you don't. I mean, how is your pet caline?"

Aidra crossed her arms and narrowed her eyes. "You know I don't talk about Madeline. Not to you, not to anyone in the press."

"All right. Your choice. Always your choice." Ugly Ben leaned forward in his chair. "How's the rest of your family? Your kid?"

"Nope," Aidra said. "Not happening. Either we talk about the current case, or we don't talk."

"Aaannnd the ice remains unbroken." Ugly Ben wagged a finger at her. "We're supposed to have a rapport, you and I. When your bosses at Fitz-Cahill set this up . . . I mean, what happens when I tell them you balked? Because that's what you're doing, you know. Balking."

"Fitz-Cahill asked me to cooperate with spinners. They don't care which ones. I could give this exclusive to Tom Griffon Junior or Marcia in the Morning."

Ugly Ben's pointer finger sank toward the floor. "You'd drag your name to that level?"

She barked a surprised laugh. "What level do you think you're on?" But it was a cheap shot and Ugly Ben knew it. As far as local spinners went, he was the best. And if she didn't respect him much, she at least trusted him. He had his own weird integrity that involved long-term planning and protecting his sources—if they remained useful.

"You, madam, have, as they say, reached a plateau. You are up on that high and windy place, thanks, in no small part, to me and my show. If you want your star to rise once more into the firmament—"

"Firmament?"

"Into the firmament," he intoned, "you will allow me to tag along. But I owe my viewers more than that. Much more. I'm going for the truth here."

Aidra leapt to her feet. "And what makes you think I'm not?"

"Truth. A good story. It's all the same to them."

She turned on her heel and made for the locker room.

"Stop, Aidra, stop."

She kept walking. "You and your viewers can stick it. I've got work to do." She wanted a shower. The sweat had cooled and pooled under her bra and she felt strangely oily.

He trailed after her. "Wait, wait, wait. Madam, please." When she didn't stop, he made a diving tackle, capturing her ankle. Some of the patrons stared, but no one seemed inclined to interfere. Aidra caught her balance with her other foot just in time to avoid toppling on top of him. She wrestled her ankle out of his grasp, but only by popping off her shoe. She took two short hops away from Ugly Ben.

He stood and held out her sneaker. "Now you'll talk to me? Because you won't get far without this."

She reached for her shoe, but he passed it from hand to hand, playing keep-away. She didn't fight long. Instead, she took off the other shoe and threw it at him. "You're an asshole, Ugly Ben."

"Yes, madam. That, I am. And you're making a scene."

"*I'm* making a scene?" But he was right. Everyone in the lobby was staring. At the front desk, Kit looked like she was about to come over and help, but Aidra waved her back.

"I'll be good," Ben said. "Okay? I'll be good. I'll behave. Come, sit. Drink your smoothie."

"Give me my shoes."

"When you sit down."

Aidra growled, but walked back to the table in her stocking feet. She'd already lost one pair of shoes today and didn't feel like losing another. She'd give Ugly Ben two minutes. Three, tops. If he stepped out of line again, Bryan would just have to find another spinner to annoy her.

Ugly Ben handed back her sneakers. "Let's start fresh, shall we? Can we do that? Start fresh?" He removed a headcam from the plastic case. "Tell me what you want to broadcast. You tell, I spin, viewers gawk, everyone wins. Give me some juice, though. I can't sell anything dry. Juice it up. Slick and wet. Slippery. Don't forget, you need this."

He's right, Aidra thought. *I need this*. She had to keep her job. She had rent, a car, Jon's tuition. She belonged to the world's most expensive gym that she couldn't afford to leave. In a way, she and Ugly Ben weren't that different. Their reputations were everything. She reached out and touched his arm, stopping him from putting the camera on his head. "Look, I'm floundering, here."

Ugly Ben put the camera down, waiting.

"I always flail around a bit at the beginning of an assignment, but it's never taken me this long to get my bearings. I don't know a damn thing right now. I know as much as someone can learn from a webzine."

Ugly Ben folded meaty hands over his round belly. "I can tell you what the general chatter on the street is."

"How many theories have you heard?"

Ugly Ben counted off silently by touching his fingers to his thumb one by one.

"Forget I asked."

"The prevailing wisdom is that Jean Claude Gascoigne resented Mackenzie Fox's success. Mackenzie was successful far longer than Jean Claude was, plus he got the girl."

"But Gascoigne could have killed Fox any time. Why do it in public?"

"He just snapped?" Ugly Ben asked. "Further proof that Exersleep plus Learning Systems is a recipe for disaster."

"It doesn't make sense," Aidra said. "Blaming the n-tech hurts Gascoigne's company just as much as it hurts Fox's."

"So what do you think it is?" Ugly Ben asked. "I bet you think the wife is involved somehow. Because the wife's always involved. Did you talk to Mrs. Fox?"

"Yes."

"Is she evil?"

"No."

"Well, there goes that theory." He crossed off an imaginary list. "My fans really liked that one, too. I'm not thrilled with you right now, Aidra. You're supposed to be telling me something. What about—"

Aidra held up a hand to forestall another question. "You've got to understand. It's not that I don't want to cooperate, it's that I can't. I've got nothing to give you."

"All right, my dear lady," Ugly Ben strapped the headcam on, hiding his scalp tattoos. "I'm going to help you. One time only. Let's do a puff piece. My viewers like you. They'd much rather look at you than me." He made an adjustment to the angle of the camera. "But I need to tell you something. Something important."

"What?"

"A puff piece has a very short shelf life. I'm going to expect some juice from you and I want it soon. You either give it to me, or I suck it out of you." Ugly Ben rounded his lips and inhaled wetly.

Aidra pointed to his head. "I can't talk to you when you're wearing that."

"And I can't talk to you without it."

"It gives me the creeps."

"It saved your life."

Aidra had a brief flash of herself lying on the ground, a dozen guns ready to fill her with bullets, Ugly Ben's voice cutting through the chaos. "That can't be the same headcam. It would be, like, four years old."

Ugly Ben touched his index finger to the strap. "It's my lucky device."

Aidra nodded. Maybe that's what she needed—some kind of talisman or lucky charm to point the way, because right now, she was flying blind.

CHAPTER EIGHT

When Noah called the next morning, she was ready to hear him strut and crow about his tremendous victory over Re-Buy's computers on Gilly's behalf. Instead, he scolded her for being on the wrong side of town, late for an appointment. "You were supposed to be at the Detroit Detention Center ten minutes ago," he said. "You're late."

"For what?" Aidra asked.

"Didn't you get my e-gram? And why are you sending me this noise, anyway? Am I your secretary now?"

"What e-gram? I've been in my car." She had work to do, clients to see, wages to earn. She'd left the Detroit Athletic Club yesterday with a renewed sense of urgency. Ugly Ben had been right, she needed to get some answers quickly. People were starting to nail down firm opinions about the safety of n-tech, and she needed to get ahead of it, before public speculation turned to certainty.

She'd spent the night doing research, trying to get enough background on the technology to separate fact from fiction. The next time someone told her that n-tech was dangerous, she wanted the knowledge to shut them down.

She'd sent all her incoming calls and messages to Noah, knowing he'd alert her if there was something truly important. What she hadn't known was that he'd wait until she was already ten minutes late before doing so.

"And exactly why am I going to the jail?"

"For your appointment," Noah said. "With Jean Claude Gascoigne."

Aidra hit the brakes and skidded into a right turn, causing the cars behind her to lay on the horns. She barreled down the side street until she could make another right and double back the way she'd come. She'd just finished dropping Madeline off at her sister's house and was on her way to another stakeout, but that could wait. If Jean Claude Gascoigne was willing to see her, *everything* could wait. She told her car the new destination and watched the map on the companel update itself.

"How did you do it?" she asked Noah.

"I didn't. You did." She could hear something like wonder, or perhaps admiration, in his voice. "Did you know they have e-verse access in jail? Nothing useful, but they get all the entertainment programming they want. Gascoigne saw you on The Ugly Ben and demanded to meet you. I got calls from three lawyers and a paralegal secretary."

"Why so many? If one lawyer asked me, I'd go."

"None of them were *asking* you."

"Demanding?"

Noah snorted. "Opposing. Objecting. Practically threatening you into not going."

She lifted her foot from the accelerator, bringing her car down to the legal limit. "If his own lawyers don't want me there . . ."

"Doesn't matter. Gascoigne wants to see you. Said he needs to set the record straight. You've been talking to spinners and I guess he can't have that. Not without telling you his side of the story."

She glanced at the readout on the companel. "Car says I'll be there in seven minutes. Contact the jail and tell them to wait."

"No, you do it."

"You call the lawyers, then. Tell them to get stuffed. I'll pay you double for that."

"Ha!" Noah barked. "I'll make those calls for free."

The Detroit Detention Center was located northeast of Cityheart, on prime real estate that nobody wanted in the last century, when the jail was built. Everyone wanted it now. There was always talk of moving the jail to someplace less desirable, perhaps on the outskirts of town, closer to the zone. But no politician wanted to make it their platform, so The Detroit Detention Center stayed on Mound Road, a sad reminder of a less prosperous time.

Aidra had just pulled into the visitor lot when her companel trilled for attention. The picture on the screen showed a pleasant-looking woman in her middle thirties, smiling widely into the camera pickup. Her credentials said she was a spinner for CI newsnet.

Aidra hesitated with a hand on the door. *Dammit.* They were expecting her at the jail. She was already late. But Bryan wanted her to be nice to reporters. She hated the fact that being seen doing her job was sometimes more important than actually doing it, but it wasn't worth arguing with Bryan about. She connected the call.

The woman introduced herself as Rosita—Aidra didn't quite catch the mumbled last name—and continued to smile a hollow, plastic smile. Her voice was flat, her motions robotic.

Aidra's first thought was of Morris. He delighted in using different MASCs, trying to fool her into thinking she was talking to someone else. But Morris would never use a MASC this bad. The multiple algorithmic scanning coprocessor was supposed to mimic facial movements, syncing with the user to provide a seamless experience. When you talked, your MASC talked. When you blinked, your MASC blinked.

This one didn't blink at all.

It stared straight ahead with dull zombie eyes. The small movements around the mouth were off as well, as if the woman had been injected with Novocain at the dentist and hadn't quite realized her lips were numb. The cheek and neck muscles weren't right, either. But it was the eyes that bothered Aidra the most. Flat, dead, with none of the bright interest humans naturally had.

"May I help you?"

"Yes," the MASC said. "I'm calling to interview you."

Aidra blinked at the screen. Why the secrecy? Spinners loved the camera. "I'm sorry, I'm going to have to end this call. I don't talk to MASCs." Which wasn't exactly true. Aidra talked to MASCs all the time—probably more often than she knew, since some of them were perfect simulations. But she wasn't talking to this one.

"Please, Ms. Scott, if I could just have a moment of—"

"You've already taken more than I care to give. If you'll remove the disguise, we can talk." She reached for the cutoff button.

"Wait."

"Please don't call me anymore."

"I said, wait."

The MASC dissolved to reveal a child with dramatically up-swept hair, blinking rapidly into the pickup camera. She wore a fuzzy purple sweater. Matching fuzzy pom poms decorated each earlobe.

"Hello, Juniper." Aidra didn't know whether to be disappointed or impressed. She thought a child as brilliant as Juniper Fox would use a better MASC. Then again, Juniper had probably programmed the scanning coprocessor herself, which was downright scary. If she was this good at age six, she'd outstrip even Morris' abilities in a year or two.

"Now can we talk?" Juniper asked.

"Why the MASC?"

"Because I thought you wouldn't let the call through if you knew it was me."

"You were right. I know it's difficult, Juniper, but I can't talk to you."

"But you're supposed to tell me about your progress."

"I'm *what?*"

"Are you still trying to prove that—"

"There is no way I'm going to discuss anything about this case with you."

"Why not? You work for my family's company, which means you work for me."

Aidra bit off a nasty retort. Juniper was mentally far above her age, but emotionally, she was still in kindergarten. Couple that with a strange childhood where she was alternately adored and hated, and no wonder her perceptions were off.

But how was Aidra supposed to answer? She couldn't talk down to Juniper, but she couldn't talk to her as a peer, either. She decided to keep it short, honest, and to the point. "I told you, I don't work for your father's company," she said. "I work for Fitz-Cahill."

Juniper nodded slowly. "I see."

"I'm glad you understand. Now, I really must go."

"Oh, I understand all right," Juniper said. "You're giving me the brush off. I'm just a little kid. It's easy to lie to me."

"I wasn't lying."

"We *own* the company."

"I know that, Juniper. But you don't own me. We need to end this call. Give my best to your mother."

"But—"

"Where is your mother?" Aidra asked. "Perhaps I could explain to her that—"

"No. You can't talk to her."

"But I think she should know that—"

"Don't tell," Juniper whispered.

"What?"

"Please don't tell her. Don't." Her lower lip quivered.

"Did she say not to call me?"

"No!"

"But she wouldn't like it if you did," Aidra guessed.

"Don't tell her. Please, don't tell." Juniper's eyes glistened but she fought back the tears. Aidra found this more moving than full-on waterworks. She could dismiss fake crying, but to both summon up tears and try to disguise them at the same time was beyond most trained actresses, much less a little kid.

Aidra sighed. "End the call right now and I'll pretend it never happened."

Juniper couldn't reach for the cutoff button fast enough.

Aidra stared at the blank comscreen. What an odd child. She considered calling Hannah anyway, to talk mom-to-mom, but she'd given Juniper her word. Aidra would tell Hannah if it ever happened again, but as long as Juniper left her alone, she'd keep her secret.

The visiting room was empty. A dozen tables were arrayed in two rows of six, bolted to the floor, as were the chairs on one side of each table. Tinted windows ran along the sides of the room, with doors on the other two sides. The door behind Aidra led back to the vetting area, the security checkpoints, the freedom of the world.

The CEO of Learning Systems stepped through the door in front of her.

Jean Claude Gascoigne wasn't a huge man, but he was a strong one. His muscles rippled under his orangeskin uniform. His neck was finely corded and though his right wrist was encased in a cast and his forehead was covered in bruises, his stay in jail had not dulled his intensity or slowed his gait.

Aidra backed off a step. She'd wanted this interview—wanted it desperately—but now that she was in the same room as Gascoigne, all she could think about was the holo-image of him shooting Mackenzie Fox at close range, and how effortless it had seemed.

The two guards who'd accompanied Gascoigne remained in the room. One black, one white, both short, and both of them staring at Aidra in a way she didn't like. Not leering, but close enough. Even so, she was glad to have them here. As calm as Gascoigne appeared, he was still a killer. She watched with gratitude as the guards shackled Gascoigne's legs to the immobile chair on the prisoner's side of the table. They left his hands free, but there was a wide slab of table between them and the chair Aidra sat in moved freely. She could leap out of the way if necessary.

Neither of the guards wore datashades or body cameras. The privacy laws extended to prisoners, too. No one could record what went on in this room. But nobody could stop the guards from eavesdropping, either. Information was currency, and information from something this high-profile would be a nice supplement to a guard's salary.

Gascoigne glared at his captors until they'd backed off a few meters. He turned to Aidra. "My lawyers don't want me talking to you."

"I received the same impression."

His voice was as featureless as the walls. "My lawyers don't want me talking with anyone."

There didn't seem to be a snappy comeback to that.

"I'm sorry," he said. "Introducing myself seemed superfluous at this point."

"And you know who I am."

"Would I have asked to see you if I didn't?"

"Dr. Gascoigne, you wanted to see me for a reason. What reason is that?"

"I don't use my doctorate as an honorific. Part of my legal team's advice on the 'public me' is to mention my PhD every chance they get. Now the guy in the cell across the aisle calls me Doc. I would call him Dopey, but that isn't a good idea."

"*Mister* Gascoigne, can we talk about the day you—" Aidra stopped herself as the guards leaned in. She waited. The two guards exchanged glances and then took up positions in the back of the room. The white guy propped himself against the wall while his partner patrolled the perimeter.

Gascoigne cocked an eyebrow. "Patience. It's one of the greatest virtues of the Supremium. They will grow tired of us soon enough. Then we can have a conversation."

Aidra doubted the guards would stay out of earshot for long. She wasn't entirely sure she wanted them to. Out of earshot meant out of arm's length. She scooted her chair back a fraction, measuring the distance Gascoigne could reach. Better. "I understand you still don't have any recollection of the incident," she said.

Gascoigne's gaze sharpened. He folded his arms and his uniform squeaked. "What you're looking for is a plausible reason for me to kill one of my oldest friends in the world." Gascoigne unfolded his arms and squeaked again. He grimaced at the orangeskin and swiped at it. "Trying to sleep in these things is infuriating."

"Mr. Gascoigne—"

"I get time for exercise every day in here. I hate to exercise. So boring. And I have to listen to this peel squawk through my every movement."

"I'm sorry, but—"

"Then there's my enhancements from Learning Systems. I download all the books I'm allowed and wonder how long before my upper level connections start to atrophy. I know all the research data, but there are variables. If I can keep using it all, perhaps I won't become as dim-witted as him." He pointed to the guard holding up the wall. "Or him." He pointed to the one prowling around the room. Gascoigne rested his hands on the table, looking Aidra up and down as if measuring her for something.

She noticed that he still held a finger outstretched, pointing directly at her. She looked everywhere but at the table, not giving him the satisfaction of a reaction.

Where was the famous Supremium charm? They were supposed to be less arrogant than this. Of course, Supremiums thought they were better than everyone else, but they didn't make a big deal of it. They held their heads up, but never felt they needed to put others down to do so.

Well, why not use it? The dumber she played it, the more Jean Claude Gascoigne would need to prove his superiority. She'd just keep asking questions, letting him talk.

"The three of you worked together," she said. "You, Mackenzie, and Hannah. Who started the original company?"

Gascoigne sighed and answered in a flat tone. "We all did. All three of us. We went to college together, and stuck with each other through grad school at MIT. It wasn't easy finding university research positions as a three-person unit, but none of us was willing to go without the others. We tried it, once. Hannah did a post-doc at Caltech while we stayed at MIT. That lasted two months. We missed her too much."

"So you started a company to lure her back?"

"Well, sure," Gascoigne answered. "Who wouldn't want to work with his two best friends?"

"So why did you split off your own company?"

"There is no possible way I could explain this technology so someone like you would understand."

"Try me."

"I will not. Except to say that our research went in divergent directions. Learning Systems and Exersleep are complementary technologies, but hardly identical."

"There were lawsuits."

"Settled." Gascoigne's uniform made a scratchy creak as he crossed his arms.

"The timing is quite a coincidence. Didn't you leave the company as soon as your two best friends announced their engagement?"

Gascoigne blinked at her for a long, silent moment. He looked over his shoulder at the guards and lowered his voice. "It's true. Long ago in a research facility far, far away I was in love with Hannah Wells, but—" His eyes found hers and his head shook the tiniest fraction, "Mackenzie was also in love."

"With Hannah."

"No."

Aidra got it then, and it didn't take a Supremium's brain to figure it out. There were only three people in this triangle, so if Mackenzie wasn't in love with Hannah . . . "He was in love with *you*."

She said the last word a bit louder than she'd intended and cut her eyes to the guards. The one by the wall seemed more intent on checking out her legs than in anything she said. The other had circled to the far corner, too far away to hear.

"After it became clear I did not return his affection, he began courting Hannah. Yes, Mack could dance to all kinds of music."

"So Mackenzie Fox stole Hannah from you, married her, and had two children with her just to spite you?" *Cock-block: level, master.*

Gascoigne nodded. Aidra sat back in her chair, seeing the links in the chain come together. Almost.

"And you're telling me Hannah never knew?" she asked.

"She'd never believe it. I tried to tell her years ago when it was fresh and I was feeling bitter. When they say love is blind, what they really mean is that it's deaf. People never hear anything they don't want to, even if—especially if—it's right in front of them."

Aidra scooted her chair back even farther. "So after Fox stole Hannah from you—"

Gascoigne shook his head. "I certainly can't claim Hannah was ever mine to be stolen. She was aware of my feelings, but had no interest in anyone but Mack. He respected her as a brilliant researcher and valued her as a colleague, but until I rejected him, he showed no romantic interest in her at all."

"That must have been difficult," Aidra said.

"Difficult? Yes. Of course." His voice was scathing. "So difficult that ten years later, brooding on how I'd been wronged, I snapped like a twig in a high wind and blew him away in front of the entire world? No."

Maybe. What had Gascoigne just said? *Patience is one of the greatest virtues of the Supremium.* Or maybe he was full of shit.

Aidra sat straighter. "You know who I'm working for. You know what I'm trying to do. And you've just made my case for me."

Gascoigne raised his eyebrows. "Have I?"

"I'm supposed to be proving that you had a motive and you've handed me one."

Gascoigne pulled back as far as his bolted-down chair would

allow. "You think I killed Mack because he stole my girl? That is a reason to hate. That is not a reason to kill."

"Then why tell me at all?"

"I'm not sure. I saw you on The Ugly Ben and you didn't seem like the other turtles, so I—"

"The what?"

He raised his eyebrows, waiting for her to catch up. Then she got it. Compared to Supremiums, everyone else was a turtle.

"Making you the hare, I suppose? Well, we all know who won that race." Aidra tapped a finger on the tabletop. "Fitz-Cahill and Exersleep are playing pin-the-tail-on-the-technology with your company. How do you think a turtle like me is going to help you?"

"Memory."

"Excuse me?"

"Memory is a funny thing," Gascoigne said. "On the most important day of my life, I have a significant measure of time that is simply gone. I have no memory of it. That bothers me. It bothers me more than it should."

"*That's* what bothers you? Not the fact that you killed a man?"

He raised his palms and his orangeskin whined with the movement.

"Do you honestly expect people to believe that the n-tech made you do it?"

"Tell me this, Miss Integral-to-the-Investigation, did they run a full analysis of the nano-machines they found in my bloodstream?"

"Why should they?" Aidra asked. "No matter how you shout it to the media or your lawyers, the fact that you had n-tech in your system doesn't affect this case one way or the other."

Gascoigne groaned and covered his face, as if he couldn't believe her stupidity. "In any event, it's too late. Any nano-machines they extracted from me are all dead by now."

"How convenient for you."

Gascoigne removed his hands from his face and stared directly into her eyes. "Convenient for someone."

She let the stare-down continue for as long as she could stand it, which wasn't long at all. "I might not have multiple PhDs," she said. "But I've read the literature your company has put out. Spent some time with the peer-reviewed studies, too."

Gascoigne's eyebrows shot upward. "You understood them?"

"I have a dictionary. I know how to use it. Looks like it's your word against the entire scientific community."

Gascoigne lifted his shoulders in a noisy shrug.

"Surely you must be mounting a better defense than this. How in the world can you blame the n-tech?"

He made a fist and set it on the table. He stared down at it. "If nano-machines are the cause, then I'm lost. Everything I've worked for my entire life will be gone, and all the people who depend on me and my technology will be hurt. I won't die, but I will feel as though I have, because my entire life will have been a lie. That's door number one."

He curled the fingers of his other hand around his wrist cast and set it on the table as well. "Door number two. If I say I was of sound mind and body when I killed Mackenzie, I am also dead. The best I can hope for—the very best—is to be in prison until they kill me."

"I knew it." Now it was her turn to make fists, although she kept them at her side. "You're choosing door number one to save your own neck. You're going to try to sell that to a jury."

Gascoigne opened his hands and laid them on the table, palms up. "I'm choosing door number one because door number three does not exist."

"Do you think I'd open one for you?" Aidra looked around the empty conference room and signaled the now-distant guards. She stood to go. "I might not be as smart as you are, or have as many advantages, but I am not slow. I am not stupid."

"I never said—"

"You didn't need to. But remember, you're the one wearing the orange suit. You killed Mackenzie Fox and I'm going to find out why." She marched to the outside door and waited for the guard to open it.

She made the mistake of looking back while he was fumbling with the lock. Gascoigne hadn't moved and his expression had barely changed, but his shoulders were slumped and his eyes hooded. The smug, superior corporate titan was gone, replaced by a man with a broken heart and a ruined life and no idea how he got here.

"Do me a favor," he said softly. "When you find out, let me know."

CHAPTER NINE

Aidra dictated notes into her datapad on the way home from the jail. Once there, she encrypted the file and sent it to Bryan. Then she took a shower. She'd already showered once that morning, but something about being inside the Detroit Detention Center made her feel extra dirty.

She was sitting down to a plate of carrot sticks and cheese slices when Bryan called. "That was quick," she said. "I just filed that report."

"And I just read it."

"Honestly, I didn't think anyone read my daily reports."

"Honestly, I didn't used to."

Aidra rearranged the carrots on her plate. Of course Bryan was watching her every move. He was getting tremendous pressure from his bosses. She was torn between making her reports more detailed to please the higher-ups and making them completely vague so they wouldn't backseat drive her case.

"So what do you think?" she asked him.

"I think Jean Claude Gascoigne is going to make bail."

"No, he's not."

"Yes, he is. The judge has every reason to let him out. Even if he disables his GPS implant, he's got spinners following him everywhere he goes. If he doesn't show up for trial, the cops can turn on any newscast and know where to find him."

Aidra bit into a cheese slice. That was a horrible line of reasoning. And also one a judge might buy.

"No matter how high bail is set, he'll pay it," Bryan said. "There's no amount of money that can keep him in jail."

"Let's say he makes bail," Aidra said, thinking it through as she spoke. "There's still a significant stretch between that and an innocent verdict. One doesn't feed into the other."

"It shouldn't," Bryan said. "But with that kind of money involved, it will."

"Let's not get ahead of ourselves, here. My job hasn't changed. I'm going to see Louisa Samahroo in an hour. I need to get some outside confirmation about Gascoigne's relationship with—"

"Yes, sorry," Bryan said. "That's why I called. I looked at your list of action items."

Another requirement of her job. Fitz-Cahill not only wanted to know where she'd been, they wanted to know where she was going next. Aidra often bullshitted this part of her reports, since she never knew where a case would take her, but in this instance, her plans were solid.

"Louisa Samahroo is taking you to lunch," Bryan said.

"No, she's not. We're meeting in her office."

"I contacted her this morning and asked her to take you to lunch."

"No."

"Why not?" Bryan asked. "It won't hurt you to eat some fancy food with a nice person in a swanky place. She's reserved a table for the two of you at the Library. Be there at noon."

Louisa Samahroo's restaurant complex was built in the massive shell of the former Detroit Public Library. It offered ten different dining options ranging from stand-as-you-eat street carts called The Cart Catalogue to a black-tie restaurant called Special Collections, complete with a personal wine steward and pastry chef for each party. The Library was always packed, and no tourist could visit Detroit without eating at one of its tables.

Louisa Samahroo had saved the building from demolition, raised the capital, renovated the site, fought off developers, protesters, and the Detroit City Council, and finally opened not one, not two, but all ten restaurants on the same day. She had accomplished this while getting her law degree and was now starting med school.

She was also friends with both Jean Claude Gascoigne and the Foxes. That's why Aidra wanted to talk to her. She suspected Bryan had a different agenda.

"How many spinners did you invite to this lunch?"

Bryan pinched the bridge of his nose with a pained expression. "I need you doing public things in public. And if you happen to be seen with the most gifted and beloved Supremium in town, all the better."

Aidra pushed aside her snack. "All right, I'll go to lunch." She had to interview Louisa anyway, so she might as well be seen doing it. It was up to the courts to convict Jean Claude Gascoigne, but it was up to her to convince the public it was the right thing to do.

Aidra walked past Translations and up steps that reminded her of childhood visits to church—high, stained-glass windows and wide marble treads with woven runners in the center. The din of the Japanese grille below faded as if she'd gone underwater. Aidra tried speaking a few words out loud. Her own voice didn't echo off the polished walls. She looked for—and found—the sound baffles above.

Louisa Samahroo's offices were in a part of the Library known as Reference. At Aidra's knock the door opened. After the cool tranquility of the hallway, she was engulfed in chaos.

She wasn't prepared to walk in on a party of twenty. The music was swing-fusion, not too loud to talk, but just barely. A few people moved in place, swaying to the music, but most seemed to ignore it. Everyone was deeply involved in conversation. Bright lights shone from wall sconces aimed at the hot orange ceiling—no, as she looked up it shifted to a cool aquamarine. The entire feel of the room changed, became less hectic. The music altered only slightly in volume and tempo, but things seemed more relaxed as the crowd changed postures. Shoulders lowered, voices became more modulated, a few smiles broke out.

"Aidra Scott."

Somewhere in her rich and varied ancestry, Louisa Samahroo must have had an elm tree. Aidra had seen plenty of vid of the creator and owner of the Library, but she was still surprised to be towered over. Louisa smiled sympathetically, reading Aidra all too clearly. Dark eyes mischievous, her host gestured toward another door. Aidra lifted her jacket with questioning eyebrows and Louisa nodded to bring it along.

On the other side of the door was a spiral staircase going up. The door closed behind them and the music cut off as if a circuit breaker had tripped.

"Sorry to take you away from your celebration," Aidra said.

"Oh, no. That was creative consultation. Happens every day."

"That was work?"

"For the Librarians, yes. That's my management staff. You ever work with the creative?"

"Hardly ever." The liars, cheats, and embezzlers she encountered in her job were crafty at times, but they were predictable. Most of them got caught in the same stupid ways.

"My upper-level people are artists. I look for someone who should be at the top of his or her field, but isn't, usually because they can't put up with the bullshit that accompanies responsibility. I give them modest salaries and the room they need to get things done without having to deal with inter-office politics and ambitious business majors."

"But down there, just now, it didn't look like they were making art."

"Not yet. They were talking about things they saw and problems they had. About things that went wrong and things that went right. Things they read and watched and dreamed. Perhaps five percent of it will go into upgrading the experience of the Library. That's a first-rate return on investment."

"Aren't the music and lights distracting?"

"I'm always tweaking their environment." She grinned down, her teeth a white flash in the staircase. "I need to play, too."

They emerged onto the roof. Aidra shrugged on her jacket. The light wind brought the chill of the river from a kilometer away. Louisa led them toward the front of the building. Across Woodward Avenue, the facade of the Detroit Institute of Arts looked like an ancient temple, its newly restored exterior almost glowing in the spring light.

"I keep the music loud to favor the assertive and goad the introverts. A worthy idea has a life of its own, needs to be heard, will get itself heard. If I can make a quiet little mouse shout, the mouse has something to say."

"And do you pay for Exersleep and Learning Systems for them?" Aidra asked. "Hard to be Supremium on a modest salary."

Louisa nodded with absent approval. "So you caught that. I make it a condition of employment and finance them in both treatments. A Supremium is worth her weight in gold. I make it so they want to work for me for the fun of it and they can pursue whatever other interests they have with everything that's left over."

Aidra thought about the joy of working at the Library with other Supremiums, the delight in talking to other people with similar ability and ambition. A conversation of the blessed. But it locked them in, too. Quit the Library, and it was back to talking to the turtles.

Louisa's pocket chirped for attention and she pulled out an ultra-slim datapad. "Just let me take care of this. Thirty seconds. No more. You can time me."

Aidra propped her elbows on the half wall and looked out over the soft, rounded skyline. Solar panels glinted in the sunshine while the muted green of eco-roofs complimented the blue of the sky.

Detroit had historically been industrial, with function more important than form. But the emptying out of the city at the turn of the century, followed by the high-tech boom, had transformed the skyline. Rugged steel and brick factories had given way to glass and greenery and neon. The brown of a city that wasn't afraid to get its hands dirty had become the white and silver and watercolor hues of a city that cleaned up after itself.

The view was only marred by the cranes jutting over the new vertical farm being built two streets over. Its specialty was going to be Asian greens that were too delicate to ship and had to be grown locally, like hollow-stem spinach and pea shoots. Aidra wondered if any of the vegetables would show up on plates at Louisa's restaurants.

She turned in the other direction and watched the gaudy holos that floated above Autumnland theme park like apple-shaped clouds until Louisa closed the cover of the datapad and joined her at the wall. "Sorry about that."

"No problem. Restaurants must take constant attention."

"Oh, that was a legal case," Louisa said. "And class notes for school. And checking in with my fiancé."

"That's a lot to keep track of."

"I manage," she said. "My gadgets help."

"I suppose Learning Systems helps, too. How often do you go?"

"I went every forty-eight hours at first. The feeling is incredible. Almost addictive. It was like waking up. I was asleep. Parts of me, important parts, were asleep and I never knew it. It's fun seeing some of my Librarians still in that initial phase—watching them realize their potential a bit more after each session."

"But you don't go as much now?"

"I've reached the maintenance level. I've made about as many new neural connections as a human mind can have. Now, I just go three times a month to keep the connections strong."

"How do you know what's enough?" Aidra asked. The research she'd been doing was highly contradictory on that point.

"I suppose we'll never know if we've reached our full potential. But does it matter? It's not what the connections do, it's what you do with them."

"Can I ask you something?"

"I can guess what it is. You're wondering if I ever have second thoughts about using Learning Systems in conjunction with Ex-ersleep." Louisa looked out over the silver and green cityscape, breathing deeply.

"So do you?" Aidra asked.

"Do I have second thoughts about being Supremium? Never. It's allowed me to live my dreams." She held up her e-ssistant with her law/medicine/relationship data. "All of them."

"And if Jean Claude Gascoigne walks free? If he convinces people n-tech is dangerous? If they outlaw Exersleep, or Learning Systems, or both?"

"My dream ends." Finally something had gotten through that calm. Louisa looked strange without her smile. Alien. "I'm haunted by the thought. I know it wouldn't happen all at once and I certainly wouldn't lose everything. It might even be so gradual that I don't notice things slipping away. But I think that's even more heartbreaking. Don't you?"

Aidra stared back silently, wondering how Louisa did it. It was such an obvious plea for sympathy and understanding, and yet Aidra found herself swallowing it whole. It was sad to think about what would happen to the Supremiums if the nanotech enhancements were outlawed. After all, *they* hadn't done anything wrong.

Louisa touched her arm "Ah, but that's never going to happen, so why even talk about it? Let's go eat. What are you in the mood for?"

"I thought you reserved a table."

"I'll let you choose. The Library is yours."

Aidra consulted her stomach. Anywhere in the building, from Special Collections on the top floor to Checkouts—the diner near the entryway. What was she hungry for? None of it. "Actually," she admitted. "I don't usually eat at this time of day. But I suppose I could—"

"Me either!" Louisa crowed. "Oh, God, that is so refreshing. People always expect you to eat—"

"At *their* mealtimes," Aidra finished for her.

"Exactly." They shared a moment that only the live-all-days understood.

"I'd love a cup of coffee, though," Aidra said.

"Splendid." Louisa led them back to the stairs. "It will give me a chance to check on the new ordering system at Dewey's. You can let me know what you think of it."

They headed for the great hall on the first floor. Dewey's was the coffee shop to end all coffee shops. You could get a plain cup of joe or the very latest in trendy, technicolor lattes. You could sit on a counter stool or sprawl on any of a dozen couches around a many-sided fireplace. Dewey's seemed crowded, but the line moved quickly.

"Excellent," Louisa said. "Wouldn't you say?"

"I give up. What am I looking for?"

"We've started offering the 'regular-faves' option on customers' datapads. You set your usual order, and when you get close to Dewey's, it sends you a query to see if you want it. If you say yes, it's waiting for you when you get to the counter."

Aidra's friend Gilly loved the feature, wouldn't shut up about it. "My neighbor insists it's almost telepathy. What was the problem?"

"Quirks in the queue. The tiniest of delays in line and you're waiting. Or if there's no one ahead of you, your order sits there, sometimes for too long. Precipitates form in the solution, or the topping melts off into goo, or the coffee is tepid. My goal is for your drink to arrive at the same moment you do."

"Did you add more baristas?"

"We tried, and it helped when traffic was heavy, but it wasted manpower on slow days."

Aidra watched the queue flow forward in a steady stream. Behind the counter, baristas were broken out into specialty. "Got it," Aidra said. "You counted the people in line. Not only the sheer number of customers, but how long each order takes to make. A five-person queue looks different if everyone is getting a plain pour than if everyone is getting a pink-and-blue cappuccino."

"Each drink has a complexity number," Louisa confirmed.

"So it's just math from there on in. Complexity times position in line divided by the number of baristas working."

Louisa clapped delighted hands. "The algorithm is a bit more detailed than that, but not by much. Where were you six months ago? We could have used your help."

Aidra smiled, pleased by Louisa's regard. Then she caught herself. All she'd done was observe. She didn't think up this system. Louisa was just being nice.

Louisa held up her e-ssistant. "What will it be?"

"Plain coffee. Hot."

"Black? Blue? Green?"

"Black."

Louisa ordered the same. They retrieved their drinks and found a table with enough visibility to be seen from anywhere in the coffee shop, but enough sound baffles to make their conversation private.

"May I join you?" A young woman approached their table. She was wearing a skirted suit, dressy shoes, and understated jewelry. Aidra assumed she was one of Louisa's Librarians. But then she noticed the minicam peeking out of the woman's pocket. A spinner. They were soon joined by a second and a third, all of them pulling in chairs and squeezing around the table.

Louisa smiled warmly at them. "What can I do for you today?"

"How are staffing levels?" the first spinner asked. "Have any of your top management quit this week?"

"No, of course not."

"They're all keeping up with their treatments?" the second one asked. "Nobody has opted out of Learning Systems or Exersleep?"

"Why would they?"

"So we can report your full confidence in both kinds of

enhancements?" the third asked. Like the first two, he kept his voice at a low conversational volume.

Aidra stared at the faces around the table. Who were these people? News spinners didn't look like this and they certainly didn't act like this. Where were the loud clothes and loud hair and loud questions?

Figures. Louisa insisted upon—and got—the best of everything, including spinners. And what did Aidra get? Bottom feeders who ambushed her in public and chased her through parking lots.

"So you don't have second thoughts about running your empire with Supremiums?" the first spinner asked. They were taking turns, nobody talking over anybody else.

"Never," Louisa said.

"Even though one of your friends is accused of murder?"

"Acquaintances," Louisa said. "And no."

The spinners took Louisa at her word, backing down from that line of questioning. They asked a few more softball questions, and when Louisa requested privacy, they left the table, even replacing the chairs on their way out.

"How did you do that?" Aidra asked. "I've never been able to make a spinner listen to a thing I say."

"I enjoy the media people. I invite them to events. I feed them meals."

"Too bad I can't cook." Aidra lifted her cup and took a cautious sip. Delicious. And just the right temperature. As if Louisa had timed the spinners' coming and going to coincide with the cooling of their beverages. But that was too perfect, even for Dewey's.

"I went to the Detroit Detention Center this morning," Aidra said. As they enjoyed their coffee, she told Louisa about her meeting with Jean Claude Gascoigne. Louisa murmured encouragement and nodded in all the right places. "So what do you think?" Aidra asked.

"About . . ."

"Any of it. Why did he do it? And why now?"

Louisa put her cup down. "I have no idea."

"Don't you have a theory? Everyone else seems to."

"I try not to make assumptions about people."

"Oh, come on," Aidra said. "We all do it. It's human nature."

"Why? People aren't going to change in response to your judgment. The whole thing makes me tired." Louisa reached for her coffee. "I'd rather try to understand people."

"Jean Claude Gascoigne is not like you."

"He is very much like me."

"So every Supremium is just one stressful event away from being a total asshole?"

Louisa paused with her cup halfway to her lips. "What do you mean?"

"I mean, I get that he's in jail where he's getting no sleep, bad food, and no privacy. But what if his circumstances are just revealing his true self?"

"Jean Claude is stressed, yes, but that's not why."

Aidra raised her eyebrows in a question.

"He's the CEO of his own company. When do you suppose was the last time someone told him what to do?"

"Um . . . never?"

"And how often do you think he's told what to do while in jail?"

"About every five minutes?"

"For a man like him, that's intolerable. I'm not excusing his rudeness, I'm saying I know where it comes from."

"He called me a turtle."

Louisa's cup clattered on the table. "He didn't."

"Yep. Turtle."

"Okay, he's an asshole."

Aidra laughed. "See? I knew you were as human as the rest of us."

Louisa held up her cup. Aidra tapped it lightly with the edge of hers.

"This weird love triangle thing," Aidra said. "Mackenzie being in love with Jean Claude. It seems a bit far-fetched. I mean, how could Hannah not know? She was their best friend."

"So you think Jean Claude manufactured this story out of thin air."

"I wouldn't put it past him." Gascoigne was Supremium. Nothing he said was off-the-cuff or accidental. If things sounded odd, he meant them to sound that way. Aidra didn't know how he was playing her, but had no doubt that he was.

She caught Louisa's expression. "But you don't think so."

Louisa took a long drink of coffee. "I've heard rumors about Mackenzie Fox."

"And rumors usually start somewhere."

"I know a lot of women who threw themselves at him, but he didn't take them up on it."

"That doesn't mean anything. Maybe he was a devoted husband."

"You've seen video of him with Hannah. Did he seem particularly devoted?"

"That doesn't mean he wasn't faithful," Aidra said.

"You know a lot about men, do you?"

"Hardly anything."

They laughed and touched cups again. Talking with Louisa was so darned easy. It was like talking to Quinn or Gilly or someone she'd known forever. She studied the other woman across the table, wondering how Louisa had won her over so quickly. *And could she teach me how?*

"You're the one who hung out with them," Aidra said. "What do you think?"

Louisa tapped her chin, a faraway look in her eye. "There was a fundraiser. An art exhibit and charity auction raising money for Slopes disease. This would have been the night before Jean Claude shot Mackenzie."

Aidra knew about the party. It was all in her case notes, from when Gascoigne and Fox arrived to what they ate and when they left. Some of the party had been recorded, although not much of it had been made public due to the privacy laws. "Did something happen between them?" she asked. "Yelling? Fighting?"

"On the contrary. They spoke together and Mackenzie shook Jean Claude's hand before they left. I think Hannah even hugged him."

"She hugged him?" Were they just keeping up appearances, as Hannah said they did? Or was that friendliness sincere?

"Hannah's a hugger," Louisa said. "Doesn't mean love."

"It probably means something," Aidra said.

"Don't you think you should be asking Hannah about this?"

"She's not returning my calls." Aidra had tried three times since leaving the jail. But maybe it was just as well. How did you ask a woman if her husband was in love with another man?

Louisa drained her cup and stood. "I have a pediatric oncology seminar to attend in forty-two minutes. Can I walk you out?"

Aidra couldn't see a clock anywhere. She wondered if circadian awareness was another benefit of having thousands more neural connections than the average person. As they left Dewey's, she had to powerwalk to keep up with Louisa's long strides, but didn't complain. In fact, she took it as a compliment. After all, you dawdled politely for strangers.

Aidra's datapad chirped. She'd forgotten to silence it. She glanced at the display and groaned.

"Thirty seconds?" Louisa asked over her shoulder. "I could time you."

"It won't even take that long. I'll tell him to call back later."

Aidra opened the connection, preparing to give a quick excuse, but Noah jumped in first. "You can't even begin to guess how tedious it is to look through arrest records. They're all indexed by *date*."

"Noah—"

"So I made a little program to help me find what I was looking for and—"

"Gotta go. Talk later." She disconnected the pad with a sheepish look at Louisa. "Sorry about that."

"He seemed hard at work."

Aidra shook her head. "My assistant doesn't really understand what I do. He's a computer guy. His solution to problems is always more data."

"When what you need is better data."

"Much better."

"If you like, I could look into a few things, talk to a few people, see what I can turn up."

"That would be great," Aidra said. "But I don't know how much I can do with hearsay. Even the things Gascoigne told me aren't things I can bring to Fitz-Cahill or the police."

"Hannah isn't returning your calls."

"No."

"She'll return mine. Let me talk to her and get back to you." Louisa stopped at the outer door of the Library. "Anyway, I still owe you a meal."

"You don't, really."

"I insist. Just be sure it's a time when you're hungry."

"Deal." She waved goodbye and walked out into the afternoon sunshine.

Her feet skipped down the steps to Woodward Avenue, feeling better than she had since taking on this case. She felt like she had a new friend. Even better, she felt like she had a new ally. Of course, Louisa also had an interest in keeping Exersleep and Learning Systems in business, but her offer of help seemed genuine and Aidra had no doubt she'd follow through. It was the puzzle. Give someone like Louisa Samahroo a challenge and she'd rise to meet it. She wouldn't be able to help herself.

No wonder Aidra liked her so much.

CHAPTER TEN

Leaving the Library, Aidra's first thought was that she should call Noah back. Driving time was wasted time and nobody could waste time like Noah Raintree. But she needed to call Pohl Erbie first.

This morning at the jail, Gascoigne had worried about the blood tests they'd done on him. But in the next breath, he claimed that any nano-machine—any evidence—would have died and left his system.

She wondered what Erbie would say about that. He had most of Gascoigne's medical information, or at least the information the lawyers had chosen to share with Fitz-Cahill. According to Erbie, everything was normal. But did he know what normal was for a Su-premium? Someone as nano-phobic as Erbie might not even know what to look for. She trusted his credentials as the lead scientific consultant on the case, but there was no harm in double checking.

She sat in her parked car and commanded her datapad to contact Fitz-Cahill. She had to talk to two e-secs before Erbie came on the line. Over his shoulder, she could see his officemates arguing in the background.

"Sure, we've got them," he said when she explained what she wanted. "We don't have the actual blood samples, but we've got all the information they contained."

"What kind of information?" Aidra asked.

"What are you looking for? Potassium levels? Glucose? Mean corpuscular volume?"

"Do those things affect the amount of n-tech in his brain?"

"Not one bit," Erbie said. "I'm just telling you how complete the tests were."

"Right."

"They took blood every two hours for the first thirty-six after Gascoigne was arrested. Those lawyers are no slouches."

"I think the tests were Gascoigne's idea."

"Sure, sure." Erbie nodded. "He's still blaming the nano-machines for the murder."

Aidra checked her notes in the case file. "Gascoigne Exerslept just before midnight on Thursday. By Saturday morning at five, he'd eliminated all of the nano-machines by the normal means." Aidra didn't know Erbie well enough to say that once the machines died off, they were considered waste products by the body and were shit, pissed, or sweated out of the system.

"So what?"

Aidra counted on her fingers. "That seems long. Don't they leave your body in twenty-four hours? Or is that just Exersleep?" Maybe it was longer for someone who habitually used both Exersleep and Learning Systems.

"That is well within normal parameters," Erbie said. "Anything could affect the degrade time, from the person's metabolism to perfectly legal drugs like caffeine or alcohol or marijuana."

"Was he tested for those?"

"No need to. There's nothing unusual here. Gascoigne had the standard dose of nano-machines and they died right on schedule."

"Mostly on schedule."

"It's not like he took an overdose."

"Because there's no such thing as too much."

"They've got it fine-tuned," Erbie said. "The standard dose is very high, to compensate for a person's weight and age and everything else. So in some sense, you're always overdosing. Who cares? Because your brain can only use a certain amount. Drink a few glasses of water and flush the rest goodbye. But it's not too high, because they don't want to lose money. You could call it the lowest effective dose."

"Why Mr. Erbie, you sound positively positive. Are you sure you don't want to use Learning Systems yourself?"

"Not a chance. There's no way I'm trusting these bugs in my head."

Aidra thanked Pohl Erbie and ended the call. She scrubbed her hand over her face, then rolled her shoulders, trying to release the tension in them. She started her car and put it in gear, thinking about driving away. But to where? It wasn't like she had to go out and catch a bad guy. Her suspect was already in jail. And all of her other work was on hold or parceled out to Noah. She didn't even need to go home, since Madeline was at her sister's house.

Part of her wanted to point her car north and not get out until she'd reached the tip of the Upper Peninsula, hang out with Jon until his final exams were done, and road trip home. But that part of herself was reckless and immature. She needed to act like an adult, including earning a living.

She counted the hours since she'd last Exerslept. Twenty-seven. No wonder she felt so on-edge and grumpy. She thought it was just the coffee wearing off, but it went deeper than that. A blood test would show zero n-tech in her body and that was the problem. She was off her schedule. Her body craved movement, her brain craved rest, and her spirit craved those sweet, sweet endorphins. Time to get to the gym.

Aidra toweled off in the locker room of the Detroit Athletic Club, wondering why a hard workout and a long shower didn't invigorate her the way it usually did. Where was the tingly, alive sensation from every muscle getting attention? Where was the wide-awake, refreshed feeling in her brain? Those things were still there, of course, but it was as if she was reaching for them instead of letting them come to her.

She finished dressing and exited the smoothly modern women's locker room into the brightly lit lobby. She approached the front counter where Kit was waiting for new customers. "Hey, there," Kit said. "Relaxing workout?"

"It was . . . different. I was wondering if I could see my recording."

"Of course." Kit scrolled through menus. "Do you want it here or on your datapad?"

"Send it to my pad, I guess." Aidra had never asked to witness her own workout before, not even as a newbie. But something was definitely different about today. She remembered Ugly Ben sneaking into her workout room yesterday and ambushing her there. What if he—or someone else—had done something like that, preventing her from getting a full cycle? That would explain her uneasy feeling.

As she sat at the smoothie bar watching the recording, she found nothing wrong. The tech had done everything right and so had Aidra.

It had been less than a year since she'd started using Exersleep, and she'd only become a habitual Exersleeper in the last six months. Had it become routine already? Would her after-exercise feeling of satisfaction become more and more elusive as time went on?

She sipped her pineapple-kiwi smoothie and stared at her pad. The answer was not in this gym. After meeting Jean Claude Gascoigne and Louisa Samahroo, there was only one thing she could do. She'd been dancing around this in her own mind all day, but the conclusion was inescapable.

Pohl Erbie's voice echoed in her head. *A little extra doesn't hurt a thing.* It was time for her own extra. She needed to know what the Supremiums knew.

And why not? Being an Exersleeper, she was already halfway there. Learning Systems was waiting for her, open 24/7 with chairs for anyone who could pay. Well, she couldn't pay, but Bryan would probably authorize the charge. Maybe.

She sent him a blip, listing all the reasons she should try a dose of

Learning Systems nanotech and all the reasons Fitz-Cahill should pay for it.

At the reception area, Kit let out a gasp and jerked her head up to look at Aidra, then waved her over. Aidra left her datapad and smoothie behind and hustled to the desk.

"Did you hear?" Kit asked. "I just saw it on the news. He's out." Kit spun her personal pad so Aidra could see. It showed the shaky cam of a live news spin. Jean Claude Gascoigne stood in front of the Detroit Detention Center, wearing the same ornate-style suit he'd been arrested in, smiling for the cameras and thanking his many supporters.

This had to be a simulation. The sleazier spinners liked to run things like this, showing viewers what *could* happen. Aidra checked the corner of the screen, looking for the legally mandated disclaimer—the words that would tell her this was only speculation, not truth.

But it proudly displayed the logo of Tom Griffon Junior. Griffon never used sims. His specialty was live broadcast and raw footage.

She focused again on a beaming Gascoigne, raising his arms in victory, much the way he'd done the day he shot Mackenzie Fox. But today, he simply lowered his arms and pointed to a member of the press standing in the front row. He was ready to take questions.

Kit muted the audio and looked at Aidra with sad eyes. "The bastard is free to walk the streets."

"He still has to go to trial," Aidra countered. "The judge didn't think Gascoigne was a flight risk. That doesn't mean the judge thinks he's innocent." But her voice lacked confidence.

Across the room, Aidra's datapad buzzed. She walked back over to the smoothie bar and snatched it up. Bryan's worried face looked back at her.

"I already saw," she said before Bryan could open his mouth. "Doesn't change anything."

"This changes everything. They're winning."

"Legal games. Nobody thinks that Gascoigne's innocent."

"Everyone thinks that," Bryan said. "That's the problem."

"So let me show them differently. You got my blip."

"Yes, I did," Bryan said. "And the answer is no."

Aidra planted her elbows on the table and held the pad in two hands, looming over it. "There are Supremiums all over this, dancing intellectual circles around me. I need to know what they know."

"Which is what?" Bryan asked. "That being Supremium is great? That people like being smarter than everyone else with all the time in the world? That tells me nothing. You want to be Supremium, do it on your own dime."

"If I had the dimes, I would. Right now all I have is a subsidized gym membership and a whole lot of speculation. I can gather secondhand information all day, but that's not what Fitz-Cahill hired me for. Theory isn't enough. I need experience."

Bryan ran a hand along the back of his neck, then tugged at the flowered lapels of his ornate suit. "Maybe you should talk to Pohl Erbie."

"I just did. And if you want to know Gascoigne's glucose level or the exact pattern of blood spatter on Mackenzie Fox's clothes, then Erbie is your man. If you want to know why Gascoigne did it, you come to me."

"It's easy for you to spend Fitz-Cahill's money. You don't file the expense reports."

"If I don't find some answers soon, neither will you." She immediately regretted the words, especially when she saw Bryan run a hand over his forehead as if trying to forestall a coming headache.

"Come on, Bryan," she tried. "If you're going to go down, go down in style." She realized—too late—how suggestive that sounded, but she just let it hang there.

"Why did he do it, Aidra? What do you really think?"

"I don't know. Maybe I'm not smart enough to know. Not yet."

Bryan tilted his head to one side, and then the other, as if weighing two options.

She looked at Bryan with raised eyebrows, hoping he'd make the right choice.

"I can only authorize one session."

"One is all I need."

"And don't do it in Detroit."

"Why not?" There were Learning Systems chairs all along the Riverfront. She'd planned to trot out one of her false names and slip into one of those.

"Too many newsies," Bryan said.

"Don't you think the spinners will be busy covering Gascoigne's release from jail?"

"It's not a chance I'm willing to take. The spinners love you."

"And whose fault is that?" Aidra countered. "You're the one who wanted me out there, you know, in public."

"You're working for Fitz-Cahill, trying to take Gascoigne down, and you're using the tech he invented? How do you think they'll spin that?"

"It's a show of faith. I trust this technology."

"I don't want you doing free publicity for LS or Gascoigne. Especially not now."

"All right." Now it was Aidra's turn to reach for the cutoff. "But out of town transportation just makes it more expensive."

Bryan shrugged one shoulder. "You'd better make it worth it, then."

Aidra ended the call and put in a blip to Noah. She instructed him to get her an appointment for Learning Systems in Ann Arbor or Toledo or Windsor. Someplace she could get to on the monorail in under an hour. She didn't have any time to waste.

CHAPTER ELEVEN

Aidra sat at a window seat near the back of the monorail car, peering through a thick downpour, watching the outskirts of Ann Arbor come into view. She was struck, as she always was when leaving Detroit, how different other cities looked. It wasn't just that Ann Arbor was smaller or older. Everything here was so square and so gray. Academic cubes and angular research buildings seemed to cut into the skyline. Buildings in Detroit were rounder, newer, and more colorful. Solar stained glass was hugely popular, and Cityheart was a riot of shaded greenery.

Of course, that beauty came at a price. The glittering jewel of a city was surrounded by the no man's land known as the disincorporated zone. No one lived there, at least not officially. In the zone, there were no city services, no schools, no police protection, and no hope. But living in Detroit, it was all-too-easy to forget about the zone and compare the best of her city with the worst of everywhere else.

As they glided toward the station, Aidra glanced at the datapad on her lap, checking the map. She was pleased to see that her destination was only a block away. Noah had scheduled her a same-day appointment in Ann Arbor at a Learning Systems facility connected to a major research lab.

The company itself was headquartered in Detroit, but they liked picking off promising university neuroscientists, and had therefore set up research labs near several colleges. Columbus had the largest R&D department, but Ann Arbor's was almost as big. Aidra wondered about the culture of the town, with the University of Michigan and Learning Systems both trying to make people smarter by different means. Did they argue among themselves? Or did they realize how much they had in common? Both college and nanotech took money, time, and commitment. Mostly money. Both methods were routes to advancement that were closed to all but a few elites.

She thought about her son. Perhaps it wasn't fair to say that college was only for the wealthy. Jon had done all right, and they were far from rich. From the moment he'd entered kindergarten, she'd started making plans for him to go to college. It had killed her to say no to things like trips and treats and techie clothes. Killed her again when carefully saved money would disappear into a car repair or an unexpected school fee. But Jon had made it to his first-choice college with some scholarships to help. *It just takes hard work.*

Her pad signaled an incoming blip, a message from Learning Systems confirming her appointment. How considerate. She opened it and frowned at the message.

[I'm happy to meet with you today, but I have to inform you that our legal counsel will be sitting in. Wanted you to be prepared.]

Aidra stared at the screen. Why would they need their lawyers? Is this what they did for all new clients now? Was the fallout from Gascoigne that bad?

Then she noticed the signature line. It was from Emerald Mathers, head of Research and Development at the research facility on Huron Drive.

Noah, what did you do?

The train pulled into the station and she hurried into the building with the rest of the passengers. She found a bench and ordered her datapad to contact Noah. She gave a cursory look around to make sure she was alone, but at this point, she was too angry to care much about privacy.

"I'm meeting with Emerald Mathers?" she blurted as soon as Noah answered.

"That's right. I did like you asked. I set up the appointment for you." He squinted at her through the screen. "You mad?"

"An appointment for a *treatment*. You were supposed to set me up as an ordinary client."

"Then why didn't you say so? You're all hot and bothered about the science of this thing, peering behind the curtain. How was I supposed to know you just wanted a regular session?"

"Oh, I don't know, maybe because that's what I told you to do?"

"You did?" Noah fiddled with something on his desk. "Oh . . . yeah, I see it now. You did. You want me to cancel the appointment?"

Aidra looked out the station window to the hulking building a block away. "I'll cancel it. In person."

"You sure?"

She reached into her shoulder bag for her umbrella. "May as well. I'm already here."

Emerald Mathers was exactly as Aidra had pictured her—flowing red hair, freckles, wearing black pants and a green sweater under her lab coat. The sweater matched her eyes and Aidra wondered if Emerald's parents had picked her name before she was born, or only after seeing those stunning eyes. Or perhaps it was the other way around. Perhaps she wore contacts to match her name.

She was about thirty, which seemed young for a director of research. But that was the benefit of Learning Systems. The smart got smarter and therefore promoted faster.

At the other end of the age spectrum was Christian Swatt, esquire. Thin, tan, and at least eighty. He had the air of someone who had seen it all, conquered most of it, and had no doubt he could handle whatever was coming next. Aidra would have been intimidated by him if it weren't for his flickering holoset that made his image sparkle and pixelate. She wondered idly where his office was and why he put up with second-rate equipment. But people his age knew the next upgrade was always right around the corner, so why invest too heavily in this one?

"I'm only here to protect Learning Systems' proprietary information," Swatt said by way of introduction. "I won't interrupt, and you can ask any questions you wish. I'll advise Ms. Mathers on whether she should answer them."

Aidra counted silently in her head. Was that two lies or three? She doubted she could ask *any* question, and seriously doubted he wouldn't interrupt. She wasn't sure about the other stuff. She kept a wary eye on the lawyer while talking to Emerald Mathers.

"This is quite awkward," Aidra said. She gestured around the oversized conference room they'd shuttled her into when she arrived. "I meant to make an appointment for a treatment. Please allow me to apologize again for taking up your time, Ms. Mathers."

"Call me Emmy." Her eyes twinkled. "Everyone does. We have a treatment facility, one building over. Unfortunately, they're all booked for today. But don't worry." She fluttered her hands as if trying to smooth things over. "I could start you right here. We've got plenty of materials and I could get you set up in one of the exam rooms."

"Absolutely not." Swatt's image crackled, but his words were clear. "You are not authorized for this. You are not allowed to give undocumented treatments."

Aidra agreed with the lawyer, which surprised her. An off-the-books session sounded great for her wallet, but bad for her brain.

"Who said anything about undocumented?" Emmy lifted an oversized pad from the desk and handed it to Aidra. "You'll still be processed in as a regular user, same as anyone else. Nobody in this building will touch you without proper disclosure forms. I'm sorry, they go on for *pages*, but one signature on the bottom and you'll be an official Learning Systems client."

Swatt made a sound in his throat, but didn't interrupt.

"So, if you'll just sign here, and then the payment screen, I can answer any questions you have before we move to an exam room."

"Shouldn't that be the other way around?" Aidra asked. "You should answer my questions before I sign anything."

"Sure. Sure." Emmy gave another wave of the hand and a sideways glance at Swatt, who made a strangled grunt.

"I've done my homework," Aidra said.

"And I'm willing to bet you still don't know the half of it." Emmy pulled out a tablet and began drawing diagrams. "The system is dynamic and elegant. We don't have to introduce any artificial chemicals at all. Your brain does all the work."

"What do you mean? You're adding *something*."

"It's really the stimulation of the mesocortical pathways that makes it work. We introduce just a few molecules of a polyphenol hydroxylase to trigger a cascade event. In the target areas, the receptors produce additional proteinase horns at an unprecedented rate."

Aidra nodded. The lawyer had not interrupted any of Emmy's explanation. Maybe he knew it would sail right over Aidra's head.

"You've heard the saying, 'neurons that are wired together, fire together,' haven't you?"

"I have now."

Emmy nodded happily. "When we learn something, groups of neurons—we call them constellations—fire together, creating electrochemical channels between themselves and other constellations. It's easier for the impulses to take the path of least resistance rather than go around. By introducing the cascade effect, we can connect more of the constellations than ever before. And here's the biggest benefit. Your brain gives a great return on investment. The building blocks are all right there in your brain chemistry, waiting to be used. It takes only the smallest trigger. Pour a glass of water off a cliff, make a waterfall."

"I thought they were pathways?"

Emmy blinked at Aidra, silent for a moment. Then she wiped her datapad's screen to start over. "It's really very simple. Think of the neural pathways in your brain as roads. Billions and billions of roads and interstates and avenues making connections all the time, okay?"

Swatt cleared his throat and glared.

"Your sense of smell is the most primal. It's hardwired to your memory."

Aidra nodded, thinking of how easily something like the scent of pig manure or fresh hay could send her instantly back to her childhood in Pinckney.

"Your sense of smell is a superhighway. Your other senses are dirt roads in comparison."

Aidra brightened. She got it now. "And Learning Systems makes all your senses into superhighways."

"And raises the speed limit," Emmy said. "After six months of treatments, every neural pathway in your brain is a superhighway and you're going at top speed."

Swatt cleared his throat. "I must advise you to stay with the facts, Ms. Mathers. Going into fanciful imagery doesn't truly represent—"

"And these treatments, they're weekly?" Aidra interrupted. She found it easier to pretend Swatt wasn't in the room.

"Usually," Emmy answered. "Although some people do it more often than that. But you're using the brain's existing chemicals after all, and there's only so much your body can make at once, so we advise people to go slow."

"You sound as if not everyone takes that advice."

"Does anyone take advice? We charge per treatment, of course, and rely on the effects of self-regulation. I won't lie to you. You're going to be one tired puppy after this. Happy, but tired."

"So after six months, you're done?"

"No, of course not. What kind of business model would that be? Let's go back to the roads in your brain. You still have to patch the potholes and sweep the streets. Remember, this is an artificial state of affairs. With all the infrastructure our process creates, a Learning Systems client would have to engage in a ridiculous amount of overstimulation to keep it active. Besides, our clients would bang down the doors and raid the place if we didn't give them regular boosts."

"Are you saying it's addictive?"

"No!" Swatt blurted.

"Of course not," Emmy assured her. "How can it be? It's n-tech, not drugs. We're just enhancing what's naturally there."

Aidra thought about her last session of Exersleep, and how the usual "runner's high" hadn't been there. Was Learning Systems the same? Did the thrill wear off after awhile?

"But people like it," Emmy said. "They like it a lot. It's not physically addictive, but you could say it's mentally so."

"No," Swatt said. "You could not."

"Fine." Emmy turned her head and slid Aidra a wink where Swatt couldn't see. "It's not."

Aidra looked down at the pad in her hand full of tiny print and legalese. Emmy gestured to it. "Your signature goes right there. If you'd just sign it, we can move to the other room and begin your treatment."

Aidra held the pad but did not sign. She scanned the fine print trying to see why Emmy was pushing so hard for her signature. "You claim it's just a tiny amount of chemicals to get the cascade started."

"That's right," Emmy said.

"Can you define tiny amount?"

Swatt's image crackled. "I advise you not to answer that question, Ms. Mathers."

"Is it true that every dose is technically an overdose?"

"Well, there's only so much—"

"No," Swatt interrupted. "I'm going to insist on terminating this interview."

"It's not an interview," Aidra said. "I'm asking things any client would ask."

"You aren't a client," Swatt said. "Clearly, you are looking for grounds with which to slander the reputation of this——"

"No, she isn't." Emmy was on her feet now. "If you'd bothered to sit in on any of these preliminaries before, you'd know that nine out of ten of our customers ask the very same thing, or worse. Let me answer."

"I'm afraid for a non-client, I can't let this line of questioning go any further."

Aidra swooped the light pen off the desk and scrawled her signature. She whipped over to the banking screen, tried not to wince at the amount listed there, and pressed her multicard to the reader. She handed the pad back to Emmy.

"She's a client, now. Goodbye, Mr. Swatt. Out, out, out." Emmy waved the datapad in front of Swatt's face and then through the pixels of his holo image as if she could break it up by force.

Swatt gave Aidra a sour glance before cutting off the connection and blinking away.

Emmy smiled into the silence. "Now we can talk freely. You're a client and therefore have a legal right to privacy. So, what's the next question?"

Aidra placed the light pen carefully on the desk. That's why Emmy was pushing her to sign. What else was she missing? She'd soon find out.

"I can only afford one treatment," Aidra said.

"No problem. You get the most noticeable benefit from the first boost anyway. If it were up to me, I'd give everyone the first treatment for free. But then Christian Swatt, esquire would really have something to say. Every batch is numbered and we keep meticulous records about who gets what, so I can't even give you a discount." She gave a tiny pout of sympathy. "Next question?"

"Are you really set up to do treatments here? This is a research facility."

"What do you think we do research on?"

"Right."

"Next question?"

But Aidra didn't have anything else she wanted to know and the legal forms had her signature on them. The time for questions was over.

"I guess I'm ready. But are you sure you don't want to hand it over to a tech?"

Emmy laughed. "I used to *be* a tech. It wasn't so long ago that I did this every day. I'm sure I remember how."

"Uh . . ."

"Kidding! Supremium brain, remember? I don't forget anything. My lab is on the third floor. Let's go."

"How will I know when it's working?" Aidra asked.

"You'll know."

Aidra leaned back into the padded contour chair and was told to relax and to let the n-tech do its job.

"No headset or anything?"

"Exersleeper," Emmy teased. "Can you feel a thin metallic strip against the top of your neck?"

"No."

"It's there. The insertion machinery is on a nanometric scale and programmed to avoid nerves. Exersleep works the same way, but because you don't process the experience there's no way to remember the nothing."

Aidra laughed. "'Remember the nothing.' That's a good way to describe it because I don't feel anything. I thought I'd at least—oh, wow."

She was glad the lighting in the room was low and diffused, because detail and visual texture had instantly sharpened until the corner of the framed print across from her was almost painful in its beauty and precision.

She took a breath and felt the expansion and contraction of

each individual muscle, the whispering shift of her blouse over her skin, reveling in the full awareness of that sip of air. Not just smells, but the actual taste of the air, her own breath—hummus on bagel, tang of the orange slice, the underlying mint of her mouthwash, but also the smell of her deodorant, her bodywash, the conditioner in her hair, the smell of her own skin below that. It didn't hit her in an overpowering cloud. She could smell each layer.

She heard the nearly silent footfalls as Emmy moved across the floor, the musical creak of the swivel chair onto which she lowered herself. The notes of the chair reminded her of a piano song her aunt had played whenever she stayed the night. Aunt Deelie had only played that song when Aidra stayed over alone, never when Quinn stayed, too.

The abstract subject of the picture on the wall, a swirl of blue and yellow against an indigo background was the looping shape of a jump rope in the elementary school gymnasium, a blur of light against the mats lining the walls. Aidra had bested everyone except Lucy Pindertile at jump rope every year but fifth grade, when she'd gotten herself too worked up over the competition and tangled out early, beaten by nearly everyone. "Lucky Lucy" had been so surprised that she had tangled out herself. The two of them had collapsed on the hardwood floor and laughed like loons as the sweating, red-faced girls still in the running assumed expressions of strain and concentration like masks of Greek tragedy.

A fan of light was refracted from a chip of mica in the granite countertop and turned into the sharp point of morning sunlight sparking from the tiny stone in her engagement ring. The morning after her wedding to Dean, the first day of their honeymoon trip and she was up before him, marveling over the light on her ring, on the simple, yet profound change in her life. *Marriage vows are like speaking an incantation, a spell that changes you forever.* Realizing she'd said it aloud, she'd turned to see Dean sitting up in bed and grinning at her. "You getting all poetic on me, girl? That ain't fair."

It went on and on. Memories of school, jobs, pets. Each sensation linking up with events Aidra had no idea she could recall. At last, the lights dimmed further and the soft, silent sounds hushed and stopped calling to her memories. The air was just air.

Aidra checked the time. She had been here for the better part of the day, surely? She was shocked to see that less than an hour had gone by while she'd been lost in a world of color, sound and memory.

"So?" Emmy asked. "How do you feel?"

"Thirsty," Aidra said. "And hungry. Wow."

"Oh!" Emmy said. "Oh, dear. Maybe it *has* been too long since I've done this. I'm sorry. People usually bring their own."

"Their own?"

"Food. The most popular one is those energy gels that long-distance runners use. You can slurp it down fast and it gets right into your body. Maple syrup is another. I once saw someone drink half a bottle, straight up."

Ordinarily, that would sound disgusting, but right now, Aidra could taste the sweetness on her tongue. She licked her lips.

Emmy had pulled her purse out of a desk drawer and found a crumpled bag of M&Ms inside. Aidra snatched it out of her hand. She ripped off a corner of the package and tipped the contents into her mouth.

"Come with me." Emmy led her down the corridor to a vending machine built into the wall. Aidra had never seen such a beautiful sight. Emmy waved her badge and it signaled readiness. Aidra slammed her finger at the sensor, ordering an energy drink, then a kid's juice box, then another. She figured liquid was faster than food. She'd get herself calmed down, then eat something.

Emmy opened the energy drink and put it into Aidra's shaking hand. "This will be a start, but you're going to need more in an hour or so. Don't fight it. Let your body tell you what it needs."

Aidra was too busy gulping liquid to answer. She finished the energy drink and reached for the juice boxes.

"The brain requires a tremendous amount of glucose to function and I'm afraid we've used all of yours. It isn't as if you can pour this juice directly into your brain. The rest of the body has to process it first. Takes time."

Aidra thought about how happy and relaxed she felt after each session of Exersleep. This couldn't be more different. She was dead tired, yet her brain was humming. It was like she was a college kid who had pulled an all-nighter before an exam, staying up way too late and drinking too much coffee. She wanted someone to challenge her to a game of chess. No, two games. At the same time.

She finished the first juice and poked the straw into the other, feeling a bit better. She was able to drink the second juice at a normal pace, even tasting it. By the time it was gone, she felt almost normal. Hungry, but normal.

"I'm going to have to leave soon, or I'll miss my train." She tilted her head, surprised at her statement. Even more surprised that she knew it to be true.

"You're right," Emmy said.

"I know. But how?" She'd only glanced at the monorail schedule once on the way here. Could she really figure out time and distance to the station and know with certainty when the next train would arrive?

"I thought this would make me learn more easily."

"And more easily synthesize what you've already learned," Emmy said. "It looks like intuitive leaps, only they're not so intuitive. You'll know things. You won't know how you know them. A few more treatments and you'll be able to trace the path from one thought to another, linking them in a chain. But at first, you get these weird flashes. Trust them."

"I already do."

Emmy walked her back to the treatment room to gather her purse and jacket. "Well, this has been kind of neat. I'd almost forgotten that initial rush. Watching you brings it all back. I know who you are and who you work for. I know why you're here. And I know you're never coming back. I just wish . . . well, it would be nice to see what you could do as a true Supremium."

It *would* be nice. Aidra felt her throat tighten and blinked back a tear. Funny, she thought being smarter would make her less emotional. But if anything, she felt more in touch with her emotions than ever before. And why shouldn't she be? Emotions were a kind of knowledge, too. Feeling and thought had synthesized into a holistic understanding.

This must be why Supremiums were usually so personable. They were in touch with themselves and therefore less likely to judge others. Yet, no matter how Aidra's emotions tugged at her, she knew it would be foolish to go into debt for something she couldn't afford in the first place.

"I'm going to have to think it over," she managed.

"Do me a favor," Emmy said.

"Sure."

"Do something active with those new connections of yours. Too many times, people get so focused on their thoughts that they don't go out and experience things. They're so much in their heads, they forget to enjoy the world."

"I don't think that's going to be a problem for me."

Emmy tapped her own forehead. "Just don't stay up here too long. Have some fun."

Fun sounded great. What did Supremiums do for fun? Climb the ladder of success? Design new ladders? She supposed she'd find out. But right now, food was at the top of her mind. She couldn't stop thinking about maple syrup. She wondered if any of the food courts at the monorail station served pancakes.

CHAPTER TWELVE

Aidra burst through her condo door and rushed to the refrigerator. She was starving. There had been no pancakes at the monorail station, and no time to eat them anyway. She'd arrived just as the train was pulling in, with only enough time to buy a pack of marshmallow candies from the nearest kiosk, which she'd nibbled all the way home.

Her newsreader had popped up story after story about Gascoigne and her queue was filling with news about his release and subsequent press conference. He was already slated to guest on five different comboviews. His lawyers were probably splintering. She ordered the companel to keep the combos for her. She'd have a lot of them to watch, if she could stomach it.

She reached for an orange juice, then put it back. She needed protein and probably some fiber, too. With a sigh, she put down the juice and took out a stick of cheese and an apple. She ate them standing up in the dark, silent kitchen.

Her condo seemed emptier than usual without Madeline. She usually greeted Aidra at the door and was happy to do whatever Aidra was doing, even if it was just sitting on the couch watching a movie. But Quinn had offered to keep the caline for an extra day, since Aidra's three- year-old nephew was crazy about her.

Aidra was down to her last bite of apple when her datapad signaled an incoming blip from Louisa Samahroo. [I promised to contact Hannah Wells-Fox on your behalf, and I have.]

[That was fast.] Aidra blipped back. [I just saw you a few hours ago.]
[We're having coffee tomorrow. Hannah may have helpful information.]

Aidra wanted to tell Louisa that she'd already tried that, but perhaps a Supremium would see things Aidra hadn't. Aidra pictured two Supremiums trying to out-clever each other, studying each other's words and body language while masking their own. Maybe it wasn't as exhausting as it sounded. Supremiums probably found it a fun game. [Call me after?] she asked.

[I still owe you a dinner. The Library? 6:00 tomorrow?]

[Sure. Meet you at your office.] Aidra marveled at her quick answer. In seconds she'd blown right past wondering why Louisa wanted to meet, why they couldn't just talk on the phone, and gone directly to understanding her motives for a face-to-face. This Supremium stuff was *awesome*.

[I've turned up something strange.] Louisa blipped after a long pause.

[Strange how?]

[Still looking. I'll tell you more tomorrow. 6:00. Wear something fancy.]

Aidra wondered what Louisa couldn't tell her on the phone. She hoped whatever it was would be worth getting dressed up for. Fancy meant her little black dress. Fancy probably also meant they were going to Special Collections.

She couldn't wait.

Until then, she would see how far she could get with her freelance assignments. One side of her condo's main room was a little dining nook which she'd turned into a makeshift office by adding a folding screen. She slid around it into the desk chair and sorted her message queue.

She shunted aside e-grams from news spinners and clipped together her personal bills to pay later. That left ongoing cases and new business.

She had a long-standing contract with the Dearborn school district for pre-screening of its job applicants. They were hiring new custodians and lunchtime supervisors, and needed background checks on each one. Aidra opened the files and skimmed them, checking against criminal databases and credit bureau information. She then turned to the hand-written application forms the prospects had filled out. That was where the real dirt was always hidden, and why she always insisted that the school send her the original applications. They would rather let the computer's handwriting recognition software digitize everything and send her neatly sanitized files, but she wanted the raw data.

She sorted the applicants into three piles—good hires, rejects, and maybes. But twenty applicants later, she saw that the "maybe" pile was empty. In fact, she'd sorted them twice as fast as she usually did. How could Learning Systems increase her reading speed so much in one treatment? Was she really that accurate now, or would she have to go back and double-check all her work later?

She immediately dismissed that thought. Work this easy would not have to be double-checked. It was obvious from one glance who had a prior criminal record, who was hiding uncomfortable secrets, and even who liked children and who did not. It was all over the page—the swift swoop of confident handwriting on the easy questions, the vague truths and half-answers on the more sensitive stuff, or the way that some people had solid recommendations from previous bosses, while one guy's only references were his mom and his pastor.

Aidra closed the file, zipped it for transmission, and added Dearborn School District to the queue of invoices to be written. In fact, now would be a great time to finish up all her outstanding jobs.

But first, more food. She headed toward the kitchen, banging her knee on the corner of the coffee table on the way. Well, being Supremium certainly hadn't made her more graceful. Or maybe it was her furniture placement. It didn't look like this configuration was working either. She'd eat first, then see if her new neural connections would help her interior design skills.

She opened both fridge and pantry, marveling at the nearly empty shelves staring back at her. This time last year, they'd been stocked with all of Jon's favorites. She was only a functional cook, but she'd always made decent meals for them both. Now, she could rarely be bothered to do more than flash cook instant soup.

After looking around a bit more, she finally opened a can of tuna. She considered dumping it onto a plate, but why dirty a dish? She carried the can and a fork to her desk, along with a second apple. She alternated mouthfuls of tuna with apple, reveling in the differences. The salty taste and soft texture of the fish contrasted with the crisp sweetness of the apple. But after three bites of each, it was almost as if she couldn't taste either of them anymore. As if her senses had learned this food and had no need of further input. She finished eating and writing reports at the same time. It was the fastest she'd accomplished either task.

She looked at her empty inbox. Emmy's reminder came back to her. *Don't stay up here too long. Have fun.* She needed to get out of her head. And she would. But she was processing things so fast, she'd be done with this work in no time. Why waste that ability?

She turned to Noah's messages, looking at the oldest ones first. Perhaps her new abilities would allow her to see them as an opportunity instead of a source of frustration. She looked at notes he'd taken on a prospective new case. It seemed that one Jeremy Hobson, esquire, lived a bit too close to the edge of the city and was a bit too worried about his property values. It bothered him that a "certain class" of people were using his street to cross in and out of the disincorporated zone. Of course, Hobson would never admit as much. Instead, he talked about increased traffic, criminal activity, gangs and militias. It was worth his while to make sure his street didn't become a pass-through into the city and he wanted to make it worth Aidra's while as well. Barriers between the city and the zone that surrounded it were not uncommon. Why shouldn't Hobson erect one on his street, especially if he was willing to pay for it?

Aidra stared at the file, noting how carefully Hobson framed everything in terms of safety and precautions, never in terms of class. But the majority of people who lived in the zone weren't criminals or gang members or anything except poor. And people who lived in the city assumed the opposite.

She saw how it could be done. As sketchy as Noah's notes were, the entire plan came to her in vivid detail. A few stakeouts, a few well-placed surveillance spiders, and she'd have a good idea who was regularly going in and out. Do a little facial recognition, match a few people to some petty crimes, and get Noah to crunch the data into a compelling story. By the time the city council met next, Hobson's wall would be all but approved.

She closed the file, stabbing the screen so hard her finger hurt. The truth was, Hobson would get his wall. If she didn't do his dirty work, he'd find someone who would. And the residents of the zone who came into the city to work or to see family or get supplies would have to take the long way around, ways that were getting longer and longer all the time. But what could anyone do? No one was supposed to live in the zone anyway.

She pushed back her chair and walked to the kitchen. She threw her apple core in the trash and the tuna can in the recycler, where it hit the bottom of the bin with a satisfying clink. Job offers like this made her remember why she gave fifty hours each week to Fitz-Cahill. Hobson would get his wall no matter what, but at least she'd know she didn't have a hand in it.

She turned on the tap and gulped water directly from the sink. Then she marched back to the desk and opened a fresh e-gram. She used her most polite, most even-handed tone to tell Jeremy Hobson, esquire, to fuck off.

The companel trilled for attention. When it automatically connected the call, Aidra knew it could only be from one person. She frowned at the face on the screen. "Morris. I've told you a million times—"

"I know, I know. You want me to wait for you to answer. But it's no trouble for me to just put myself through."

"Trouble, no. Rude, yes."

"It's not like I can count on you to pick up."

"What if I'm in the middle of something?"

Morris lifted his eyebrows. "Are you? I know you work odd hours. And that's cool, but you could at least return my e-grams."

"I was just about to." *Later. Maybe.*

"You're awake twenty-three hours a day. If you're Exersleeping to gain more time, what are you doing with all of it?"

"I told you, I'm *busy*."

"Are you okay?"

"I'm fine. Why?"

"Nothing. You just seem . . . twitchy."

"I'm trying to work, Morris. In case you missed the spins, I'm up to my elbows in the Fox-Gascoigne murder and I'm trying to keep my hand in on the freelance side, and I've got to do more things by myself thanks to that half-wit you sent me."

"Are you talking about Noah?"

"Who else?"

Morris sat back in his chair. "Noah is one of the smartest people I know."

"If he's got an intelligent side, he's hiding it very well."

"Did you know he's writing an AI?"

"So?" Aidra asked. "You do that all the time."

"I realize you have no other frame of reference, but I feel I should remind you: I am exceptional."

She pressed her lips together, holding back a sarcastic comment. There was no way Noah was as smart as Morris. And even if he were, it did her no good unless some of those brains were used on her behalf. "I don't think Noah is going to work out," she said. "I know corporate cases aren't exactly his speed, but he always acts like he's phoning it in."

"Can you blame him? You don't pay him enough to do more."

"I pay him plenty. I pay him what I used to pay you." Aidra brought her hand to her mouth. *Oh. Oh, dear.* She got it now. She didn't know if this was another gift from Learning Systems or just her brain finally having all the information it needed to understand. It wasn't her fault. Not really. She didn't have a frame of reference for this, either. She'd paid what Morris had billed her because she'd assumed that was the going rate for his expertise.

She put both hands on the desk and leaned into the screen. "Why didn't you tell me I underpaid you?"

Morris shrugged. "Technically, you didn't. Technically, I undercharged you."

"It doesn't matter what you call it, you screwed over the next guy. I know you thought there would never *be* a next guy, but you had to know our arrangement wouldn't last forever. I can see why you did it. It's sweet, and I love you for it in a way. I even get why you're telling me this right now. It's endearing, and that's what you need, isn't it?" She was talking too fast. She could feel the words spilling over themselves to be heard, one thought tumbling out upon another. "Because I know that things haven't been the greatest between us, but I've got it all figured out. I'm sorry you can't figure it out, too, but things are quite clear to me at the moment. What you want from me—from us—and what you need, what I need, and what I'm able to give. Those are four different things, Morris."

Morris blinked at her through the screen. He reached up and brushed a hand over his bristle-short hair. "How many cups of coffee have you had?"

"None. My coffeemaker is broken. Why are you changing the subject?"

"So you decided to go directly for the hard stuff." He peered more closely at her. "It's not flash. You're too coherent for that. Flashers babble. But man, this looks like something from the street."

Aidra pointed to her head. "I haven't squirted a single chemical into my brain."

Morris' eyes widened. "Oh, shit. You boosted. You did Learning Systems."

"Oh, shit? More like oh, *yay*."

"Yay," Morris said with a straight face.

"Why can't you be happy for me?"

"Because you're no longer you."

"You should talk!" Aidra glared at Morris. He carried a chip in his head that was illegal in several countries and highly restricted in this one. Thanks to the NSA, he was practically a cyborg. His brain was in constant contact with the electronic universe. You could say his brain was *part* of the e-verse.

At least Aidra was certain that every thought rattling around in her skull was her very own. Morris couldn't even be sure if he was thinking or computing. And he was worried about a few nano-machines?

"Hey!" Morris protested. "I didn't choose this. This was done to me."

"You like it," Aidra said.

"Sometimes," Morris said quietly. Aidra knew that his chip came with numerous side benefits. He was a computer. He was a clock. He was a GPS and a library and a security program. More importantly, he knew new ways to handle his fears. He'd once suffered from crippling agoraphobia that kept him housebound. Now, he had the occasional panic attack and a few behavior quirks that made him more eccentric than broken. Whether he had chosen it or not, she could bet he liked it more than *sometimes*.

"Do you like this?" Morris asked.

Aidra started to speak, then hesitated. Did she like it? She'd only had one treatment of Learning Systems. It wasn't enough to become Supremium, no matter how much she wanted to.

She sat with that thought. *Did she want to?* She was getting more done in less time than she ever had before, even with Exersleep and coffee. But that wasn't the best part of Learning Systems. When she made a decision—what to eat, which train to take, which job to decline—she knew it was the right one. She could go upstairs right now and plan her wardrobe for the entire year, knowing she'd look flawless every day. She could pick winning stocks and effortlessly time a boiled egg and know when to bring an umbrella. And she'd be right. No wonder Supremiums always seemed as if they had their shit together. They actually did have their shit together.

But the cost was high, and not just in money. It was one more way for society to become stratified, the haves and the have-nots, making it even more impossible for anyone to rise above the circumstances of their class. And she couldn't forget how she'd felt after the Learning Systems treatment. She'd emerged frantic and shaky, as if coming down from an overdose. It wasn't something she ever wanted to experience again, much less on a regular basis.

She focused on Morris. He probably hadn't noticed a gap in the conversation. She was processing so fast, it was as if the thoughts came in layers, each one piled atop the last. So much better than thinking one thought at a time.

"Sometimes," she echoed back at him. "I might like it a little. Look, I gotta go."

"No, you don't. You're ending the call so you don't have to answer my question."

"I thought I just did."

"Not that question." They both knew he was talking about the job. The one he'd found for her in D.C. The one he'd been sending her e-grams about several times a week. Would she take it?

Aidra fiddled with a piece of peeling laminate on the edge of her desk, trying to push it back into place. Morris had tried. He'd done a tremendous amount of legwork and research to find her an entry level job in a big PI firm. "I don't know," she told Morris. "I'm not sure this job is worth uprooting my life for."

"It's corporate work," Morris said. "It's just like what you have now."

"It's nothing like I have now. They know me at Fitz-Cahill. I have a reputation. I have contacts. People trust me."

"They'd trust you here, too."

"Eventually." Until then, she'd be monitoring security systems and other grunt work. True, much of what she was doing at Fitz-Cahill these days was routine, but not all of it. They gave her the important stuff, too. This current case could affect the entire n-tech industry.

Silence stretched between them. Long enough that surely Morris would notice this one. He'd also notice that she was pretending the job was the only thing she had reservations about.

"I can't make this decision overnight," she said finally. "I need time to think." She looked over each shoulder in turn, as if she could determine where those words had come from. Not five minutes ago, she thought she knew the answer to everything.

But that was the problem. Normal relationships were complicated enough, even for Supremiums. And a relationship like theirs, where neither one of them knew exactly where they stood and so much was left unsaid? Impossible.

"All right," Morris said. "I get it. I understand you've got obligations. But there's a downside to playing it safe. When you start coasting, you get sloppy."

"I'm not coasting."

"You're afraid."

"Excuse me?"

"I know what that feels like. I know fear so bad it will paralyze you. But trust me, that is no way to live."

Aidra ground her back teeth together. She was beginning to regret not ending the call when she'd had the chance. "I'm not coasting, I'm not afraid, and I'm not getting sloppy. I'm a single mom, working my butt off to put my son through college. And if that means working for Fitz-Cahill, then that's what I'm going to do."

"Sure." One side of Morris' mouth quirked up in a half smile. "How is double-Y these days?"

Aidra practically growled through the screen. "I told you not to spy on me."

"Technically . . ."

"I told you not to spy on Bryan Lynch."

"I was simply asking after your friend in a friendly way. Since you guys are, you know, so friendly."

"That was a jerk move, Morris." But her anger was tinged with pity. Morris would always be needy. It was just how he was wired.

His head chip and his job and his medications kept him functioning, but his emotions remained raw.

"Sorry," he said in a way that meant he was anything but. "Go solve double-Y's problems. Make him satisfied. Who knows? Maybe you'll satisfy yourself, too."

"Don't mind if I do." Aidra said goodbye to Morris and ended the call, thinking about how nice it would be to make him eat his words. She was already composing the e-gram she'd send him once Gascoigne was found guilty and sent to prison.

She stood up from her desk chair and paced around her condo. She didn't want to think about Morris. Or about moving. Or her current cases. Or the hundred other things on her mind. Too bad Madeline was gone or she'd take her out for a nice long run. That was good for turning off the brain.

So was sleeping.

She tugged at the edge of the couch, pushing it to the middle of the room. She fussed with the alignment. Now what? For the first time, she was seeing the downside of being Supremium. There was no escape. You were always awake, always processing new thoughts and replaying old ones, and nothing could distract you—at least not for long. How did people get used to this?

She sat on the couch, then immediately jumped to her feet. What was she doing? She was finally Supremium and she was wasting it sitting on her ass doing paperwork and having awkward conversations. She was supposed to be having fun. She should call a friend, go out. She opened the curtains to look across the condo courtyard, checking to see if there were any lights on at Gilly's place. Gilly knew how to have fun.

Gilly.

She knew how to have fun.

A very special kind of fun.

The naked kind of fun.

With someone not her husband.

Aidra didn't know how her mind had made the leap but she

knew it was correct. Gilly wasn't being blackmailed over stupid bids on contracting jobs. She was having an affair.

Aidra lifted a palm to her forehead. She should have seen the truth the moment Gilly called her. She was a PI for chrissake. She dealt with this stuff every day. But she wanted to think the best of her friend, wanted to believe Gilly was an innocent victim.

Aidra grabbed her car keys and two protein bars for the ride. She hurried out the door.

CHAPTER THIRTEEN

Aidra set the electronic locks behind her and headed for her condo's parking garage. The rain had stopped and the night was still, with not even a breeze to stir the damp air. It was the kind of weather that would plump up her curls until they puffed around her face like dandelion fuzz. She smoothed both hands over her head as she ducked into the garage.

As she reached the lower level, she glanced over her shoulder and scanned the rows of cars. Something felt off, but she couldn't say what. Her eyes and ears gave her nothing. Was it a smell? Did Supremiums know things because of subtle scents, perhaps below the threshold of consciousness? She breathed deeply as she got closer to her car. She looked on all sides of it, then bent to look underneath.

"There you are!" Ugly Ben popped up from between rows, headcam in place. "I've been waiting forever. Where to, my lady?"

Aidra straightened and gave an inward groan. She didn't have time for spinner shenanigans. "Go away."

"No can do. I warned you, didn't I? Yes, I did. I told you that you're going to have to give me something juicy."

"I don't have to give you anything."

"Yes, you do. And you want to, don't you?" Ugly Ben ran a hand over the snug fabric of his white track suit. His jacket was unzipped most of the way, revealing a bright pink tank top with an overgrowth of chest hair bursting from the top of it.

Aidra tilted her head up, glaring at the headcam. "I said I'd share when I had information about the Gascoigne case."

"And?"

"Nothing yet."

"Boy, are you a terrible liar. Where are you going?"

"Produce store."

"Come on, Aidra. Tell me. That way I won't have to follow you so closely. Won't that be nice? You can do your grocery shopping or whatever in peace. Do you think I like lurking in parking garages? You think I like being this obnoxious?"

"I have seen your show."

"Ouch. C'mon, I like interacting with you. We make a great team, don't we?"

"No."

"But I don't like hounding you."

"So don't be a hound."

Ugly Ben brought a meaty paw to his forehead and swiped away the moisture gathered there. "My dear lady, you and I both know you are not going to the produce store."

Aidra leaned against her car door. "And you and I both know that I can give you the slip. I don't even need a head start. A couple of false circles, some playing with traffic lights, I can shake your tail in less than two kilometers. So don't even bother."

"Oh, it's no bother at all."

"I promise you, this outing has nothing to do with Gascoigne. I'm working on something else and you'll only be in the way. I'm asking you nicely to leave me alone for a bit. Please."

"Please?"

"Pretty please."

"I don't believe anyone has ever said that to me before."

"No surprise there. But seriously, Ben, from one professional to another . . ." She tried not to choke on the word *professional*. "Can you give me an hour to myself?"

Ugly Ben scratched his chest. "You're sure you're not holding out on me? Because if I find out—"

"I'm sure."

"And you'll give me something I can use. Soon."

"Tell you what." Aidra sighed. "I'm having dinner at the Library tomorrow with Louisa Samahroo. Any new information I get will be yours. Meet me afterwards."

"Time?"

"Around eight."

"Place?"

"Front steps."

"My competitors?"

"None. They can watch impotently from outside the magic circle."

"Deal." Ugly Ben removed the camera from his head. "An exclusive! My favorite." He opened her Octave's door for her. "In you go, now. Goodbye."

Aidra removed her datapad from her purse with a do-you-think-I'm-stupid look at Ugly Ben. She touched the scanning program and held the pad several centimeters above the car, running it back and forth over the most likely hiding places. The sweeper on her pad wasn't all that great, not as effective as driving through a carwash, but spinners tended to use cheap throwaway spiders that were easy to detect.

"Not that I don't trust you . . ." She kept scanning.

"You'll have to work harder than that to offend me."

Aidra nabbed two surveillance spiders from the bumper and one from the frame around the license plate. She held them out to Ugly Ben. "You want these back?"

"Why, wherever did those come from? Ah, well. Waste not, want not, I always say." He snatched the tiny devices from her palm and tucked them into his pocket. "Off you go. I'll be waiting for you at the Library tomorrow."

"Aidra?"

Leaning against someone's car door was aggressive enough, but with arms folded and no answering smile, Aidra projected as much anger as she could radiate. When she'd called Gilly's phone, her e-sec said she was working late on a job site. Since the only renovation Gilly's company was currently involved in was the One Detroit Center building on the corner of Woodward and Congress, Aidra headed directly there instead of leaving a message.

She waited while Gilly stammered through greetings that trickled into a heavy and guilty silence.

Aidra kept her tone neutral. "How long have we been neighbors? Eight years?"

"Yes."

"I know you guys pretty well."

"Yeah . . ."

"And you're the gambler, not your husband. He's concerned about appearances, but you're more likely to tell anyone who looked at you cross-eyed to kiss your ass. Now, maybe this PI comes to you because you're a woman and maybe more easily intimidated, but I'm having a hard time seeing why you didn't just tell him to go to hell."

Gilly's expression hardened and she started to speak but Aidra cut her off.

"Don't. Just don't. There's a reason this guy came to you and not Mitsu and we both know what that reason is."

She watched Gilly crumble and shooed her into the car. "All right," she said. "Tell me."

"It started just like I said. I came into work early and he was sitting behind my desk. I threatened to call the police and he told me Mitsu had hired him." Tears spilled out of her eyes. "It wasn't overbids on contracts. It was an affair, Aidra." She looked up, probably to see if there was anything judgmental in Aidra's expression.

Aidra didn't remark on the fact that Gilly still wasn't owning it. There was a big difference between *it was an affair* and *I had an affair*.

"I know it's terrible," Gilly said. "I know I'm terrible. I ended it. It's over."

"So this piece-of-shit PI claimed your husband hired him. He offered to keep quiet about the affair if you outbid your husband."

"Yes," Gilly whispered. "But when you told me my vendors hadn't hired him, I realized Mitsu never hired him, either. If Mitsu knew about me and Raymond, he wouldn't have hired a PI. He would have come to me."

"So why get me involved?" Aidra asked.

"I want to save my marriage. I realize that now. And this PI could ruin everything. I don't even know how he found us!"

"I do. You and your boyfriend met at a hotel. Probably the same one. Regularly."

Gilly was taking small, shallow breaths. "The Edgemont. The one on the Riverwalk. So many tourists come and go, we thought we'd be anonymous."

"Some of the lower life forms among PIs make contacts at the hotels, slip a few bucks to some clerk to keep an eye out for someone who might be worth shaking down. Gets the clerk to put you in a room where he's already got spiders planted. He watches you and boyfriend for a bit. Then comes to see you."

Gilly's shoulders shook. "He has pictures. He showed me a few of them."

"Yeah." Nothing terrified people more than tangible proof that they were not what they appeared to be. She couldn't say that to Gilly right now. It was easy to see how close to the edge she was.

Aidra considered. "Does he have a Re-Buy bid for you right now?"

"Yes. An empty Coke bottle."

"Give me the lot number."

Gilly read the number into Aidra's datapad and looked up at her with wide, terrified eyes. "What are you going to do?"

"Get to him before he gets to your husband. I hope."

* * *

As she drove toward the Riverfront, Aidra tried to moderate her distaste for the whole situation, her mixture of disgust and anger at Gilly for starting the situation in the first place. Aidra liked Mitsu just fine, but she had no idea what their marriage was like from the inside. No one ever knew everything about someone else's relationship. It was none of her business.

And if it wasn't any of her business, it certainly was not the business of the PI who called himself Jay. Gilly had made a mistake, no doubt about that. But for a slimeball like Jay to try to profit from that mistake made Aidra want to beat him until he cried for his mama. Sure, Private Investigators did sneaky, deceitful, low things sometimes. She'd done a few of them herself. But always in the service of her client and always with a better outcome in mind. Jay's only motive was to enrich himself.

And that would be his undoing.

She put in a call to Noah. No visuals in a moving car, but all she needed was information. "How are you coming on that Re-Buy thing I asked you about yesterday?"

"It takes more than a day to hack that kind of company."

"So what you're saying is, you haven't even started."

"I'm saying I haven't *succeeded*. Doesn't mean I didn't try."

"Sure," Aidra said.

"I don't live all day like you do."

Aidra worked her way through the maze of small streets near the Riverwalk, avoiding strolling pedestrians. "What if I don't care who's selling this junk?"

"Huh? You told me you needed his name."

"I'm halfway to finding the guy myself. I just need you to get the money back."

"Hmm. Why didn't you say so?" She could hear Noah clicking keys. "That's easy."

"It is?"

"I can process a refund on all the items Gilly bought. I'll convince Re-Buy they've been returned. We'll say they were defective products. The automated system at Re-Buy will shoot the money right back into her account."

"You can do that?"

"Mmm Hmm." Noah's keyboard clacked as he typed faster. "This isn't even a hack, don't you see? It's more like an exception to the rules. I don't have to break any of their security protocols to do it."

"In that case, don't just mark Gilly's stuff as returned. Make the computer think it's getting returns on everything this man ever sold on Re-Buy."

"Finally, something squeezy."

"Do we like squeezy?"

"We love squeezy."

"I'm glad you're experiencing job satisfaction. How soon can you do this for me?"

"How soon? I just did it. I wasn't thinking out loud. I was working, here."

Aidra glanced at the companel's blank screen, wishing she could see Noah's face. "Are you messing with me?"

"Not this time."

"You know, Morris says you're smart."

"I am."

"I think he might have left the word 'ass' off the end."

"I'm that, too."

Aidra slowed her car and crept into the Edgemont's parking lot. "Good work today, smartass. I mean it."

"Later, boss." She could swear she heard him smiling through the phone.

The tourist-friendly Riverwalk was a mix of high-end shops, small souvenir stalls, restaurants, entertainment, and hotels for every budget. Aidra crawled her way through throngs of pedestrians, bikes, and strollers to the Edgemont.

At the front desk, Aidra had a short but very persuasive chat with the clerk that involved a little bit of tempcash and a lot of threats. Yes, he knew Jay the PI. Yes, he sometimes gave Jay information about regular clients. Yes, Jay was outside the hotel tonight. The clerk told her Jay drove a newish Ford, which Aidra found parked in the middle of the row facing the front entrance. A man matching Jay's description sat low in the driver's seat.

She did a wide circle of the car, waited until he was looking the other way, then approached the car from the back. She opened the rear door and slid inside in a single motion. "Don't turn around." She pressed the muzzle of the Rockston Diamond hard against the base of his skull. The buzzing whine of the electronic firing mechanism hummed loud in the quiet car.

He was a big guy, broad of shoulder, barrel-chested, thick necked. His right hand was moving by centimeters into his coat. She let the gun dig in and a bit of Pinckney twang enter her voice. "Show me two fingers, big fella." He did. "Reach in with thumb and index and pull it out slow. Because your next of kin is gonna have a hard time re-selling this craptastic car with your brains splattered all over it."

She could feel the seethe coming off him as he teased out a semi-automatic.

"Ah, a boy and his Smith and Wesson. Slowly raise it and press it against the ceiling." Before it was halfway there, Aidra snatched it with her left hand. She saw a trickle of sweat run down the side of his thick neck. "Relax, fella. You play along and we're just gonna have a chat."

"I got nothing to say to you."

"Why, Jay—it is Jay, isn't it?—you don't even know what I want to talk about."

"You want to rob me, is that it? Good luck, bitch. You'll get nothing."

"Funny that's where your mind should go," Aidra said. "We could probably have a nice long discussion about robbery, but we ain't gonna. You look like a hip-pocket man to me. Reach your left hand around for your wallet and pull it out."

"You will die for this."

"No, I won't. Now pull out that wallet or I will aerate you and make looking at it unnecessary."

He reached for his wallet. She'd been right—hip pocket. He handed it over the seat.

She took it slowly, and then ordered him to place both hands on the dashboard where she could see them. He did so, making fists with both middle fingers outstretched.

She kept an eye on him while flipping open the wallet. He had two multi-cards with different names, but his PI license was the same as one of the multi-cards and a health club ID.

"Bart Jefferson Klaver," she said. "So that's where the Jay came from. It wasn't J-A-Y, it was just your middle initial."

Klaver didn't respond.

"I'm Aidra. Aidra Scott. Take a look in the rearview. Hi." His eyes flicked to the mirror and she saw recognition there. He'd probably seen her on the newsnets. In the last few years, she'd ended up there a lot more than she wanted to. She didn't give him time to think about it. She dropped the slow Pinckney drawl and became all Detroit. All business.

"I have some news for you Mister Bart J. Klaver. Your days as a blackmailer are done. Over. You are officially out of the business. You understand me?"

"I don't know what you're talking about."

"Let me spell it out for you. I represent your victims. All of them."

"Victims, my ass. Do you know what kind of sleazeballs—"

"Stop it. You can't seriously be trying to take the moral high ground here."

"You're in the same line of work. You know what we do."

Aidra's finger itched in the trigger guard of her Rockston. She didn't want to shoot him, not really. But it would be awfully satisfying to clock him with the butt of the gun. Extra hard. Sadly, she'd have to get her satisfaction another way.

"Two things, Klaver. First, don't you ever—*ever*—compare yourself to me. Second, I want you to think about how easy it was for me to find you. You thinking about it? You have to be thinking hard. I can hear the hamster spinning that little wheel for all it's worth."

"You got lucky," Klaver said.

"No, I'm actually good at what I do. And you know what I do, Klaver? I help people. Right now, I'm going to help you."

"You want to help me? Hand me back my gun."

"That's not what's going to happen here. In a few minutes, I'm going to leave. And when I do, the first thing you're going to do is look at your bank account. It will be empty."

"Bullshit."

"I didn't just take the money, Klaver. I gave it back to its rightful owners. Turns out, using Re-Buy as your go-between wasn't the best move. So now everyone has their money back and everyone is happy—well, not you, but I don't really care about that."

"You fucking cunt bitch whore. I will kill you."

"You *had* to go there," Aidra said. "The holy trinity of gendered insults. You know, I don't mind the foul language, but you could be a little more original."

"Fuck you."

"Not much better. But hey, I said I was going to help you and I will. I'm going to help you stay out of jail. Because last time I checked, extortion is illegal. And using your PI license to do it means it falls under the racketeering laws and can be prosecuted at the federal level." She waited. "Did you know that, Bart J. Klaver?"

His hands twitched on the dashboard but he didn't answer. The back of his neck was shiny with sweat.

"So, you sit here and think it over." She opened the door. "You will come to realize that the best thing to do is just walk away. And maybe consider a career change. I'll keep your weapon safe for you. You can pick it up at the Cityheart police station."

She could anticipate his next words. So far, the little dirtbag had reacted exactly the way she'd expected him to.

"You'd better hope I never see you again, bitch."

Bingo.

She was halfway out of the car, but leaned back in for some last words. "That's right, you twinkie-dick, muscle-headed, buttcrack-humping son of a jackhole. You better hope we never meet again. Because the next time I have to track you down, we're going to do more than chat. Next time, I'm going to blow your shriveled little nutsack off with your own gun."

She brandished his Smith for emphasis, then slid out of the car and used it to shoot out the back tires one by one. The pop-thump, pop-thump reverberated against the other cars and she half-hoped someone would recognize the muted crack of electronic gunfire and call the cops. *Let him try to talk his way out of this.* She blew him a little kiss, then scurried to her own vehicle and drove away.

As she high-tailed it out of the Edgemont's parking lot, she thought of Emmy Mathers. The Learning Systems tech had told Aidra to have fun with her new abilities. Aidra stole a look in her rearview and caught a glimpse of Klaver, out of his car now, examining his shot-out tires.

Yes, this certainly qualified as fun.

CHAPTER FOURTEEN

It was nearly dawn by the time Aidra made it home. Dropping Klaver's gun at the Cityheart police station was a huge pain in the ass, especially since he'd probably never claim the thing. But she couldn't keep it, so she'd filled out the forms, waited for the weapon to be taken into custody, and then made the long drive home.

She'd sent Gilly a blip along the way, but not being able to share things directly with her friend made her victory seem hollow. Or maybe she wanted to share it with someone who would really understand. Someone who knew how cool it was that she'd anticipated every one of Klaver's moves and was already ten steps ahead of him. Someone like Louisa.

Stop it, she told herself. *Next thing you know, you'll be calling Gilly a turtle.* She sent Gilly another blip with extra hearts.

She'd only been home a few minutes when her WelcoMat announced a visitor. This was followed by a distinctive knock on the door and the turning of Quinn's key in the lock. Aidra's sister always did that—knocked to let Aidra know she was coming, and then let herself in anyway.

Madeline pranced through the door wearing her collar and leash, the other end held by three-year-old Parker. Aidra traded glances with Madeline, then smiled at her nephew's proud face. He probably thought he was walking the caline instead of the other way around. Quinn followed behind, carrying a bakery box and a basket of toys.

"You're here early," Aidra said. She'd expected her sister this morning, but was surprised to see her at six-thirty.

"Parker was up at five and I knew you'd be awake, so here we are." Quinn brandished the bakery box. "I brought doughnuts. I was going to bring those Chinese buns, but the guy in line ahead of me bought all the taro ones."

"I like doughnuts." Aidra took the box. "No coffee, though. The maker is broken."

"I'm off coffee anyway," Quinn said. "Makes me nauseated."

"Are you sick?"

"Only in the morning."

Aidra dropped the box on the kitchen table and rushed to hug her sister. "You're pregnant? That's wonderful! How far along?"

Quinn released her and smoothed a hand over her belly. "Not even twelve weeks. I just found out last night."

Aidra squealed and hugged her sister again. She scooped up Parker and included him in the embrace. Madeline danced around their feet, grinning and cooing, dragging the leash behind her as if to say, *Hey . . . a little help here? You with the thumbs?* Aidra laughed and bent to unhook it, then set Parker in a kitchen chair and poured him a glass of milk. "You're going to be a big brother, buddy. What do you think of that?"

Parker shrugged and grabbed a chocolate doughnut.

"I don't think he even knows what that means," Quinn said.

"Sure he does. You've seen him with Madeline. He's so good with her."

"I think he's Madeline's *little* brother," Quinn stage-whispered.

"Maybe," Aidra said. "For now."

They both looked at the caline, who sat patiently under Parker's chair, waiting for him to drop crumbs. Aidra did some math in her head. The way calines' genes were mixed up with human DNA and God knew what else, estimating their intelligence was a challenge. Madeline was far smarter than any dog, but putting her abilities into terms of child development was tricky. There were some things she did astonishingly well. There were other milestones she would never reach.

Aidra surveyed the half dozen doughnuts in the bakery box and inhaled, her senses alive with sudden need, her mouth salivating. She grabbed a maple glazed and sat across from her sister at the tiny kitchen table and took a bite.

She felt some icing on the corner of her mouth and worked her lips together, the sticky feel of it crossing a sudden bridge of memory. Mom didn't let her not-yet-teenage daughters use actual make-up, but she and Quinn had pretended on Sunday mornings with doughnut glaze. She used her finger to dab it across her lips and caught Quinn's eye, wondering if she remembered. She saw the recognition on Quinn's face and they shared a microsecond smile.

"That's an adorable basket," Aidra said, nodding toward the tote full of toys. It was just the right size to carry comfortably and looked like it held a lot. The sides were decorated with barnyard animals made from a child's thumbprint. "Did you make it?"

"I made it!" Parker said, spraying chocolate crumbs all over himself. "With Mama."

"That's right, we did." Quinn wiped him off with a napkin and then turned back to Aidra. "Kind of. It was a kit. We put it together. I've become one of *those* moms."

"What moms?"

"Crafty. I've even started subscribing to *JJToday*."

"So?" Aidra reached for another doughnut. The crumb cake looked tasty.

"I hate her."

"Hannah Wells-Fox?" Aidra asked around her mouthful. That had to be what her sister meant. Surely Quinn didn't hate little Juniper. The child was only six.

Quinn nodded. "I can't stand her. And I hate myself for watching her. And then I go out and buy everything she's selling and I make everything she tells me to make and I'm thinking about growing out my hair so I can try some of her hairstyles."

"Oh."

"I fantasize about having a girl just so I can dress her like Juniper Fox."

"That's not so bad."

"It's *disgusting*. And when I try to make something and it doesn't turn out as nice as Hannah's . . ." Quinn covered her face with her hands. "I start to think it's because I'm a dimwit or my fingers are too fat or something. It's never that Hannah has a staff, and a nanny, and a stylist, and probably doesn't even make those crafts herself. It's always my fault."

"I don't think she does."

Quinn pulled her hands away from her face. "See what I mean?"

"No, I mean, I don't think she has a staff. Well, she certainly has people for her charitable foundation. And she probably has house cleaners and gardeners, but when it comes to the comboviews, she does it all."

"Because she doesn't sleep."

"Right."

"Fudge." Quinn's sideways glance at Parker meant she'd like to say another word but couldn't.

"I'm done," Parker announced. He slid off his chair and grabbed the toy bag, dragged it into the living room, and upended it, spilling plastic cars and smart blocks onto the floor.

Aidra looked in the bakery box. The raspberry-filled was calling her name. She took a bite. Delicious.

Quinn gestured over the counter that divided the kitchen from the living room. "Still looking for that perfect *feng shui*, I see. Wasn't the couch over there the last time I was here?"

"I like it better this way. I think." She was experimenting with a floating arrangement, putting the couch in the center of the room with its back to the door. It made for a nice sort of front hallway, even if the small living room now looked even smaller.

"Are you going to replace the chair next?" Quinn asked.

"Nope. The coffee table." The words just popped out of her mouth, but now she could see it perfectly. She'd tried so many configurations of the existing pieces, but the answer was there all along. The couch and the chair were both fine. All she needed was a smaller coffee table.

Quinn looked back at Aidra and raised an eyebrow. "You, uh . . . hungry?"

Aidra's hand was reaching into the bakery box again, it hovered guiltily. "I'm sorry. Did you want the last one?"

Quinn put a hand on her stomach and made a sour face. "The doughnuts looked good until I saw you eat three of them. Where are you putting it all?"

Aidra bit into doughnut number four. Chewed. Swallowed. "Right into my brain."

"Come again?"

"Now that I'm Supremium . . ." she wanted to see how it sounded out loud. "Sugar and fat taste really good to me right now."

"Ha ha. Supremium. Are you going to start making comboviews too?"

Aidra licked frosting off her fingers, waiting.

"Oh, my God. You're serious." Quinn leaned across the table and lowered her voice. "What did you do, sell your soul?"

"I only got one treatment, so I'm not actually Supremium, but I don't have another word for it." And who was to say she wasn't Supremium now? This wasn't like Exersleep, which temporarily changed the chemical balance in the brain, reversing its effects as soon as the n-tech died off. With Learning Systems, she was making new neural connections. They might stay permanent if she kept them active enough.

"Why stop at one session?" Quinn asked. "Why not keep going?"

Aidra caught herself looking at the empty bakery box. "Because then I really would have to sell my soul. Or at least my condo. Fitz-Cahill paid for this treatment. Reluctantly."

"So what's it like?"

"Interesting." Aidra slid her plate to the side and swiped at some crumbs that had spilled on the table. It was more than interesting, but that was the only way she could describe it. She wanted to tell Quinn everything at once—the way her thoughts seemed to crest in ever-higher waves, the thrill of predicting what people would do next, the way she accepted the wisdom of her emotions. But where to start?

"I know things," she said at last. "And I can't explain how I know them. It's like my five senses give me information without me filtering the thoughts first. I see and I know."

"So you have ESP now?"

"No! Not at all. I still process things the same way everyone else does. I just process them *better*."

"I see."

"I didn't say I *am* better."

"Yeah, you kind of did. If you think I'm too stupid to understand—"

"I would never say that. I would never even think it." Aidra placed her hands flat on the tabletop. "It's not that you're dumb, it's that you're inexperienced. You've never even tried Exersleep so—"

"Oh, God, not you, too. Half my office wants me to Exersleep. Then I can go back to work full time."

"It's not just for your job," Aidra said. "With a second baby coming, you'll need all the hours you can get."

Quinn reached for the half doughnut Parker had left behind. "I don't know . . ."

"Don't believe that stuff you hear on the newsnets," Aidra said. "Just because one guy went nuts doesn't mean the technology is dangerous."

"Of course not. That's just legal talk. Gascoigne's lawyers trying to make a case. But Exersleep . . ."

"What?"

Quinn took a bite of what was left of Parker's doughnut and chewed thoughtfully. "I like snuggling up with my family at bedtime. It's kind of the best part of my day. Maybe it's different if you're single."

"Thanks."

"I didn't mean it like that. I just, you know, worry about how it would change my life."

"Lives always change, whether you want them to or not." Aidra watched Parker stacking smart blocks, clapping when he got the sequence right, and then knocking them over for another go. She remembered Jon doing the same thing.

She also remembered singing to him at bedtime, rubbing his back if he had a nightmare, making sure he always had his favorite blanket. She was sure she'd had a cuddly toddler just yesterday. But then she blinked and he was in college.

No wonder she didn't like sleeping anymore. It was too easy to miss things.

After Quinn left, Aidra watched some newscasts. They were still full of Mackenzie Fox and Jean Claude Gascoigne. A story like this didn't fade away, no matter what else happened in the world. Wars, politics, disasters and crime all played on the news, but nothing like the CEO of one of the country's fastest-rising companies killing his rival.

His rival? That word hardly seemed enough. Aidra tried to reconcile what Gascoigne had told her about Fox with what Hannah had said. Were any of the rumors flying around her marriage true? Aidra turned it over and over in her mind, trying to see how the love triangle fit in with everything else she'd learned.

She checked the time—from habit more than actual need. Ten o'clock. Hannah was probably having coffee with Louisa Samahroo right now. What were they talking about? Louisa had hinted that she'd found new information. What was it?

But Aidra didn't have to ask Hannah anything. The entire life of the Fox family was broadcast in hundreds of comboviews. She turned to her companel and told it to open the latest episode of *JJ Today*.

Mackenzie Fox's face filled the screen. Alive, handsome, smiling. His eyes twinkled as if he were about to laugh at a joke. Aidra wondered when the photo was taken. How many days before his death?

She gasped as the photo blinked and moved. Not a photograph. A holo. Music swelled in the background—lots of strings and a smattering of French horn. Juniper was right, the song was beautiful.

Aidra changed the field of vision. The dead man was too close, his face filling the entire screen. She backed off and rotated the view until she was looking at Fox from a few meters away and at a slight angle. Better.

That's what people loved about combos—the ability to change the field of vision. The 360 cameras allowed viewers to see from all sides at any depth. People could peer into corners, look down from above or up from below, and move about the scene as if they were in it. Easter eggs abounded and fans loved finding little surprises.

Aidra didn't do any of that. Once she found an angle she liked, she kept the viewpoint static and allowed the comboview to unfold as Hannah had first envisioned it, letting the family's brutal grief wash over her.

Aidra sat still, completely focused on the scene as Hannah's voiceover recalled her husband's early life, his education, and most of all, their courtship. His parents adored her. Her parents adored him. They had hundreds of inside jokes. They shared a passion for their work. They spoke the language of science and the language of love. She called him "Maximum." He called her "Poodles." The births of their children were the happiest days of their lives.

The music and visuals added up to a loving portrait that built and built until Aidra's throat closed and she had to turn away. She stared down into her empty hands. She saw how Hannah had done it, knew exactly how her emotions were being manipulated, and none of it mattered. Mackenzie Fox was dead and it was far too soon. His wife and children would never get over it. She felt their loss as keenly as if it were her own.

She let out a shallow sigh and replayed the combo from another angle, hoping it wouldn't affect her so much a second time through.

After five replays, she realized her foot had fallen asleep where she'd been sitting on it. She shook it out and scrolled through the *JJToday* menu. She searched the older combos for any references to Mackenzie Fox.

Three hours later, she was no closer to the answer. Thanks to the endless flexibility of comboviews, she was able to skip over recipes, fashion advice, and home decor segments to only watch family scenes. Mackenzie Fox rarely appeared on camera, but she'd assumed the sheer number of combos would give her enough views of the man to build a complete portrait. Instead, she felt like she'd barely glimpsed him. Even the memorial tribute was filtered through Hannah's experience, focusing on her vision of her husband.

Aidra had no illusions that she was seeing the real Fox family. Hannah had told her as much the day they met. Mackenzie wasn't perfect any more than Juniper or Jovan were perfect. But viewers would never see the children's dirty diapers or temper tantrums or even mismatched socks. And they wouldn't see Mackenzie burping or drinking milk out of the jug.

But it was more than just carefully chosen images. Mackenzie simply wasn't a part of the combos. Was he even a part of their lives? Sure, the CEO of a powerful company was always busy, but in most of the combos, he didn't even rate a walk-on part.

Was he edited out? That didn't make sense either. Even though Hannah and the kids were the stars of *JJToday*, viewers still preferred the whole family unit. The combos Mackenzie appeared on were the highest rated, so why not do more? Hannah had done the editing herself and was showing her family to the greatest advantage. This was the best she had to work with.

Aidra left the comboview proper and slipped over to one of the fan sites. She could break down each episode herself, but why not let the fans do it for her? Combos were powerful and the 360 cameras practically begged for remixes and mashes. The fandom had already picked apart each video, endlessly dissecting every detail on the screen, drilling down frame by frame into the tiniest of micro-expressions.

She gathered stills of Mackenzie Fox and used her holo-unit to project them on the wall. She focused specifically on times when he was talking to, talking about, or interacting with Hannah. It was nice to see how much he liked her, and Aidra's stomach unwound a bit at the thought that Mackenzie and Hannah had started out as best friends, and seemed to remain so. That love triangle story Gascoigne told himself to sleep better at night was probably just a story.

Probably.

Some little nagging doubt made Aidra pull a few more stills from the combos, and then a few more, until she had an entire army of Mackenzies projected on her wall.

What's wrong with this picture? She pressed her hands to her temples as if she could wring a few more electrical impulses out of her neurons. Mackenzie Fox was best friends with his wife. What could be sweeter? He truly liked her.

He *liked* her.

Aidra got it then, and looking at a few more stills for comparison made it obvious. It was something she'd missed entirely when running the video at normal speed. She only caught it when she froze the video at key moments.

Mackenzie looked at Hannah with an open expression, with warmth, with smiles. But the way he looked at other things told the whole story. The half-closed eyes, the exposed neck, the subtle wetting of the lips were things he did often, but not for Hannah. Mackenzie Fox *loved* his children. He—sadly—loved his datapad and his car.

He *liked* his house, his clothes, his kitchen, his favorite coffee cup, and his wife.

Well, Mackenzie Fox was a private person. And they'd been married eight years. Maybe this was the natural cooling of passion to mere affection. Or maybe he didn't want to show his love in front of the cameras.

But she was seeing Mackenzie Fox's most unguarded micro-expressions, something below the threshold of conscious thought. Something even a Supremium couldn't hide. And what she was seeing wasn't love.

Did Hannah know? She'd lived with the man. She'd made the comboviews. But did she put them together frame by frame? Of course not. Obsessive fans might have time for that, but Hannah was always moving on to the next combo.

At least, Aidra hoped she never saw it. As heartbreaking as this was to watch, it would be even more heartbreaking to think that Hannah somehow knew.

Poor Hannah. Played for a fool by a man who found revenge more satisfying than love. Hannah had hung her entire life on a man who only saw her as a prize to be stolen from his opponent. Gascoigne might have lost, but at least he knew what game he was playing. Hannah likely never had a clue.

Aidra thought about her own ex-husband, the day Dean had said those famous words to her. Those words that every man on the planet says when a relationship is over. Those words that might have hurt if she thought he meant them. *I never loved you*. Only in Hannah Wells-Fox's case, those words were true.

Gascoigne had tried to tell her. And she didn't listen.

Was it enough? What would Bryan think? She would take this to Fitz-Cahill tomorrow morning. But first, she needed to talk to Louisa Samahroo. Louisa had hinted that she knew something, and whatever she suspected would either be confirmed or denied once she talked to Hannah. Louisa was probably onto the same thing she was.

By itself, this wasn't enough to convict Gascoigne. But Aidra had been hired to seed doubt, to raise questions, to make a jury think twice.

And this was certainly something to think about.

Aidra stood at the door and swept her eyes around her condo. She'd been home all day and it showed—plates in the dish rack, sofa pillows askew, Parker's muddy footprints near the door. Usually, the only things she had to clean were the dust bunnies in the corners. She thought about Quinn's house with toys everywhere and the constant parade of laundry and the churning dishwasher. She remembered when her own home looked like that.

Time to go. She had an Exersleep session scheduled for four o'clock, giving her a chance to shower and change before meeting Louisa at the Library at six. She wondered if Exersleeping would feel the same now that she had Learning Systems n-tech circulating through her body as well. But why should that make any difference? The two kinds of tech did such radically different things—one of them chemical, one of them neurological.

She patted Madeline and told her to watch the house. She had one foot outside and was setting the locks when the companel chirped for attention. Aidra was ready to let it forward to her car or her datapad, but Madeline sprinted across the room, hopped onto the couch, and pawed at the connect key. She'd recognized Jon's face on the screen and answered the call.

"You are a very clever girl," Aidra said, patting the caline's head. When had she learned to answer the phone? Did she and Jon have regular chats while Aidra was out?

"Mad-dog!" Jon grinned into the pickup. "Who's a good girl? You are. Yes, you are. Yes, you. Good girl."

Madeline grinned back, tongue lolling.

Aidra sat next to Madeline and put her arm around the caline. "Hey, baby."

"Hey, Mom. I'm just calling to check in."

Jon never called to check in. He contacted her a couple of times a week but always for a reason—he needed money, laundry instructions, advice about roommate troubles. As the school year progressed, the calls had come less frequently. *As they should*, Aidra reminded herself.

"I saw you on the spins," Jon said. "You shouldn't frown so much. You're getting the mom-lines on your forehead."

"I think everyone gets those lines when they're talking to Ugly Ben."

"Are you going to do more?"

"I'm probably going to have to. I'm sorry."

"Nah, it's airy. My buddies want to make a drinking game out of it. It's a sip every time you roll your eyes. Finish the cup when you sigh heavily."

"Hilarious. You're nineteen."

"Just kidding. My roommate thinks you're cool."

"That's a relief."

"I think you're cool, too."

"Thanks, baby." Aidra checked the time. She was going to miss her Exersleep appointment if she didn't leave soon. But she wasn't about to cut Jon off in the middle of a conversation. "You doing okay?" she asked.

"Squeezy," Jon said. "That summer internship keeps sending me more forms to fill out and I'm finishing everything up before finals and I'm trying to pack up my stuff so I can move out."

"Can you fit everything in your car?"

"It's smooth. Lenny will take the fridge for the summer so all I need are my clothes and my datapad. And my guitar."

"Your what?"

"Oh, yeah, check it out." He held up a scratched acoustic guitar. "Guy on my floor was getting rid of it."

"He was just throwing it away?"

"He got a new one for his birthday, so he didn't want this one.

Said it wasn't worth taking downstate." Jon strummed a few out-of-tune notes. "It's weird. Feels like spring just got here and it's time to go home."

More like spring finally got here and you'd better get yourself home. "You've still got finals," she said.

"Yeah, but that's it. And then I'll be gone."

"You'll be home for less than three months," Aidra said. "Then you'll be right back there. Same dorm, same friends, ready for year two."

"Actually . . ."

Here it comes.

"I was thinking." Jon moved his fingers up a fret and experimented with a few more notes. "I'm thinking of taking an apartment next year. Me and Lenny and a couple of the other guys. They have these houses near campus and—"

"I thought you liked the dorm."

"The food's not that great, and it gets noisy sometimes, and it will be cheaper off campus."

"No it—"

"I could bring Madeline, too. The guys are all cool with it."

"You want to take Madeline to Houghton?"

"Why not? I mean, you're so busy anyway. You won't even notice that she's gone."

"Well, besides the fact that she'll be the most mature person in your house—"

"Hey, now."

"What about your scholarship? It pays for your dorm. It won't pay for off-campus housing."

"What do you think, sis?" Jon asked Madeline. "Want to go to school? Do you? Huh, girl? Want to go to school with me?"

"No!" Aidra leaned into the comscreen. "This is a terrible idea. You can't just turn down free room and board."

"About that . . ."

Aidra's heart lurched. "What happened?"

"It wasn't my fault, Mom. I swear, it had nothing to do with me."

"I thought that money was guaranteed."

"For a year," Jon said.

"Well, yes, you have to reapply for the scholarship every year, but I assumed—"

"They had a lot of applicants this year, Mom. Like, twice as many as usual. The fellowship committee gave it to someone else. That's all."

Aidra wondered if the scholarship was given to someone more deserving, or someone more improved? Say, someone who used Learning Systems?

Well, so what? It wouldn't change anything. Jon had always competed against kids with more advantages—two supportive parents, more money, more enrichment activities. Learning Systems was just more of the same. Jon was doing fine.

"Maybe if I don't do that internship this summer." His shoulders drooped and the guitar sagged in his arms. "I could find a job and save up—"

"Out of the question."

"There are jobs up here, too. I could take fewer classes every term and—"

"And then your academic scholarship will be cut, too." His partial academic scholarship was designed to get him in and out of college in four years. That meant hard classes and plenty of them. Even if he got a job on campus, he could never earn as much as his scholarship paid. Staying a full-time student was the only option that made financial sense. Now, she just had to get him housing.

Aidra rested her cheek on the top of Madeline's head, once again grateful that her job came with a subsidized gym membership. If she was going to pick up more side jobs, she'd need Exersleep more than ever.

"We'll work it out," she told Jon. "Maybe your dad can pitch in a little." There was nothing in their divorce agreement about college costs, and Dean was living paycheck to paycheck, but wasn't everyone these days? It wouldn't hurt to ask.

"A small job," Jon said. "A few hours a week. Or a loan or something."

"Just keep getting those A's for me, baby. That's your job right now. Let me worry about the money."

"Okay, Mom. But Lenny and I are going to look at rental houses tomorrow."

"You can look. Looking's free. And do it after you study."

"Sure. After. Bye, Mom." Jon blew Madeline a kiss and waved to Aidra before hitting the cutoff.

Aidra grabbed her keys and purse and gave Madeline one more pat. Unless she experienced the miracle of the green lights, she was going to miss her Exersleep appointment, which she literally couldn't afford to do. If she didn't have time to Exersleep, she didn't have time not to. Maybe she'd settle for a half cycle today, just a top-up, until her life was calmer and she could get back to her regular schedule.

CHAPTER FIFTEEN

"Well, well," Louisa said, smiling down at her. "When did this happen?"

"When did what happen?" Aidra asked, trying for nonchalance.

"You know what. Since when are you Supremium?"

"I've only had one session of Learning Systems." Aidra craned her neck to look at Louisa, who had played up her height by wearing platform shoes. Something had made Aidra wear cute flats with her black dress. Maybe she sensed how much Louisa enjoyed towering over her. Maybe she was thinking about all those stairs to the fourth floor. She couldn't say exactly what it was, but her gut said the flats were perfect.

"Anyway," Aidra said. "That was a lucky guess. You can't tell by looking at me."

"Yes, I can."

"No, you can't."

"Yes, I can," Louisa insisted. "It's written all over you."

"Liar."

"So . . . how is it?"

Aidra grinned. "It's *amazing*."

"Told you."

"Not in a way I could hear."

"Sure I did," Louisa said. "You tried it, didn't you?"

"Ohh, arrogant much?"

"Arrogant the exact right amount."

They laughed, but there was something tentative in Louisa's mirth, as if she wasn't quite in on the joke, or there was something else on her mind. Of course, there was always something else on

Louisa's mind, but this looked less like multitasking and more like worry. *If I were a little more Supremium, could I see what it was?* Aidra put that thought aside. No sense longing for what she couldn't have. And if Louisa had something to say, she'd say it soon enough. Supremiums didn't waste time—ironically enough, since they had all day to waste.

"Shall we go down?" Louisa asked.

"Down?" Special Collections was on the top floor. Eating anywhere in the building was a treat, but they both seemed overdressed for Hardbacks, the sports bar on the second level, or even the international restaurants on floor three.

"To the Archive," Louisa said. "Unless you wanted something else?"

"Once you invite me to the Archive, there *is* nothing else." The ultra-exclusive steakhouse was built around the Library's extensive wine cellar. Aidra had always wanted to see it, but had never been able to convince herself it was worth the price. Now, she would not only see the Archive, but dine there with the owner.

"So what did you want to tell me about Mackenzie Fox?" Aidra asked when they were in the private elevator. "Did Hannah give you more information?"

Louisa seemed to be struggling with something.

"Are you okay?" Aidra asked. A connection formed. "Are you glad that Gascoigne is out on bail or are you worried?"

Louisa seemed to shake it off. "We should have our meal."

The elevator doors parted, but instead of turning right, toward the hostess stand, Louisa turned left and opened an unmarked door.

Aidra followed. "Where are we going?"

"Kitchen."

"Now that *is* exclusive. What do you need to check on this time?"

Louisa didn't answer. She strode down a long corridor and Aidra scrambled to catch up. They passed the receiving area, where crates from the day's deliveries stood empty. In the server station, rows of plates and wine glasses stood on industrial racks. After that was the salad station, where prep cooks were putting together elegant dishes of micro-greens. A few people looked up curiously, but Louisa never acknowledged them. She seemed to be mumbling something under her breath.

"I'm impressed," Aidra tried. "But you could have just showed me the dining room."

Louisa said nothing. She led them past the grill area, where white-jacketed chefs were expertly turning steaks. The smell was intoxicating. Even with the industrial fans blowing away the smoke, the scent of seared meat was almost like having it in her mouth. Her taste buds were alive with anticipation.

Louisa was noticed by all the cooks and greeted by some. She ignored them all. Aidra tripped along behind, wondering where her funny, charming friend had gone.

A chef's knife, long and thin with a sharp point, sat on the end of the prep counter. Aidra spotted it a moment before Louisa did. Then it was in Louisa's hand, slicing through the air and toward Aidra's face.

Aidra yelped and stumbled backwards, trying to maneuver around the hot grill. "What are you doing? Are you crazy?"

Louisa's only answer was to stab again, this time aiming for Aidra's belly.

"Watch it!" Aidra said to the cooks. She hated knives. In some ways, they were worse than guns. It took no skill to use them and they were deadly in close quarters. This was the kind of knife used for stripping fat from an aged steak and Aidra had no doubt it would just as easily cut through her own flesh.

On Louisa's third attempt, Aidra swung her purse off her shoulder and caught Louisa's wrist in the strap. She spun the purse like she was twisting a tourniquet, holding it and the knife as far from her as possible. If she could numb the arm, Louisa would lose her grip.

Louisa jerked her arm up and Aidra's feet left the ground as she was pulled forward and into her attacker. *Damn, she's strong.* For a fraction of a second, they were kissing close, and Aidra saw the hideous blankness on Louisa's face.

"Have to do this," Louisa mumbled. "Have to do this. Have to do this." She raised her other arm and transferred the knife to her left hand.

Aidra aimed a kick at Louisa's shin, let go of the purse, and rolled backwards. She was up again in a second, her hands outstretched. She might have to try for a grab, but she had already seen how quick Louisa was. If she missed, Louisa would bury the blade deep before Aidra could try again.

Louisa shook her right arm to free it from Aidra's purse, flailing it away and behind her.

Chaos had erupted on the grill line, with chefs dancing around, some moving forward as if to help, others removing hot dishes and trying not to burn themselves or the food in the confusion. A gabble of noise was coming from farther away, questioning voices coming from the prep area. No one near them spoke, either afraid to attract Louisa's attention or afraid to break Aidra's concentration.

Aidra's hands wanted to reach for the purse she was no longer wearing, to go for her weapon, but that was wrong. She'd carried a ladylike purse to go with her little black dress. No room for a gun in there, so she'd left it at home. She vowed never to make that mistake again.

Louisa lunged forward and Aidra spun away, putting thoughts of the gun out of her mind. If she didn't find another weapon, she'd never make *any* mistake again. Maybe she could grab one of the cast iron searing pans. But the only ones in her reach were on the hot grill. Could she lure Louisa toward the other knives? No. Even if she got one, she'd be no match for the larger woman in hand-to-hand fighting. Her best bet was to stay out of the way.

One of the grill chefs circled behind Louisa. He caught Aidra's eye and gave her a nod. Aidra wanted to shout at him to get back, but her throat closed in panic. Any warning would only tip Louisa off, and if Louisa saw him, she would spin around and gut him.

The chef lurched forward and grabbed Louisa with strong arms. She stomped on his instep with her heel and drove her elbows into him. She slashed with the knife. The chef bellowed and grabbed his wrist where she'd cut him, making the mistake of turning away from her. The knife flew, slicing him again and again as he tried to fight her off.

A second man approached from the other side, but Louisa was too fast. A line of blood emerged from his elbow to his wrist as Louisa cut his arm.

She turned to her original victim, already curled in a fetal position. Red streaks marred his perfect whites as Louisa stabbed his back, his hands, his neck. He screamed once and was still.

She cut a third man across the palm as he tried to grab the knife, nearly severing his thumb.

"Back!" Aidra shouted. "For God's sake, get away from her. Don't give her a target. Louisa! Louisa!"

But Louisa was beyond hearing. There was nothing of the brilliant, vivacious woman in her now, nothing of the Supremium. She was still mumbling "have to do this" and her eyes had an eerie vacuity that Aidra had seen once before—dusty marbles in a slack face.

"Someone call the cops."

"I already did," a prep chef called from the back of the room.

But they would be too late. Louisa's shoulders relaxed as she stood in the circle of cooks, her victim bleeding to death at her feet. Her head tilted ever so slightly, as if listening to something, or perhaps recalling something.

"Have to do this," Louisa said. Her hand moved slowly, deliberately, over, across. The knife met her throat and opened it from ear to ear, silencing Louisa Samahroo once and for all.

CHAPTER SIXTEEN

At least it was Sofia Gao.

That was the thought that kept Aidra together in the hours that followed. The shock and trauma blurred many of the details for her, but a few moments stood out with haunting clarity. One of the unhurt chefs had covered Louisa and her victim with tablecloths brought in from the dining room. The restaurant manager, a man with a red-gold burr of beard stubble, screamed into her face. She could remember his anger but not what he said. One of the Librarians from the creative consultation paced in a tight circle muttering, "Paradigm shift. Complete paradigm shift."

Sofia Gao's voice had been the first thing she could really hold onto. Aidra met her eyes and gave her a nod of recognition. Sofia thanked the restaurant manager for clearing the dining room and getting all the customers out of the way. She detailed six Detroit City cops to secure the kitchen. "And for Pete's sake, Kimble, station someone at the back stairs. We've already chased three spinners out of there."

Aidra supposed it was a good thing that the entrance to the Archive was a private elevator. She could imagine the mayhem if Louisa had killed herself in one of the restaurants in the main hall. This was chaos enough, with the wounded chefs being treated by paramedics, the rest of the kitchen staff waiting to make their statements, and Librarians milling around the small space while the police tried to establish a perimeter.

Aidra sat in a chair that had been pulled into the server station. The sight of half-done steaks sitting in bloody pools on the prep counter had made her sick to her stomach and she'd asked to go sit down by the plates and silverware.

Sofia was taking her time. She'd gloved up and peered under the tablecloths covering both Louisa and the dead chef at her side. Several officers, including a few carrying equipment cases, waited respectfully.

Sofia turned to the techs. "Not much room for a circle here, but do what you can. I want in and out access and make sure you get scenics on all the witnesses."

Some officers unspooled scene tape while those with cases began setting up tripods topped by holo-cameras. Aidra thought of the viewing room at Police Headquarters. In a few minutes, anyone with access to that room would be able to visit this scene in detail. How efficient. How cold. Sofia gave instructions for securing the entire basement and spoke into her datapad.

As the motions were performed, the procedures followed, the protocols enacted, Aidra lapsed back into her own head.

The Louisa Samahroo who was lying dead on that floor, the one who had stabbed a man to death and used the same knife to slit her own throat—that was not the person Aidra had known. Something had changed her, and Aidra was terrified that she knew what it was. The combination of Exersleep and Learning Systems had tangled themselves in Louisa's brain and made her homicidal.

It had been so easy for her to dismiss Jean Claude Gascoigne as an anomaly. She told herself he was using the nanotech as an excuse. He'd meant to kill Mackenzie Fox all along and blaming the n-tech meant he'd get away with it.

But poor Louisa hadn't wanted to kill anyone. Aidra was sure of that. The chef who'd died at her hands was in the wrong place at the wrong time.

Maybe Mackenzie Fox was, too.

Who else was going to be in the wrong place today? Who else would die at the hands of a Supremium? The Library was full of them. Were they all ticking time bombs waiting to go off?

Was she?

Aidra curled forward in her chair, hugging herself. Her knees tapped against one another as a fresh set of the shakes overtook her. *Jon. I have never been so glad that my baby is so far from home.* She had to stay away from him, and anyone else she loved. At least Morris was all the way in Washington.

She stared at the floor, trying to clear her head. She was thinking nonsense now. Morris had nothing to fear from her because Morris wasn't currently a part of her life. At least, not a physical part. They hadn't gotten physical in quite a while.

Focus, Aidra. She'd only had one session of Learning Systems. She would never do it again. She'd be fine. Just fine. She had to be fine.

At least it was Sofia Gao.

Sofia had finished with the bodies and her circuit of witnesses and stood before Aidra.

"I thought you were under suspension," Aidra said.

"Board cleared me this afternoon," Sofia said. "One of the nice things about all the publicity is they couldn't just put it on a shelf and forget it. How are you doing?" she asked gently.

"Fine," Aidra answered.

"Really?"

"Not remotely. Please tell me that you're closely monitoring Jean Claude Gascoigne and his new-found freedom."

"We're monitoring him 24/7 anyway. Subcutaneous GPS and beacon, both."

"And now?"

"Now, it's going to be more." Sofia's eyes were flint. "I've already requested we re-arrest for public safety, but that decision is about three tiers above me." She lost a fraction of her intensity. "Tell me what happened."

"Are you recording?"

"Of course I'm recording."

Aidra spoke clearly for the datapad's microphones. She went

through the entire evening, from making plans with Louisa for a fancy dinner to the moment it ended with two dead people and the entire restaurant staff in shock and mourning.

"I liked her," she finished and realized it wasn't enough. "I really liked her. I mean, I barely knew her. Just met her."

"But you were on the road to friends."

"Yes. Anyway, I can't tell you much more. I felt light-headed and I thought I might throw up, but after I sat down here . . ." Her hand wandered into the air in a shrug.

The junior detective called Kimble trundled over to them holding out a delicate china cup of coffee. "For you, boss," he said.

Sofia waved it away, so he tried giving it to Aidra.

"No, thank you." Her stomach felt like someone had drawn it taut and knotted it.

"You sure?" Kimble asked.

Sofia pointed to the cup. "Where did you even get that?"

"One of the waiters made a fresh pot." Kimble took a healthy sip and let out a satisfied sigh. "I'll say this for the Library, they sure know how to cater a crime scene."

"Didn't I tell you to watch the back stairs?" Sofia asked.

"You told me to send someone, yeah." Kimble took another sip.

"Well, now I'm sending you."

"Okay, okay." He nudged Aidra. "Pot's over there if you change your mind."

Sofia waited for him to bumble away and then turned back to Aidra. "Three of those cooks thought they saw you and Samahroo fighting hand-to-hand *before* she picked up the knife to defend herself. Relax." She showed a palm. "Kind of thing happens all the time. Eyewitnesses see things that aren't there." She consulted her datapad. "We've already cross-linked the security footage. It's just 2D-single perspective and the angle isn't great, but it clearly shows what you told me."

"Glad to hear it."

"I know this is difficult but—"

"What was his name?" Aidra asked. "The chef. The one Louisa killed. What was his name?"

Sofia consulted her datapad. "Marco Arturo Rodriguez. They called him Marc. Single, no children. Worked here for five years."

"Marc Rodriguez," Aidra repeated. "Marc Rodriguez."

"I need to know everything you and Louisa talked about."

"That's just it," Aidra said. "We didn't talk. She wanted to tell me something. That's why we were meeting. She was acting so strangely. But I couldn't figure out why. At least not fast enough." Aidra's throat closed with sorrow. Her eyes prickled and she blinked up at the ceiling.

Sofia patted her shoulder. "It's not your fault."

"It feels like it is."

"I know."

She remembered the expression on Sofia's face when they watched the holo recording of Gascoigne killing Fox with Sofia's gun. She was probably wearing that same look.

Sofia's pad chimed. She listened to her earbud and nodded, turning the display toward Aidra. "Why did you call a taxi?"

"I didn't."

"This guy claims he's your ride. You know him?"

An irate Patrick Sullivan was glaring out of the pad.

"Never seen him before in my life."

As Aidra descended the broad front steps of the Library, the wind hit her first. One of those humid spring breezes that seemed to smother rather than refresh. After that was the noise. She was immediately surrounded by spinners shoving video-audio pickup wands in her face, shouting questions, connecting through uplink spikes to the vans that littered the sidewalk, and from there, to the world. They all spoke at once, interrupting one another and trying to be the first with a complete question she'd actually answer.

"Ms. Scott!"

"Ms. Scott!"

"What happened in—"

"Are all Supremiums—"

"Over here, Ms. Scott."

"Look this way, Ms. Scott."

Aidra blinked and said nothing. She recognized most of the local spinners, Tom Griffon Junior, Marcia in the Morning, and of course, Ugly Ben. But this was national news. The big guys were here, too, the household names like C.J. Monroe and Tally Tits.

"What did she—"

"When will you—"

"Did you mean to—"

"Exclusive!" Ugly Ben shouted above the babble. "Ex. Clus. Ive. You promised."

Aidra felt like he was talking from some remote patch of long-ago and far-away, but it was only yesterday. Grief was like a wind, blowing through anything she might have said in the past. She'd given her word. So what? What did it matter now?

The others ignored Ben and kept bellowing their questions. "Was the n-tech in her blood the source of her unnatural strength?"

"You can clearly be heard on the security cameras telling everyone else to back off. Were you and Louisa Samahroo a coordinated hit squad?"

"Why were you protecting a murderer?"

"What did you have against Marco Rodriguez?"

"If Louisa couldn't finish the job, were you going to do it?"

"Enough!" Sullivan elbowed his way through the crowd. "You nutwads know better than this. Don't the privacy laws mean anything to you jerks?"

"We need to hear it from her," Tom Griffon Junior said.

Sullivan rounded on him. "You're hearing it from me."

"No comment," Aidra said.

"There, you see?" Sullivan took her arm. "Now move on, jizz-wipes, or you'll get nothing but my fist."

The spinners backed away to the legally mandated four meter limit. She could bet every one of them could pace off the distance down to the half centimeter. They couldn't hassle her anymore, and if they broadcast her image, they had to alter it by at least fifty percent. The law was quite clear on that. But the law couldn't make them leave, and it couldn't make them stop recording.

Ugly Ben was the last to back away. He didn't say anything more, just regarded her with sad, disappointed eyes.

Sullivan glared around the circle. "Don't you turd-stains got better things to do?"

"Don't feed them," Aidra said softly. "Don't give them new things to spin."

"I'm going to give them my boot up their asses. Shoo, jackals."

As unnecessary as Sullivan's intrusion was, Aidra was glad to see him. He was one of the few people who understood how this felt. To be coming up on something good, to be close to breaking a case, and then have it snatched away. To have someone die right in front of you, and never be certain it wasn't your fault. She didn't know if Sullivan had been through this exact experience, but she could bet he'd gotten close. He would give sympathy, advice, and wise counsel, dressed up in tough talk and cursing that sounded almost like poetry.

She wanted to throw herself into his arms for one of his classic bear hugs, but held herself back, and not just because of the spinners. What if she hurt him? What if she went completely crazy and did something terrible? She had both kinds of nanotech in her now and therefore could not be trusted. "Are you carrying?" she murmured.

Sullivan took a step away from her. "You know a PI who doesn't carry? Didn't I teach you anything?"

Apparently, not enough. Aidra thought of her own gun sitting in its desk drawer back home. While fighting Louisa, she'd desperately wished she had it. At this moment, she was glad she did not.

Sullivan led her toward his car, parked in a restricted area at the curb. He referred to the vehicle as his Hotrod Lincoln. During her apprenticeship, he'd incessantly sung an old tune by that name. The car was still carefully maintained, without a drop of road slush on it, but the finish was not quite as shiny as it once was and the tires were balding. One wing mirror had been broken off, and was now bolted on with a mismatched bracket from the hardware store.

He opened the passenger door. "We need to get away from this."

Aidra hesitated, making sure the door was between her and Sullivan. "How did you know where I was?"

He pointed to the spinners who stood in a semi-circle on the other side of the car. "Everyone knows where you were. These bum-chewers had access to the security cam about five minutes after the cops did. It hit the newsnets five seconds after that."

"Since when do you believe a single thing spinners have to say?"

"They ain't always wrong."

"You know what I think? I think you knew where I was before the spinners did. You've been tracking me. Where did you hide the bug?"

Sullivan scoffed. "A digital assistant is like no assistant at all."

"So you were following me?"

"How many times do I have to tell you? Never work harder than you have to. Getting someone else to do the legwork is the smart way to go."

Of course. An apprentice learning the trade. She had followed plenty of dead ends so Sullivan wouldn't have to. He was still "passing it on," as he put it, teaching someone the ropes in exchange for their time, their energy, their youth.

"So you've been keeping an eye on what I do." She gripped the top of the car door. "I offered to share."

"And if I had something worth sharing, I'd share it back."

"If you spent more time working instead of sitting on your butt and letting me bird-dog for you, perhaps you—"

A short whistle made her turn toward the spinners. They were trying to get her attention in order to film her face. Another one barked out a cough while a third cleared his throat. Tally Tits held up an oversize pad that read, *"Are you working for Gascoigne?"* The spinners weren't allowed to talk to her, but you could always count on them to exploit a loophole. Tom Griffon Junior also held up a pad. *"How long had you and Louisa been planning this murder?"*

"That's it." Sullivan slammed the car door and advanced toward the spinners. They kept the four meter perimeter, moving with him to form a human bubble.

"I told you ass-wipes to get the hell away. Do I have to show you?" His Smith was out of its shoulder holster and in his hand before Aidra could blink. The spinners scattered, ducking behind nearby cars or retreating to their vans. Aidra rushed forward, ready to wrestle the gun away from Sullivan.

He waved the weapon in a wide arc, saw he was without a target, then grunted in satisfaction and put it away.

"What do you think you're doing?" Aidra demanded. "You *never* take out a gun you don't intend to fire. You taught me that."

"Who says I wouldn't fire?"

"Are you completely flipped?"

"Not at people." Sullivan smirked. "But shooting out some tires would be fun."

"*No shooting.*"

He raised his eyebrows. "You asked me if I was carrying. And now you don't want me to use the piece I have. But it worked. They're gone."

"They're not gone." None of the spinners had left the scene, and the video-audio pickup wands jutting out from their hiding places meant they were still recording. "You're just giving them material."

"Well pardon me if you've got a better idea."

"Pretty much anything would be, wouldn't it?"

They glared at each other a moment, breathing heavily. Sullivan broke eye contact first, running a wrinkled hand over tired eyes. "Ah, look at this shit, will you? This mess has the two of us growling and circling. That's not right."

Aidra sighed. It *was* a mess. And that was also as close to an apology as she'd get from Sullivan.

"Some night, huh?" he said.

"Don't you think it's quite a coincidence that the Supremium I happen to be talking to about Supremiums going berserk just happens to, you know, go berserk?"

"Wrong place, wrong time. Just the law of averages working itself out, if you ask me."

That sounded logical and lazy at the same time, but Aidra couldn't say which one it was. Tonight's events had her too scrambled to think straight.

Sullivan jerked a thumb toward the Library. "This thing is going to shake out with or without us. You have already done your time front-and-center for Fitz-Cahill. Could have gotten yourself killed. No way those pricks can object if you just pilot around a desk chair until the dust settles."

"Is that what you do? Sit until you get dusty?"

"Only when it's too dangerous to move. Listen to your Uncle Sullivan and keep wide of those Supremium freaks. Sooner or later, they'll all end up in jail or the bughouse." He opened the car door. "Come on, kiddo, I'll give you a ride home."

Aidra froze. "My car is around back, in the ramp."

"So get it tomorrow. You shouldn't drive tonight."

She wanted nothing more than to sink into the cracked leather seats of the Hotrod Lincoln and fiddle with the music system, or stare up at the rolling skyline while nagging Sullivan about his horrible driving.

And then she'd probably lose her mind and kill them both. Locked in a moving car with a loaded weapon did not sound safe. Not now.

But Sullivan was right. She shouldn't be driving. She couldn't go with him, she couldn't drive herself home, and she couldn't tell him why. She felt awful about not sharing when she promised she would, but it wouldn't help Sullivan. She needed him to go away. Without her.

"Look at this clunker," she said. "What is it, twenty years old? Is it still street-legal?"

"Twelve, and it's already a classic. Since when do you mind my car?"

"Since it started looking like a death trap."

"What are you talking about? This beauty is the safest thing on the road."

"And the oldest."

Sullivan's shoulders slumped. "Like me."

"I didn't mean it like that. But your car—"

"Look, kiddo, if you don't want to be seen with me, just say so."

"I promise not to drive," Aidra said. "I'll talk to the detective in charge. She'll get a uniform to take me home."

"You're going to let them put you in the back of a squad car?" Sullivan gestured to the spinners, who had gathered once more, although at a safer distance. "Those turd-kissers are going to love that."

"I'll risk it." Right now, being in the back of a nice, secure police car sounded like the perfect place to be.

CHAPTER SEVENTEEN

Home.

Sanctuary. Away from the spinners, the police, and the world. Even if a newsie knew her address and knew she was at home, they could not invade her privacy once she was inside.

Madeline greeted her at the door, prancing around her feet with a doggie grin on her face. Aidra made all the proper noises, greeting Madeline and petting her. She took care of Madeline's food, water, and a quick trip to the back yard, but the motions felt hollow. Madeline didn't understand humans—their ambitions, their accomplishments, and their endless capacity for cruelty. She was made for companionship and love. That was all she knew.

But perhaps that was all she needed to know. Aidra sprawled on the floor with Madeline and snuggled next to her, feeling her warmth, matching her breath for breath. The spicy-sweet scent of caline washed over her, relaxing her. Madeline seemed happy to provide what comfort she could, lying still as Aidra ran her hand over and over her silky coat.

Calines were supposed to be custom-made for their owners and Madeline had been made for someone else—someone Aidra had nothing in common with. But somehow, she and Madeline were always in harmony. She attributed it more to the caline's sweet nature and dog genes than anything she herself had done. Madeline was one of the many blessings in her life, one of the wonderful things she had that she didn't earn.

Her life had been good. Better than good. Yet, somehow, she'd convinced herself she needed an upgrade. Why had she ever wanted to try Learning Systems? A single treatment wasn't enough to improve her mind. All it did was make her arrogant and impulsive.

Next to her, Madeline had fallen into a contented doze. Aidra wished she could join her, curl up right here on the floor and pass out. But between Exersleep and her churning emotions, she knew she wouldn't be able to sleep.

The companel trilled for attention. Aidra got up carefully, trying not to disturb Madeline, but of course, the caline woke up and followed her to the couch.

She expected Quinn or Noah or even Gilly. But looking back at her from the companel were the bright green eyes of Emmy Mathers. "Hey, I'm just calling to check on—"

"I want them out," Aidra said.

"The nano-machines?"

"Yes. I don't care how. You put them in. You take them out."

"There's really no way to do that."

"I need them out!" Hot tears dripped out of the corners of Aidra's eyes and she swiped them away with the heels of her hands.

"I can't. I am so sorry. I saw the newsnets. That's why I called. Tonight didn't look like much fun."

Aidra sniffled. "It wasn't."

"But it wasn't the n-tech's fault."

"What if it is? Maybe this is really happening. Maybe Jean Claude Gascoigne is right. We're just seeing it in long-time users first. Soon it will be everyone."

"You're jumping to conclusions," Emmy said. "You don't know what happened."

"Yes, I do. I was there."

"But you don't know what was going on in Louisa's brain. The autopsy will show brain damage or a stroke or genetic abnormality or something to explain this."

"I can think of a simpler explanation."

"Even if this were some kind of nanotech malfunction—which it's *not*—you don't have to worry. You had a single treatment. If we're all going to turn into killers, you're going to be the last one."

Aidra flashed on those zombie games that Jon liked to play. A world gone crazy, with only a few normal survivors as the heroes.

"This is nonsense," Emmy said. "Two people are dead while thousands are healthy and alive. I like those odds. Would you stop worrying? Drink some water, wait until morning. There's nothing you need to do. The n-tech will degrade on its own."

Emmy gave a few more words of encouragement, then made sure Aidra had her contact information before ending the call.

She tried to listen to Emmy's words. Tried to believe them. Nanotechnology was designed to degrade and leave the body within a day, with a small chance of some machines lasting a few hours longer. It had been thirty hours since her trip to Ann Arbor.

Wrong. She had to stop thinking like an Exersleeper. Exersleep played with the chemicals of the brain, but once it was over, the brain returned to its normal state, unaffected. Learning Systems made new neural connections and strengthened ones that were already there. Even when the n-tech was gone, she couldn't undo what was done to her mind, no matter how long she waited.

She looked at Madeline, happily waiting for whatever Aidra wanted to do next. Was Madeline safe with her? Should she send her back to Quinn's? This late at night? There would be no way to explain it that wouldn't worry her sister half to death. Aidra made sure the door to Jon's room was open in case Madeline had to run and hide. That was all she could do.

She collapsed on the couch with the weary twitchiness that she now thought of as the true mental state of the Supremium.

She turned on the newsnets. "What do you think, Madeline? Should we see how bad it is?"

She started with local news, more out of habit than anything else. On CI newsnet, Tom Griffon Junior looked back at her, all sleek hair and toothy smile. As usual, he was broadcasting live updates. Griffon didn't believe in retakes, edits, or reflection. At least she didn't have to watch herself—or the legally altered version of herself—on his show.

"So you're saying that all Supremiums are dangerous?" Griffon said.

"That is precisely what I am saying." The person talking was identified as Dr. Evan Banks, professor of neurology at Wayne State University. Banks looked the part, with a lab coat over his shirt and tie and round glasses on his face. What kind of man wore a lab coat for a broadcast interview?

"Got yourself a real try-hard, Griffon," she told the screen.

"What can be done?" Griffon asked, wide-eyed.

"Well, we can start with an immediate outlaw of all nanotechnology." Banks pushed his glasses up his nose.

"Sources tell me that Congress might be in emergency sessions about this very issue," Griffon said.

Aidra blew a raspberry at the screen. *Sources? Might be?* Typical spinner.

"Precisely," Banks said. "That is precisely what they should be doing. Quarantine of Supremiums would be a logical next step. Perhaps even putting them in protective custody in jails, to protect us from them."

"Do you think it will come to that?" Griffon asked.

"The danger can't be overstated," Banks said. "If we don't—"

Aidra commanded the companel to switch over to headlines, hoping for something a little more sympathetic. Or at least a little more human. She scrolled through news stories that the nets offered, skipping past the ones that promised to show her Louisa Samahroo's last moments, or for that matter, the murder of Mackenzie Fox, which was news again after the latest killing.

As she was scrolling, Ugly Ben's newest essay popped to the forefront. The headline read, "A Call for Personal Responsibility."

Ugly Ben's tattooed head filled her screen. He had already broadcast the action, interviewed the witnesses, and talked to the experts. Now was the time for his own opinion. This was what he was famous for. Most of his fans skipped the rest of the news cycle entirely, waiting for Ugly Ben to tell them what to think.

"Exersleep," he said. "Learning Systems. Supremiums. Humans have always wanted this. Yes, we did. We want exactly this. We want to be faster, smarter, and more efficient. We want to be *better*. And if there is a shortcut to get us there, you can be sure we'll take it. So who is surprised that Supremiums happened? Are you surprised? I'm not surprised."

He looked away from the screen for a moment, as if consulting cue cards, but Aidra could bet he had this whole speech memorized. Or he was making it up on the spot. Hard to tell with Ugly Ben.

"We outlawed chip-heads. Too dangerous, our government said. Too prone to failure. And oh, did they ever fail." He twitched and flailed in an imitation of someone with a defective chip.

"Then, after the chromosome plague, we outlawed most forms of genetic engineering. Modify *food*, they said. Modify *animals* if you want to. But don't you dare touch a human. Humans have souls, don't you know. So here we are, aren't we? This was inevitable. We were destined to go down this road. Because there was nowhere else for us to go."

Aidra hesitated with her finger on the cutoff button, hypnotized and irritated at the same time.

"But if you're going down that road, for the love of all that is holy, would you people please take some responsibility for your actions? You wouldn't drink and drive, would you? So why do you want to mix those two technologies in your brain pan?"

Aidra cut off the playback in the middle of Ugly Ben's next sentence. She got a large glass of water from the kitchen and gulped it down, trying to flush the little bots away.

Everyone said the n-tech just enhanced the neural connections that were already there. Did that mean that Louisa was already a killer before using n-tech? Was Jean Claude Gascoigne?

Aidra wrapped her arms around herself and rocked in place. She was a trained fighter in hand-to-hand combat and self-defense. She went to the target range twice a month and was an accurate shot under most conditions. She already knew how to kill. Was the nanotech just waiting to give her a reason?

She scrolled through the rest of the headlines, knowing she wouldn't find what she was looking for. None of the newsnets knew the answers because there weren't any. Jean Claude Gascoigne had killed Mackenzie Fox. Louisa Samahroo had killed Marc Rodriguez and then herself. This couldn't be a coincidence. Yet, they'd both used technology that everyone from the FDA to congressional oversight boards had declared safe for humans.

An alert popped up on the corner of the screen and she stared at it a moment, trying to make sense of it. She'd almost forgotten the keywords she'd programmed in at the beginning of the case. But of course, nobody could report on tonight's events without talking to Hannah Wells-Fox, and here she was, giving a statement.

Hannah stood on the front steps of her cute farmhouse, wearing a hand-knit sweater over a crisp white shirt—homey and professional at the same time. Her hair and makeup made her look both fresh-out-of bed and flawless. Hannah held a small pad, which she consulted before speaking into the many video-audio pickup wands aimed at her.

"Tonight's events have rocked our community. Louisa Samahroo was a visionary artist, a savvy businesswoman, and a personal friend. She will be missed by all who knew her. The fact that she took another's life as well as her own has made us sorrowful, afraid, and filled with questions. We will probably never know if the combination of n-tech in Louisa's brain made her do what she did. How can we ever know?

"Nanotechnology has given us powerful solutions to everyday problems. But nanotech straddles the line between biology and technology in a way that genetic engineering does not. Perhaps it's time we return these solutions to therapeutic, rather than recreational purposes.

"To the family and friends of Louisa Samahroo, to her many employees, and to the people of Detroit, I offer my condolences.

I am sorry for any harm that this technology might have caused, either through regular or extraordinary use.

"My friends of the press, thank you for coming. I will not be taking any questions at this time and will not comment further."

And with that, the spinners and anchors were dismissed. Once someone said "no comment," the newsies had to back off. They wouldn't like it, but no meant no. Hannah went into her house, closing the front door in their faces.

A blip popped into her box. Ugly Ben. **[Get Ready.]**

She blipped back, **[For what?]**

[We're interactive, baby!]

[What did you do?]

[Wasn't me. I'm just the messenger. Telling you what's what.]

Aidra's comscreen filled with overlapping notices. Some came from spinners and newsies, but most were from fans of Hannah Wells-Fox. Aidra had been tagged in every spin, and the comment section of Hannah's comboview was exploding.

Aidra read through a few. They were evenly divided between the outraged technophobes and the sarcastic technophiles. Some of them blamed her—misspelling her name—for Louisa's death. Several people remarked that Aidra had been driven away in a cop car, and they assumed she'd been arrested. But a surprising number seemed convinced that Aidra had been desperately wounded and were sending her their thoughts and prayers.

Aidra turned off the feed. Ugly Ben was getting his petty revenge for being edged out on his exclusive. Now she could be reached by anyone with a computer and a waveguide. She'd have to get Noah to put up stronger shields. It wouldn't be the first time she'd had to hide her e-verse identity and it wouldn't be the last, but what a colossal pain.

The companel chirped a private call. Very few people could get through after she'd cut her feed, and Aidra turned toward the screen, expecting Jon, or Morris, or her sister. Instead, Bryan's worried face looked out at her. She told the panel to answer the call.

"Hi, Bryan."

"Look at this." He brought up video of Hannah Wells-Fox's press conference.

"Seen it."

The press conference disappeared and Bryan's face was back. "How could Hannah do that? She all but admitted that the n-tech made some kind of toxic soup in that woman's brain. What is she thinking? Is she trying to kill her company? How could her lawyers let her do that?"

"I doubt she asked them," Aidra said. Hannah was a media superstar. She probably thought she knew exactly what to say to a camera and how to say it. Even if her lawyers disagreed, they'd be hard-pressed to talk her out of it.

"She's like a toxic volcano," Bryan said.

"Hannah?"

"Louisa Samahroo. But instead of lava, she's going to bury Fitz-Cahill in feces."

"Louisa didn't kill herself to spite you."

"No, of course not. It's got nothing to do with us at all, but we're going to pay for it."

Aidra's heart moved south, bottoming out somewhere near her feet. She knew what was coming next.

Bryan ran a hand over his forehead. "Worst case scenario, Exersleep is going to be sued by every Supremium and Fitz-Cahill will be facing the biggest payout we've ever had."

"Best case scenario?" Aidra asked.

"Fitz-Cahill will decide that Exersleep is too dangerous to insure and we'll lose our biggest client."

Aidra put one hand on Madeline, waiting for the inevitable. "I'm guessing that's the reason for this call."

"I'm sorry, Aidra, I didn't want to do this now, on the phone. I know you need this job."

"No, Bryan." The words squeaked out. "Don't do this. Please."

Bryan worked his jaw as if he was grinding his teeth, "I don't have a choice. Have you seen the spins?"

"Since when does Fitz-Cahill make hiring decisions based on *spins*?"

"When our lead investigator gets hauled off by the police—"

"I wasn't *hauled off*. I asked for a ride."

"I'm just saying that public opinion—"

"I knew it," Aidra spat. "You only hired me to make yourselves look good. It didn't matter what I did, or where I went, or what I uncovered, as long as the spinners paid attention to me."

"That's not true."

"Come on, Bryan. You know as well as I do that the spins are always first and always wrong. By tomorrow, they'll be singing a different tune. The anchors will weigh in and we'll get a better story."

Bryan ran the fingers of both hands over his temples. He looked over the top of the comscreen and she wondered if he was looking at pictures of his mom and brother.

It hit her then, and she felt hollow, as if all her anger had been blasted away, leaving behind an empty shell. It wasn't Bryan's fault, and getting angry at him wouldn't help. She could imagine the awful conversations at Fitz-Cahill, and the horrible calculations that Bryan had to make.

"You wouldn't believe how hard I fought to keep you on," he said.

"Yes, I would. I know you did everything you could. But are you okay?"

Bryan lowered his head and pulled in his shoulders as if trying to make himself smaller. "Fitz-Cahill wants me to stay on at least until this thing with Gascoigne comes to some kind of resolution. They're bringing in the white coat brigade, hoping the medical experts can sow the seeds of doubt before Gascoigne goes to trial. I'm coordinating."

She was grateful that it hadn't been a full-scale housecleaning. A tiny part of her wanted it to be. Misery loves company and all that, but Bryan being unemployed wasn't going to change her own situation. If he could keep his job by dropping hers, she would try to be happy for him.

"They're going to be sorry," Bryan said. "I'm going to make sure they are. I'm going to fill your queue with every freelance assignment that comes up. Your full rate. No discounts."

Aidra nodded and thanked him, but she knew it wouldn't happen. Bryan would try, and the top brass would insist on cheaper alternatives. They'd probably get interns to do most of her job. They would get poor results, argue about it for months, and eventually regret letting her go, but that wouldn't put food on her table today.

They exchanged a few more pleasantries. Bryan promised to call her the moment he had a new assignment for her, although he was vague as to when that might be. They agreed to get together for drinks when they had time. Aidra ended the call as soon as she politely could.

She groaned and flopped back on the couch. It wasn't just that her working hours had gone from more than full-time to zero. It was also the hit to her reputation. This was the highest-profile case she'd ever had. Everyone knew who she was working for and everyone would know when she got fired. It was a lot harder to demand top dollar for her services when she looked like a failure.

She still had to pay for rent and food and car and taxes and insurance. Jon's college costs still needed to be paid. None of her creditors cared if she was employed or not. And without Fitz-Cahill and Exersleep, her job just got a lot harder.

She looked out the window at the darkness, thinking about the day ahead—all the days ahead. She mentally shuffled through her pending and unfinished caseload, already regretting turning down that offer from Jeremy Hobson, esquire. Stopping people from going through a boundary wall at the border to the zone was just the kind of low-stakes, high-paying assignment she could use right now.

She leapt off the couch and marched herself to the kitchen. No. She would not start thinking like that. This case had gone to hell.

Some cases did. She'd lost her job. There would be others. She just had to find them. There was no reason to start thinking about ethically sketchy cases simply because pickings looked slim. Time to put on her big-girl panties and deal with what was in front of her.

She messaged Noah the news, telling him to line up any new leads and shoot them to her inbox. She reached for the coffee maker's start button. Time to make a big pot of wide-awake.

Nothing happened. It wasn't until she pushed the button a second and third time that she remembered it was broken. She used a can opener to pry off the lid and peered into the inner workings. Every tube was clogged. That was the problem with these modern makers. They brewed fresh, delicious coffee on demand, but they had to be used every day or the whole thing would gum up. She yanked the pot from the wall and threw the entire machine into the recycle bin. A truck would come and take it away, and some other machine would break it down into its useful parts.

Some things couldn't be saved.

CHAPTER EIGHTEEN

Aidra jerked awake. She rolled over on the couch and blinked at the gray pre-dawn light coming in the living room window, trying to get her bearings. When had she nodded off? How long was she out? She checked the time. Five o'clock. It had only been a few hours. But *sleeping*? She wasn't a sleeper. Then again, yesterday's Exersleep session had only been a half cycle. Add in an exhausting night and the crash was inevitable.

She stretched and went to the kitchen for some water, turning on the newsnets along the way. By the time she'd taken care of Madeline and got herself showered and dressed, she'd heard enough of the headlines to form a basic picture.

The tide of public opinion had turned, as it always did, and now people were dissecting Louisa's personal life, trying to figure out why she'd do such a thing. Because of course it wasn't the nanotechnology that made her homicidal. The tech had been around for years, and experts were showing people why it was safe to use. So it had to be Louisa's own fault. Even Tom Griffin Junior and Ugly Ben had softened their original opinions.

Too little, too late. She'd told Bryan this would happen, but it hadn't happened soon enough to save her job.

She snapped off the companel in the middle of a tearful interview with Louisa's fiancé, who didn't understand how this could have happened.

Aidra didn't understand it either. Poor Louisa. What had gone wrong in her brain? But having a second killer would open up a new avenue for Erbie and the other consultants at Fitz-Cahill. Instead of trying to find out why Gascoigne was homicidal, they could now try to find what Gascoigne and Louisa had in common. It might turn out to be chemical, or genetic, or something strange about their brains that made n-tech a bad idea for them.

Or it would be the n-tech itself.

But either way, she couldn't sit at home, waiting for her brain to go boom. Emmy was right. She'd had *one* treatment. Learning Systems had already made changes to her brain and the nanobots had left her body.

And she'd slept away precious hours when she could have been productive. When it came to those extra neural connections, it was use-it-or-lose-it.

But standing in her kitchen eating a bowl of cereal over the sink, she couldn't say she regretted her small nap. The rush of neural connections from Learning Systems had been intense. It was like puberty all over again, where every emotion felt like it was on the surface of her skin. Now, in the light of morning, she felt less frazzled, as if she'd tucked away those raw feelings, leaving room for more subtle ones.

Now that she could think straight, she knew what to do. She needed to work as much as possible, before those last few neural advantages faded away. Without a steady paycheck, she'd have to piece together small assignments. She'd tell Noah to sort incoming jobs by priority, the highest-paying ones first. As soon as he sent her the list, she'd start making calls.

But first, she'd need a taxi to take her to the Library to fetch her car. And coffee. Lots and lots of coffee.

"Why are you at Blackstones?" Noah asked.

Aidra balanced the large cup and opened her car door. "Because that's where the coffee lives."

"There are a dozen coffee shops closer to your house."

"Thank you, human GPS." Aidra set her cup in the holder as

Noah's call automatically transferred to the Octave's companel. "I'm not near my house. I had to go get my car. Besides, the other coffee shops aren't as good."

"Intriguing." She could hear Noah clicking his keyboard. "How far would you drive for Blackstones? What's your outer limit?"

"Does that matter? Please tell me why you called so I can enjoy my drink. And when I say 'tell me why you called,' I really mean, 'tell me you've got fabulous new jobs lined up for me.'"

"I found him," Noah said.

"Who?"

"Zach Wilson."

"New client? Excellent." Aidra put her car in gear and pulled out of her parking spot. "Now, I'll need you to schedule me pretty heavily for the next six weeks or so until—"

"Zach Wilson isn't a client."

"Then who is he?"

"I told you I remembered something about a guy who killed his family, right? So then I set up a program to scry through arrest records. I told you this, remember? And I found him. Right where I said he'd be."

"Which is where?"

"Jackson State Prison. Claims not to remember a thing. If he's the same as Gascoigne then—"

"Noah, can you please keep up? Fitz-Cahill fired me last night. I sent you multiple messages to that effect."

"I know, I know. But look at this. No, wait, you're driving. Don't look. Listen."

Aidra turned onto Warren Avenue, blending into the early-morning traffic. She sighed and listened to Noah talk while she drove. It wasn't like she could stop him.

The details were bleak. Zachary F. Wilson, husband, father of two, wiring specialist for Detroit Gridline Energy, guilty of homicide, matricide, infanticide. Two years ago, at his daughter's sixth birthday party, after cake, but before presents, Zach Wilson had gone to his basement to look for more party napkins. He had returned up the stairs with a loaded shotgun and opened fire, killing the other three members of his immediate family and his own mother. He'd also injured several neighbors, two of them children invited to the celebration. Wilson had then attempted to turn the shotgun on himself, but was prevented from taking his own life by his wounded father, who had hurled a heavy wooden cutting board at him, fracturing his skull and knocking him unconscious.

Aidra wondered why she hadn't heard of Wilson before. Mass shootings tended to make headlines. But she'd been in the hospital at the time, close to death. She'd missed a lot of news. She ran a hand over the scar on the side of her head and focused on what Noah was telling her.

"At Wilson's trial, he claimed to remember nothing of the incident. I didn't find him in my first searches because his amnesia *could* be explained by his head injury. But what if he's like Gascoigne and Samahroo?"

Aidra swallowed a gulp of hot coffee. "A blue-collar working man? How could he be Supremium?"

"Hear me out. Hear me out. There is nothing in his file that says he tried either Exersleep or Learning Systems, but there isn't anything that says he didn't."

"That makes no sense. That's like saying that grass isn't pink so it must be orange."

"Grass is green, Aidra."

At that moment, she was glad for the car's safety feature that made all incoming calls voice-only when the car was in motion. She didn't need him seeing the expression on her face. She turned the car toward home, already thinking about a hot breakfast and the long day ahead.

"Listen, listen, listen." Noah started talking faster, as if sensing that he was losing her. "Wilson was working the overnight shift at DGE. Eleven at night until seven in the morning. He was an excellent worker, on track for a promotion. He was also taking two classes at Wayne State."

"So?"

"At his trial, one of his character witnesses was his daughter's first-grade teacher. She said he was a regular volunteer in her classroom. One of the most involved parents."

"Again. So?"

"So this guy was everywhere. There's only one way to bend time to your will like that. Exersleep. Come on, Aidra. No one else is looking at this guy."

"Of course not."

"Which is why you should talk to him."

"Noah, I swear, you pay attention like camels ice skate."

"Like camels . . ."

"Not often and not well. Even if I wanted to talk to Wilson, I can't."

"You work for yourself. You can do what you want."

"*You* can, maybe. I can't. I'm not on this case. Which means that nobody is paying me for my time. And even if I didn't care about the money, even if I wanted to chase down this sketchy lead for . . . oh, I don't know . . . funzies, I don't have a nice big insurance company to give me clout with people. Would I like to interview this Wilson fellow? Sure. Am I going to? No. That's the PI business. Sometimes things don't get resolved. They just end."

"I'll work off the time," Noah said. "I will be your little cyber-slave until I've paid you back for the hours you've spent on this."

"I don't *have* hours to spend on this."

"Then find them! I'm making you an appointment."

"What?" Aidra had been lifting her coffee cup, hoping to sneak in a few sips at a red light. She dropped it back in the holder. "Last time I checked, you work for me."

"Check again."

"Are you kidding me? You're quitting?"

"Let's just say I'm on vacation."

"No, no, no. Noah, don't do this to me."

"I'm not doing anything," Noah said. "I'm especially not doing your billing, your booking, and your hacking."

"I don't believe this." Aidra squeezed her frustration into the steering wheel. *I would fire him for a dollar.* Problem was, no one was offering her a dollar right now. She was trapped and he knew it. She couldn't fire Noah. She needed new work and plenty of it. But she couldn't both line up new jobs and do the jobs she already had. Not without living all day. Once she was on her feet financially, maybe. But now? Impossible. As irritating as Noah was, breaking in a new guy would be worse.

Dammit, Morris. He was the one who got her into this mess. Why did he have to go off and work for the government? She knew it wasn't his fault that he'd been chipped by the NSA, but she'd give anything to have him on the other end of the phone, casually solving all her problems.

"Just talk to Wilson," Noah said. "It will take what, an hour?"

"Plus travel time." She was thinking about the best way to get to the prison outside Jackson. There was no convenient way to do it, since nobody was interested in making it easy for visitors. The monorail only went as far as Ann Arbor and then cut north to Lansing. So she'd have to drive. The highway would only take her an hour and five, but a private car needed four passengers to be allowed on the highway. So she'd have to take Michigan Avenue, one of the few reliable routes for getting through the zone and out the other side. From there, it was a straight shot west for two hours.

A honk behind her brought her back to the here and now. She'd missed a green light. She put on her signal and turned. If she went back the way she came, she could circle the block and pick up Michigan Avenue from the other direction.

"I'm sending you my credentials," she told Noah. "You get me a visitor's pass."

"So you're going to do it?" She could hear the glee in his voice.

"Let's go back to that part where you're working off the time."

"Only if I'm wrong. I'm telling you, Aidra, this guy is . . ."

She tuned out whatever Noah said next because of the startling sight in her rearview. A silver classic Lincoln had made the turn with her and was following her around the block. Only one person she knew drove a car like that. The day was overcast, with some lingering morning fog, but even through the haze, she could spot the mismatched bracket holding up the wing mirror. Sullivan was following her.

But why? She was off the case. He had to know that. And why do it himself? She entertained the notion that it might be one of his lackeys, but that was impossible. Nobody drove the Hotrod Lincoln but Patrick Sullivan himself.

Construction warnings ahead—echoed by her dashboard. In the run-up to the Olympics, the already-complex traffic situation was becoming a nightmare. She turned down a side street, waiting until the last minute to dart across a lane and around the corner, to see if Sullivan would keep up.

He barreled after her with all the stealth of a charging rhinoceros. He didn't care if he was seen. Maybe he *wanted* to be seen. Well, she might as well call his bluff. She hung up on Noah and commanded her car to contact Sullivan. Time to see what game he was playing.

No answer.

Another signal from her dash. Another construction zone. She wove down a few more side streets and called Sullivan again. Still no answer, but she was invited to leave a message.

"Hey, Sully, I don't know what your issue is, but there is no need for the cloak and dagger. We can talk any time, since we're no longer working on opposite sides of the same case. I'm on my way to Jackson. My assistant thinks I need to see someone named Zach Wilson. I'm heading there now, more to pacify Noah than anything else. Want to come along? Call me when you—"

Slam!

The corner of her vision caught a blur of movement and her

world narrowed to the interior of her car as it spun out of control. Her foot fumbled for the brakes and she shrieked with surprise as the airbags blossomed around her, cushioning the blow from the second impact. The car shuddered to a halt with a rending screech of plastic and metal as inertia brought a flush of warmth to her face.

Aidra sat for a moment, stunned, struggling with the passive restraints of the airweb. She reached for the door and realized sudden pain in her hands. Her grip had been wrenched off the wheel, her arms jerked around as she'd tried to regain control of her car.

She shook her head, trying to clear her thoughts. Mistake. Her head felt like it was being torn from her neck. She sat still until the pain went away, then tugged at the door latch and heard a *thunk*. The door moved five centimeters and stopped, jammed against something outside the window. Her car had come to rest against a steel cable rising to support a utility pole and it was blocking her exit. She looked across the shrouds of deflated crash balloons and saw the crushed-in passenger side.

Something had clipped her bumper, spinning her car out of control, and then slammed into the side of it. The windows on the passenger side were nearly opaque with crazy-cracked safety glass, but she could see a silver hood beyond—the other car. The Lincoln? Sullivan wouldn't do that to her. He wouldn't do it to his car, either. He worshipped that car. It had to be an accident. *What the hell just happened?*

She saw movement, a figure coming toward her.

"Noah. Noah. Can you hear me?" That wasn't right. She'd said goodbye to Noah a few moments ago. She remembered now. She'd been leaving a message for Sullivan. Oh, God, was he okay?

[*System backup only*] her car replied.

She found the dashboard screamer and used it to call for help—ambulance, police, whoever could get here soonest.

The car probably acknowledged, but Aidra never heard it. Glass exploded around her, stinging her forearm, cheek, and neck like a million wasps. She threw up her arms to shield her face. The other window vanished outward.

All she could do was stare out her passenger window. Was someone shooting at her car?

But in the next moment, she'd regained her senses enough to duck for cover. *Holy shit, someone is shooting at my car.*

She could only think of one person who would attempt to shoot her in broad daylight. Bart Klaver had sworn vengeance on her and now he was out to get it. What was it he'd said in that motel parking lot? *You'd better hope I never see you again.* She'd dismissed the words as the bravado of a defeated man. She never imagined he'd hunt her down.

Would he actually do it? Kill her right here on Seminole Street in front of who knew how many witnesses? She reached for her purse and found only the empty seat. Where was it? She needed her gun. She spotted the brown strap in the passenger footwell. She slid lower on the seat, trying to fit under the steering wheel, knowing she'd have no cover at all if Klaver got any closer. It had been mere seconds since she'd tapped the screamer. No police would get here in time. She was dead. She was—

She heard another sound. Not shots this time, but a yelp and a thud. Sounds of a struggle. She stayed where she was, still trying to reach her gun, feeling her heart beat so hard her ears hurt. But when no more shots came, she gathered the courage to lift her head and peer out the window.

Two men—witnesses to the crash, she assumed—had hurled themselves at the PI lying on the ground. The larger of the two men was sitting on him while the other held his Smith and Wesson in shaking hands. But hadn't she taken Klaver's Smith to the police station? Had he reclaimed it already?

She flinched when a head rose into view. A dark face with huge and bewildered eyes. "You hit?" a man asked.

Another man rose to look anxiously at her as well. "Are you okay?"

She drew in a shaky breath. "No. Yes. I don't know. Can you get me out of here?"

The two men helped her wriggle through the shattered window without flaying off her hide. She marched over to where the other witnesses had the shooter subdued. A small crowd had gathered—a mom with a stroller, an elderly woman with a tiny dog, a guy in running clothes. Datapads were out, recording the spectacle.

The figure on the ground was not Klaver. He was battered and bruised, and had curled in on himself, but it took only a brief glimpse of his face for Aidra to recognize him.

She whipped her head around, looking for the one who got away, thinking there must be some mistake. But there was no mistake. There was a single shooter on the scene and if the man currently sitting on him had not come along when he did, Aidra would now be dead.

Sullivan.

Her friend, her mentor, her solid rock in difficult times, had just run her off the road and tried to kill her.

CHAPTER NINETEEN

"And I'm telling you, I don't remember a fucking thing!" Sullivan insisted.

"Keep your voice down or they're going to drag me out of here." *And I will smother your foul mouth with a pillow if I don't get some answers.*

Aidra had tiny bandages dotting her right side. She was going to have some fascinating bruising on her left shoulder and hip. Although she had a biting bitch of a headache, she didn't have a concussion. The police hadn't liked the idea of Aidra riding in the same ambulance with Sullivan. And if they'd known about the gun in her purse, they'd have liked it a whole lot less. But when she insisted, they assigned a uniform to ride along with them.

Sullivan had been unconscious all the way to the Detroit Medical Center. Aidra's rescuers had broken his right arm, given him matching black eyes and re-arranged several fingers. He also had internal bleeding due to the many kicks aimed at his midsection.

He didn't look much better now. She glanced at his left arm, past the IV tubes and to his wrist, which was handcuffed to the bed. Once the monitors saw he was awake, the cops would be in to question him. She didn't have time for his innocent act. She needed answers.

"This chair is hard as rocks and I've been sitting in it for hours, waiting for you to come around. You'd better start talking."

"I got nothing. It's a huge black hole, dark and empty as a whore's snatch."

"What's the last thing you remember?"

He fumed, but seemed to be thinking it over. "I watched some stupid vee last night, flipped through some of the chat shows, went to bed. Next thing I know, I'm in the cock-flapping hospital, you telling me I tried to kill you."

She pulled out her pad and did a quick search of the spins. "CI Newsnet has the vid." It was cut together from a dozen traffic cams and store security monitors. There were also some hand-helds from the gathered crowd and some from morning commuters who had stopped to record and upload. Most were in flat-file, but a few had single-view holo for a 3-D effect.

The newsnet had patched together as much of the incident as they could, making a coherent narrative—or at least a narrative that would play well on the spins. It started a kilometer back from the accident site. Aidra realized that all the time she'd been listening to Noah, Sullivan's Lincoln had been pacing her. Ghosting alongside her in the morning fog, just barely off her Octave's quarter panel.

"What the . . ." For once, Sullivan had no words.

Now the Lincoln broke off and looped across two more lanes of Michigan Avenue, accelerating to charge the Octave from the side. The crash looked eerie from the high angle of the traffic cam, cars swirling in and out of mist. They watched the Lincoln plow into the smaller car at its right front wheel, driving it first into the curb of the median, and then to a sudden lurching stop against the guywire for the utility pole.

Aidra felt her throat tighten as the Lincoln's door opened. The view switched to hand-held phone cameras and she could see Sullivan—or at least enough of him to be recognizable. Most of it was from the back or the side, but there was no mistaking his yellow t-shirt and faded leather jacket. And his walk. People had strides as distinctive as fingerprints and she'd know Sullivan's anywhere.

He was shaking his head again as the figure raised a gun and fired through Aidra's car window. "Shit! Holy twisted scrotum and balls."

They watched Aidra disappear below the dashboard. The video cut to the two bystanders coming from behind Sullivan, catching him off guard enough to hurl him to the ground and stomp the gun out of his hand, then kick the crap out of him.

"Who the hell *is* that?"

Aidra wondered which one hurt more, the betrayal or the fact that he tried to deny it. She clutched the datapad tighter, resisting the urge to smack him with it. "Don't even try to tell me you had some kind of Supremium blackout. There's nothing in that thick head of yours but your own gray matter so don't even try that one."

On her pad, the newsnet ran video from the previous night showing Sullivan waving his gun at the spinners outside the Library. They had enlarged the weapon for effect, making it look as though Sullivan was waving a small cannon. Sullivan had only threatened the spinners, but it fit the narrative. Crazy loner shooting at people.

"Who are you working for?"

"What?"

"Is it Bart Klaver? Is that who hired you? I never thought you'd sink so—"

The door opened and two people barged into the room. Sofia Gao was right on the heels of Galen Browne, as if she'd been trying to stop her boss from coming in.

Aidra felt suddenly slow and stupid. There were a dozen questions she should have asked Sullivan. She'd done this in the wrong order, caught up in watching the re-enactment, trying to prove to Sullivan what he'd done, when they both already knew. She should have been trying to figure out *why*.

"In the wrong place at the wrong time," Galen Browne said. "Again. As much as it would please me to jail you for impersonating a federal operative, I will have to content myself with seeing you thrown out."

"It's okay." Aidra slowly lifted her palms. "Don't hate yourself for falling for those false credentials. Everyone does."

"I assure you, Ms. Scott. I do not hate myself." Browne's expression told her exactly who he reserved his hatred for.

Sofia stepped between them. "Don't we need to ask her—"

"Sergeant Gao, please station yourself outside this door and make certain that the prisoner has no other unauthorized visitors. I shall escort Ms. Scott off the hospital grounds."

Sofia looked furious for an instant before resuming her professional mask. Browne watched her with satisfaction, then nodded. "Allow me to make it clear, Ms. Scott, if you so much as say a single word of protest, I will cuff you and stuff you." He was obviously considering how satisfying that would be. "If, however, you possess more intelligence than you have displayed thus far, and go peacefully, then you may return home where you have, no doubt, been sorely missed. By someone."

"You practiced that in front of a mirror on the way over, didn't you."

Browne reached for her arm, but Aidra avoided his grip. "Hey! I'm wounded here!" She glanced at Sofia, who stared at the opposite wall. "All right. I'm moving."

Aidra settled her purse strap over her shoulder, ostentatiously laced her hands on top of her head, and walked down the hall. If she had to go, she was taking Browne's dignity with her. There were a few startled expressions from nurses and visitors, but Browne wore his badge on his shoulder so no one said anything.

Browne frowned at her playing the crowd. "Has anyone ever pointed out how irritating you are?"

"Every day of my life."

He hustled her to the elevator at the end of the hall, but there was a group waiting so he held Aidra back, gesturing the others to go ahead. The other visitors looked relieved, the doors closed and they were alone.

"You can put your arms down now."

Lacking an audience, Aidra did so. "What are you so pissed about anyway? No one's tried to kill you today."

Browne stared at the elevator call buttons. "My department has this situation well in hand. Or rather, we did. But every time I turn around, you're on the scene, stirring the pot."

"You got me, Browne. Pissing you off is my new hobby."

Another elevator carriage arrived and Browne herded Aidra into it.

"It's so nice of you to offer me a ride home," Aidra said when they reached the main lobby.

"As a matter of fact, you are on your own. I feel that once you are out of the hospital, my civic duty has been discharged."

"Ms. Scott? Aidra?" Juniper Fox stood in the two-story lobby. Small and alone, she should have looked lost, but, of course, she didn't. She was dressed like a well-to-do child on a field trip to a museum. The little girl looked Browne over and dismissed him. "Are you all right?" she asked Aidra.

"Juniper." Aidra looked around for some sign of Hannah. "Are you here by yourself?"

"Jovan saw you on the spins. I've been told not to watch them without guidance, but no one's noticed his interest yet, so no one's forbidden him to watch. He keeps me up to date. He saw you were hurt, so I came."

A few people walked through the main doors, stopping for a double-take when they recognized Juniper. Aidra glanced at Browne who was frowning down at the charming little apparition.

"I know you're eager to see the back of me," Aidra told Browne. "But this seems like a more urgent problem."

Browne nodded and touched his earlobe, moving away to murmur to his pad.

"So spill it," Aidra said.

Juniper looked up at her with wide brown eyes.

"Cut the act, Juniper. You know I'm not buying it. You didn't come all the way downtown just to make sure I was okay. What are you doing here?"

"Have you learned anything about my father's death yet?"

"Nothing we didn't already know."

"I was hoping you'd find out more. Working outside the system." The last seemed directed at Browne, who had finished his call.

"Hannah Fox is already on her way. Saw the girl was missing and tracked her through the GPS on her pad." Browne looked down uncomfortably. Aidra guessed he was not a parent. "Hello, Miss Fox. I'm Deputy Chief Galen Browne."

"I've seen you on the newsnets." Juniper wore the face of an angel statue—beautiful, but remote. "You were there when my father was killed. But the investigation seems to have stalled. Are you still in charge? Why is that?"

Browne glanced around the lobby. "I'll wait by the doors for Mrs. Fox."

When he was out of earshot, Aidra said, "That wasn't especially nice."

"No. I suppose not." Juniper's face showed genuine curiosity. "Have you noticed how our culture wants those with little or no power to be *nice*? How long do you suppose I shall carry that expectation?"

"The way you're going, I'd say about twenty more minutes."

The lobby doors parted and Hannah Wells-Fox flew through them. She breezed past Browne, who was trying to intercept, and straight for Juniper. The heels of her tall riding boots clattered on the tiles as she ran to her daughter. She scooped Juniper into her arms and held tight, closing her eyes and murmuring into the girl's ear.

Juniper squirmed and protested. Hannah put her down, but her hands were everywhere, testing all of Juniper's limbs and rubbing her head. Hannah dug through all her pockets, came up with a tissue, wiped her eyes, and then hugged Juniper again.

Hannah finally let go of Juniper and stopped dabbing her eyes. She turned to Aidra with an expression of such intensity that Aidra cringed, ready for the verbal smackdown.

But instead, she got a maternal hug of her own. "I can't thank you enough for watching over Juniper. If you hadn't—I was so worried—Oh my God, I don't know what I'd do."

Aidra stiffened in Hannah's embrace. "I really didn't—"

Hannah tried to step back. "Ooops, I apologize. Hold on."

Aidra's hair was caught on something. Hannah's sleeve button? She could only imagine how much her curls were sticking out. She hadn't seen a comb since that morning.

Hannah disentangled herself and dropped her arm. "I can't understand what got into Juniper. If you hadn't been here . . ." She turned toward Browne as if she might hug him too, but only held off because of his badge—*and perhaps his face*, Aidra thought.

Browne stared at Hannah as if she were crazy, but Aidra understood the mother protector instinct and how relief from worry could make someone seem a little nuts. Once, her son had been kidnapped and nearly killed. Aidra had slept on a chair in Jon's room for a month after. So if Hannah was feeling extra huggy and was babbling, Aidra wouldn't judge.

Browne sighed and pulled up menus on his datapad, mumbling something about more paperwork. "Mrs. Fox? I'm going to have to ask you some questions."

"Of course."

"Maybe we can get the hospital social worker down here to help us out."

"Is that necessary?" Hannah asked. "This is the first time my daughter has run away and I promise you it will be the last."

"I wasn't running away!" Juniper protested.

"She's six years old," Browne said. "In the city alone."

"I'm perfectly capable of riding a public bus," Juniper said. "That is what they're for."

"That is *not* what buses are for."

"How did you even know how?" Hannah asked. She was running her hands over Juniper again. "We've never ridden a bus together. What were you thinking?"

"It isn't difficult, mother. If everyone else can ride the bus, I can ride the bus."

"I believe that's my point," Browne said. "Juniper, don't you understand? It's not safe for children to wander the city by themselves."

"I didn't wander. I came straight here. And don't you think it should be your job to make it safe for children in the city?"

Galen Browne closed his eyes and his lips moved a little. Perhaps he was saying a prayer, hoping for a less crappy day, or maybe the patience to deal with this one. He opened his eyes and glared at Aidra.

"Don't worry about me," Aidra said. "I'm going home."

"I'll make sure of that," said a voice from behind her.

Aidra turned. Bryan stood a few meters away, wearing his work clothes and a happy smile, looking too fit and rested and polished for a hospital. She self-consciously smoothed down her hair. "What are you doing here?"

"Apparently, taking care of you. I went to your room, but you'd signed yourself out. Looks like I got here just in time."

"I don't need taking care of."

"Then how about a ride?"

"I can drive myself."

Bryan raised his eyebrows, waiting for it to sink in. Aidra's car was still back at the accident site.

Browne cleared his throat. "Straight home, Ms. Scott."

Aidra nodded. Of course she was going home. She had no car, no job, and nowhere else to go.

CHAPTER TWENTY

Bryan took her hand and walked her through the hospital lobby. Aidra let herself be led past the front door information kiosk and down a quiet hallway toward the elevator heading to the underground parking lot. "I'm going to make sure you get safely home," he said. "See you settled in."

"Thanks, but I'm okay."

"You don't seem okay."

"I don't need a babysitter."

"No, you don't."

"I don't work for you anymore."

"I know."

"So why are you here?"

"Because you need a friend." Bryan opened his arms and stood waiting.

After a moment's hesitation, Aidra moved into them. She closed her eyes and rested her head on Bryan's chest, enjoying the feeling of warmth and protection. Unlike Hannah's urgent embrace that had pulled Aidra in and held too tightly, Bryan's hug was soft and undemanding. It made her feel safe. It was an illusion, but one she'd believe as long as Bryan held on.

He patted her back a few times, gave her one more squeeze, and held her at arm's length. "Two people attacking you in two days. What is going on, Aidra?"

"I wish I knew."

"I thought with your Supremium advantages . . ."

"Ha. Yeah. I'm so smart. I'm so stinking smart that I can't make sense of things even when they happen right in front of me."

"Did Sullivan tell you anything?"

"Nothing useful."

The elevator doors parted and they got on, exiting at the parking ramp. Bryan pointed out his Sinfonia and opened the door for her. "I called Ugly Ben," he said. "Told him you'd be in touch."

"Ah, hell, Bryan, would you quit doing that?"

"It was either that or have a spinner infestation right here at the hospital. Why do you think the others left you alone? They know who your story belongs to."

"You're telling me that spinners practice professional courtesy?"

"To a point. You'll have to talk to Ugly Ben soon."

Aidra closed her eyes and rested her head on the leather seatback. "I don't want to talk to him."

"Then talk to me. Start at the beginning."

"The beginning? Let's see. My sister is pregnant, I need to start paying my assistant more money, I've got some useless extra neural connections, Jean Claude Gascoigne is walking around a free man, and I need to find out when Louisa Samahroo's funeral is so I can pay my respects. Also, I need a job."

"Congratulations," Bryan said.

"For what?"

"You're going to be an aunt."

"Oh, thanks."

He exited the Detroit Medical Center's sprawling complex and drove into the flow of traffic. "But what about today?"

"I guess that's the important part."

He patted her hand. "It's all important."

She sank into the seat, wishing she could lean against Bryan as he drove. He was so easy to talk to. She found herself giving more and more details, telling him everything that happened from when they spoke last night until Sullivan ran her off the road this morning. Bryan took it all in without judgment, and understood what was going on without a lot of explanation. He just listened, letting her spill the whole story as he steered the car to Aidra's condo.

Aidra watched him deliberately leave his datapad behind when he locked the car.

"Don't you need that?"

"Nah. Whatever's in there can wait until tomorrow."

"No, Bryan. Don't do that. There's no sense in you getting fired, too."

"You need me more than work does right now."

On the way up from the condo's underground parking deck, Bryan put a comforting arm around her shoulder and she smiled up at him. The WelcoMat recognized her and let them in.

Madeline met them at the door and pranced around Aidra's feet. Aidra sank to her knees and buried her face in the ruff of long hair around Madeline's neck, calming herself with the caline's spicy scent. "Hello, girl. Hello, my good girl. I'm back. I am so sorry I left you alone all day."

Madeline nosed Aidra's cheek, then nodded politely to Bryan.

"This is Bryan," Aidra said. "He's a friend."

"Do you think she understands that?"

"Of course."

"Is there anything you need?" Bryan asked. "Do you want me to cook you something? Pour you a drink?"

"You cook?"

"Yeah. You hungry? It's past seven. Have you eaten today?"

"I'm not . . . I just . . ." Aidra hugged Madeline's neck, ashamed to feel her throat tighten and her eyes burn with tears. She was supposed to be stronger than this.

"Hey," Bryan said softly. "Why don't you sit on the sofa? I'll bring you some water."

"No. I need to take Madeline out."

"I'll do it. Where's the leash?"

Aidra pointed to the leash hanging from the door knob and stumbled to the couch, her back to the door. She heard Bryan hook Madeline up and take her outside.

She sucked in a shaky breath and swiped at her eyes. Dammit, she shouldn't be so spun up. Talking it over should have made her feel better, not worse. But even after spewing all the details to Bryan, her thoughts still circled back to Sullivan.

He was working for the other side. Was it as simple as that? He was working for Westrock. But why attack her? She didn't know anything that Sullivan himself didn't know. She'd been removed from this case and while she had others pending, none of them were important or high-profile. It didn't make sense.

Unless Klaver had somehow gotten to him. She'd emptied the slimy little PI's bank account so she didn't know how Klaver was paying Sullivan. But even if Klaver could pay, how could Sullivan turn on her like this?

It was as if Sullivan was a piece from a different puzzle she was trying to fit into this one. No matter how she turned it, the edges wouldn't line up.

What would happen to him? An incident like this would end his career. Sullivan couldn't work as a PI with a felony on his record, and a private investigator in a one-man shop probably didn't have much of a retirement fund set aside. What would he do now?

The door opened and shut and Madeline came to sit at her feet. Bryan stood behind the couch and gently put his hands on her shoulders, massaging the tension out of them. Aidra sighed.

"What are you thinking about?" he asked.

"Sullivan."

"Don't."

"It's useless to ask me not to think about someone. I can tell you right now not to think of The Duchess of Elba and guess who you'll be thinking about?"

Bryan's hands dug more deeply into her tight muscles. "You need to stay away from him. He's obviously deranged."

"He's always been a little off, but until today, he's never been homicidal."

"Do we have to talk about him?"

"No. In fact, I'd rather not talk about anything at all."

Bryan's hands became less about massage and more of a caress. Warm, inviting. He leaned over and kissed the top of her head. Aidra turned her face up for a more earnest kiss. Bryan's lips were tentative at first, then more insistent as Aidra reached a hand behind his neck and pulled him closer. Their tongues met in a dance that electrified Aidra's extremities.

Part of her wondered if she should be doing this, but most of her brain—and her hormones—cheered her on. This wasn't just a delayed reaction to a near-death experience. This was real attraction. She'd liked Bryan for a long time. She liked his boyish face and barely thinning hair and broad shoulders. She liked the way he listened to her, focusing completely on her when they were together.

Bryan leaned over the couch and half-jumped, half-fell into her arms. He kissed her again. Their kisses became nibbles became licks and back to kisses again. Bryan shed pieces of clothing one by one and helped Aidra do the same. It felt amazing to be skin-to-skin with him. But it felt even more amazing to *let go*. She didn't have to think or plan or decide. Bryan was running his hands and lips over her body and all she had to do was receive his touch.

And then she was touching him in return, letting her hands move where they wanted to, caressing and stroking down his chest and over his buttocks and back up between his legs, enjoying the perfect muscles that Exersleep had given him. She had nothing to worry about, nothing to figure out or unravel. Their destination was a given and they could take all the time they needed in getting there.

Bryan groaned and pulled his hips away from her, out of her reach.

She opened her eyes and sat up. "What's wrong?"

"Are you . . . prepared?" he asked. "I wasn't expecting this, so . . ."

"Yes. Upstairs." It had been awhile since she needed them, but she had still optimistically stashed condoms and other fun things in her bedside table.

"I'm glad," Bryan said. "Because I don't want to leave."

"And I don't want you to."

He stood and pulled her to her feet. Aidra led them up the stairs and to her bedroom, Madeline right behind them.

Bryan looked down at the caline. "Um . . ."

"It's okay. Just close the door."

"But what about—"

"Madeline, go to bed." Madeline would sleep in Jon's room, the way she did every night. Aidra closed the door behind her and turned back to Bryan.

"Just like that?" he asked.

"Yes, just like that. She's not a dog."

Bryan smiled at her. "Aidra, go to bed."

"Ohh, you're going to order me around now?"

"For the moment, yes." He put his arms around her waist and half-lifted her onto the bed.

"Hmm," Aidra said. "You ordering me about. Let's see how that works."

It worked wonderfully well.

Aidra jerked awake. She checked the time. Three o'clock? She tried to make sense of that number. She'd been sleeping for five hours—long enough to make her feel groggy and out-of-sorts, but not long enough to feel refreshed. She'd been at the hospital all day yesterday and had missed her usual Exersleep time. And the day before she'd only had a half cycle. No wonder she'd fallen asleep.

She looked over at Bryan, whose face was slack and carefree in slumber. She lifted one side of the covers and slid out of bed.

"Five minutes," Bryan mumbled. He rolled over.

She grabbed her robe and headed to the shower.

In the bathroom, she examined her body in the full-length mirror. She'd developed some harsh bruises along her ribcage and both shoulders. Her arms were a mess of scrapes. She wondered how

Bryan could have overlooked them in bed. Then again, she'd overlooked a lot herself.

Last night, she was scared and sad and lonely, and Bryan was there for her. For a few precious hours, she didn't have to be in charge, or the grown-up, or the boss. She could give in to the moment and just *be*.

But that was her true mistake. She was responsible for her own life and her own choices. She needed to make better ones. Right now, she felt both more involved and less involved with Bryan than she wanted to be. Last night was almost perfect, but there was a lot bound up in that *almost*, and she didn't want to start a fling with Bryan, much less anything more serious. She cared about him. He was such a sweet man.

And so wrong for her.

She turned the shower to extra hot and jumped in. She scrubbed herself the best she could with her sore arms, thinking about the events of yesterday. Names and faces swirled in and out. Louisa. Sofia. Hannah. Klaver. Sullivan. And a man named Zach Wilson whom she'd never met.

She knew what she had to do, where she had to go. She'd been telling herself that it didn't concern her, that her job was done here, that she should move on. But none of this would get resolved if she didn't resolve it. Feeling sorry for herself, hiding at home, sleeping with her boss—sleeping at all—would not give her the answers she needed.

She threw back the shower curtain and dried as fast as she could. She went back to her room and swatted Bryan's arm. "Bryan, get up."

"Huh?"

"Please get up. Can you get dressed? I need to go to Jackson."

Bryan ran a hand over his face and blinked at her. "What time is it?"

"Three-thirty."

"Jesus, I can't remember the last time I slept that long."

"I can't remember the last time I slept, period."

"Don't you doze after sex?"

Aidra thought it over. She honestly didn't know. She hadn't had a partner in the six months since she'd taken up Exersleep. She decided not to mention that to Bryan. "I gotta go," she said instead.

"You need a ride to Jackson?" he said with bleary eyes. "Okay. Just let me—"

"Actually, I need a ride to my car, to the impound lot the cops towed it to."

"Is your car even driveable? Your airbags deployed. You can't take it anywhere."

"I have an idea." Aidra handed him his pants. "Can we go?"

Bryan tugged on his pants and reached for his shirt. "Why Jackson?"

How to explain? Did she even have to explain? She wasn't working for Bryan right now. She didn't need his approval. "Can you just take me to the impound lot?"

"Sure." He drew the syllable out as he buttoned his shirt. "Where are you going after that?"

Anywhere I damned well please, she wanted to snap. But that wasn't fair. Bryan was trying to help. She took a breath. "I need to see a man named Zach Wilson."

"Why?"

"Honestly? I don't know."

"Is he connected to a case?"

"I'll find out."

"Why do you need to go to Jackson to see him?"

"Because yesterday morning, Patrick Sullivan almost killed me trying to stop me."

CHAPTER TWENTY-ONE

Bryan convinced her to dry her hair and eat something before they went. She put on her interview suit—boxy black pants and conservative jacket over plain white shirt. It was the kind of outfit that could fit in anywhere, yet it was immediately forgettable. Perfect for the impersonation she had planned for today. She straightened her hair and pulled it away from her face.

Madeline seemed just as confused as Bryan at their early rising, but consented to breakfast and a walk.

When she came back, Bryan stood next to the front door, head in his datapad.

Aidra lifted her chin toward the pad. "I thought you left that in your car."

"I went to get it while you were fixing your hair." He took a step closer to the door. "I can't drive you to Jackson."

"I never asked you to."

"I missed eighteen calls," Bryan already had his coat and shoes on. He gestured to the door. "I've got a meeting with Mason Cahill himself in two hours."

"I'll get a cab," Aidra said.

"No, I'll take you to the impound lot." He cleared his throat and put his datapad in his pocket. He brought his hands together and looked down at them as if they were the most interesting thing in the room. "It's the least I can do."

Aidra thought she should try to decode that sentence, but now was not the time. She needed to go see Wilson and then go back to the hospital to finally get some answers out of Sullivan.

Bryan shifted awkwardly in place, but didn't move from the doorway. "Aidra, I don't want last night to define our relationship."

"Uh . . . it won't?" Aidra was dismayed to hear her voice go high and thready. *Relationship? Who said anything about a relationship?*

"Because we're friends, right?" Bryan finally looked at her. "I mean, you're a fine person and it would be perfect if we were right for each other, but . . ."

"We're not."

"I'm sorry, Aidra. Last night was so . . . And I was . . ."

"Yes?"

"And it was very . . . I mean, it was *extremely* . . ."

Aidra wondered if Bryan would ever finish a sentence again. He'd probably rehearsed the first part and had run out of lines. She decided to let him off the hook. They didn't need to unpack their emotions. They didn't even need to discuss it. They both knew they weren't going to be lovers. She touched her fingertips to his arm. "Don't worry. If our friendship can't survive this, it wasn't much of a friendship, right?"

"So we can put this to bed—"

"Really?"

Bryan ducked his head. "Bad choice of words. Can we pretend this never happened?"

"Sure." Forgetting about it implied they were sorry it happened. And maybe Bryan was sorry, at least a little. But she wasn't. It was a mistake, no doubt, but not an unrecoverable one. After the life-threatening errors she'd made, a merely awkward one was a welcome change.

She gave his hand a reassuring squeeze and shooed him out the door, locking it up behind her. In Bryan's car, she whipped out her datapad. There were three messages from Morris, which she ignored with a guilty pang. She commanded her pad to call Noah.

Noah's e-sec said he was still on vacation with an unknown return date.

She sent him a blip, knowing it would show up in his feed. [**I'm on my way to see Wilson so you're back on the job. It had better be worth it.**]

She paused, then sent him another, three word blip. [**Do. Not. Gloat.**] [**Wouldn't dream of it**] came the immediate reply.

She closed the datapad with a click and leaned on the door.

Bryan looked at her out of the corner of his eye as he drove. "How do you know Sullivan's involved? How do you know what he was trying to do? Wasn't the timing just a coincidence?"

"Could be. I'll know when I talk to Wilson."

"Do you think he knows anything?"

Aidra didn't answer, just looked out the window at the buildings that lined the roadway.

"Hey," Bryan asked. "Are you okay?"

"I'm fine."

"Will you call me later? I have these meetings, but they can't last all day. You can buy me a beer. Many beers."

"You're the one with the job."

"Okay. I will buy you many beers."

Aidra smiled at him. "I'll call," she said. "I promise."

"I don't like dropping you off in the middle of nowhere."

"The impound lot isn't in the middle of nowhere. I am a grown-ass woman. With a plan." That last part was a lie. She didn't have a plan. She didn't know what the hell she was doing. She no longer had that rush of self-assurance she had right after visiting Learning Systems. She thought she knew things, she didn't *know* she knew them. No wonder Supremiums liked to get new nano-machines every week. The boost in brainpower was nice, but the boost in confidence was the real benefit.

Aidra forced down the tide of anxiety she was feeling. As scary as it was to go with her gut instinct, it was all she had right now.

It felt weird to have Sullivan's advice in her head, but there was no escaping it. "Half of impersonation—hell, more than half—is looking like you belong someplace. You could be on your knees in the dirt, blowing a giant Yeti with hairy nuts the size of bowling balls, but if you act like that's what you're supposed to be doing, people will leave you alone. You know how it is. People doing something they're not supposed to do, stick out. Maybe they look around too much, or maybe they stand too rigid, or maybe they slouch down like they're trying to hide."

So the trick is to convince yourself, Aidra finished. She wasn't Aidra Scott, PI. She was Aidra Scott, Executive Assistant to the Regional Agent-in-Charge, Department of Justice. She flashed the ID and waltzed through the visitor entrance.

The bogus credentials meant that Aidra wasn't shown into the visitation arena used by friends and family of the inmates of Jackson State Prison. The privacy laws demanded that prisoners have soundproof rooms to confer with their lawyers and that's where she was sent. A heavy, broad table took up most of the room with one chair on either side. She sat in the one without the steel post bolted to the floor in front of it.

While she waited, she used her datapad to confirm that there was no evidence of electronic information gathering. A tiny green light winked in the field. It would shade red and give a squawk if that changed during the interview.

It took ten minutes for them to bring Wilson from solitary confinement. Finally, the door slid open and a guard appeared, towing a long, lean figure in an orangeskin. A second guard stood in the doorway with his zapper drawn and ready.

The first guard mumbled an apology to Wilson as he maneuvered him into the chair and pushed the linking chain between his cuffs into the latchpost rising out of the floor between his legs. The guard turned to Aidra and asked if she needed anything else.

She lifted her chin toward Wilson. "What was the apology for?"

"The cuffs," the guard answered. "Standard procedure, but he don't need them."

Aidra raised an eyebrow. Wilson had come from solitary. You

didn't land there without a good reason. She thought her voice came out quite normally. "That should be fine for now. Thank you."

Zach Wilson slumped in his chair. He showed no interest in her or what she might want from him. That was almost as disturbing as the chains.

When the guard was gone, Aidra opened a file on her pad and looked Wilson over as she decided a federal officer would. His face seemed to hang from a long, white forehead. His pale eyes were red-rimmed and puffy as if he lacked for sleep. His hair was drawn back into a complicated man-braid that he'd probably done himself. It hung crookedly and wisps had escaped at the sides.

Aidra put the pad on the table. "Not going to ask me my business?"

"Why should I?" His voice was a husky whisper, like paper rubbed on paper.

"You were pulled out of your cell before breakfast on a Saturday, meaning my questions won't wait. You're not curious about that?"

"No, ma'am."

"Most prisoners jump at the opportunity to talk to anyone with legal authority. Don't you want another chance to plead your case?"

"Nothing to plead." He leaned forward as much as the chains would allow. He closed his eyes and Aidra had to strain her ears to hear what he said next. "This is the worst day of my life."

Aidra didn't fall out of character, but she did check his bio again for the hometown. He sounded like every guy she'd ever grown up with in Pinckney. His address was listed as Stockbridge, Michigan, not more than a few cornfields away. "What happened today?" she asked.

He didn't answer. Didn't look at her.

"I'm here to listen to your story."

"Can't help you. Don't remember anything."

"And *that* is exactly what I want to hear about."

She'd caught his interest. Not a lot. He wasn't willing to give much, but he turned his head to regard her from the side of his leaking eyes. "You wanna hear what I don't remember?"

"Please."

"I don't remember . . ." his voice trailed off. He stared at the floor, working his wrists inside the restraints as if testing their strength.

"Whenever you're ready," Aidra prompted.

"We needed more stuff for the birthday party. Napkins. Plates." He closed his mouth and swallowed, painfully. "Next I know, I'm in the back of a cop car with my arms zip-tied behind me and a trooper's spit running down my face." His voice all but disappeared. "I killed them. I killed them all."

Aidra recalled how Gascoigne's orangeskin had squawked with every restless move he'd made. Wilson's didn't make a sound. "You don't remember any of it?" she asked.

"No."

"But you know you did it."

"My wife liked to set her companel on watch and wipe, y'know?"

Aidra knew. Originally a security feature, the companel would watch the activities in front of it for a number of hours and then wipe the stored data if there was no command to save it. A lot of people kept moments of a party for holo-albums or business meetings for company archives.

"You watched it." Her lips felt numb. The room felt smaller. He'd killed his wife and daughter and mother, injured several other people, knowing it would all be recorded to watch later.

His face was still, but tears brimmed and spilled again. His voice was a haunted whisper. "I saw enough."

Aidra lifted the datapad, pretending to consult it. She had to get this right. There wouldn't be another chance.

"You were an Exersleeper?"

Wilson blinked, shook his head—not in negation, but as if to clear it. "My lawyer tried to get it admitted but the prosecution showed the judge all the tests they did on me . . ."

"I Exersleep myself." It seemed out of character for a fed, but it might help create a bond.

Zach Wilson didn't seem to notice. "I started so I could work on another degree," he said.

According to the file, his job with Detroit Gridline Energy was helping people convert to solar, or handling the complex wiring that Musk batteries demanded. He had good performance reviews, no history of hostility or confrontation. A company memorandum included in the file mentioned him in a list for possible promotion. He was back in the might-have-been of the past, the land where his family and his future were still alive.

Aidra didn't want to pull him out of it, but she had to. "Did you ever try Learning Systems?"

"No. I'm a working man."

"But Exersleep isn't cheap either."

"When they give you a chance to do it for almost nothing, you take it."

Aidra understood that, having taken that same deal herself. Interesting, but not very useful. Maybe there wasn't anything here that would help her. She asked a few more questions, things she already knew from the briefing file. Had he ever had a violent experience before that day? Had he eaten anything unusual, maybe drunk something that could have given him an allergic reaction? Had he ever experienced losses of time before? He answered everything with a single word. "No." Wilson was turning to stone again, ossifying word by word, withdrawing into the persona that served as a remnant of a soul in here.

Finally, he stopped speaking to her at all. He just stared at the floor, murmuring something over and over.

"Mr. Wilson, do you know Jean Claude Gascoigne?"

No response.

"How about Mackenzie Fox? Did you ever meet him?"

A flicker as Wilson's eyes met hers for a short second, and then he was back to staring at the floor.

"Mr. Wilson?"

Nothing. He continued to talk softly to himself. She leaned over the table to listen, careful not to get too close.

Wilson's words were the only sound in the otherwise silent room. "This is the worst day of my life."

She waited, but he said nothing more. Aidra admitted defeat and rose to leave. She tapped on the door and three guards came in. One stood aside while the other two unstrapped the prisoner from his chair with unexpected gentleness.

"Thank you for talking with me, Mr. Wilson," she said to his back. Wilson said nothing.

Aidra caught the eye of the guard in the doorway. "Can I ask you something? What happened to him today?"

He holstered his zapper and allowed a human expression into his features. "What do you mean?"

"Did Wilson get in a fight? Is that why he was in solitary?"

"Him?" The guard shook his head. "Wilson's not in solitary because he's dangerous. He's in solitary because he's on suicide watch."

"He said this was the worst day of his life."

"So?"

"He said it more than once."

"Yeah, I know. He says that every day."

CHAPTER TWENTY-TWO

Aidra bypassed the entrance ramp to the highway and ignored the gaggle of fourths lined up for rides. If she were still on Fitz-Cahill's payroll, she'd hire three of them to round out her carpool so she could take the highway. Now that she was on her own, she had to economize, so she took the surface streets home.

The lights on Michigan Avenue were expertly timed and Aidra let herself get swept into the flow of cars, sailing through green after green. The temptation was always to go faster, especially when the mid-day traffic was light, leaving ample room between her and other cars. But she maintained a steady pace and let her mind wander as the borrowed car ate up the kilometers to Detroit.

All she could think about was Zach Wilson. Day after day, alone in his prison cell, Wilson had to live with himself and what he'd done. *This is the worst day of my life.*

Whatever reason Sullivan had for running her off the road yesterday, she didn't see the connection to Wilson. Wilson didn't fit. He'd used Exersleep, but not Learning Systems. The timeframe was all wrong. Two years ago, when Wilson killed his family, Exersleep had been well-established, but Learning Systems had barely gotten off the ground. Wilson wasn't Supremium. He was a normal guy—well, not entirely normal. Something had caused him to kill his family. And he would pay for that the rest of his life.

She commanded the car to play music but couldn't find anything she liked on the set playlists. She shut it off and eased into another lane. She tried to enjoy the scenery, but there wasn't much to enjoy. A straight road on flat land scrolling past houses, stores, and churches, back to houses. A thick blanket of gray clouds hid the sun, adding to her dark mood.

There was something wrong with Wilson. He'd barely talked to her. The man had told her nothing. As if there was nothing to tell.

This is the worst day of my life.

When you find out, let me know.

She gave her head a shake. Those were Jean Claude Gascoigne's words, not Zach Wilson's. The two men couldn't be more different. Gascoigne had killed his former friend and business partner, and seemed as arrogant as ever. But killing his family had left Wilson a shell of a person. He was guilty and he knew it.

She was only thinking of them both because of the jails, the handcuffs, and the orange uniforms. And the way both men seemed so bewildered.

And that little flick of Wilson's eye when she'd asked about Gascoigne and Fox. She hadn't imagined it. For the briefest of moments, she'd had Wilson's attention. Was it because he'd seen the murder on the newsnets? Or was it something more?

When you find out, let me know.

She changed lanes and smashed the accelerator, leaping ahead of two cars, knowing it would disrupt her careful rhythm and make her stop for the next light. So what? It would give her a chance to call Noah. She fumbled with the unfamiliar dashboard system and finally got through.

"Wait," Noah said. "Your signal isn't coming in too clearly."

"Not surprised. This ancient car took forever to sync with my datapad."

"What are you driving?"

"A Lincoln Navigator. Belongs to Patrick Sullivan."

"How?"

"Don't even worry about it." As she'd expected, she hadn't been able to start her Octave. Even if she got it going, it wouldn't have been much fun to drive with two shot-out windows. But Sullivan's car was in the same lot, dented but drivable, and she knew where he hid the spare key card. It had been easy to convince the impound lot that the Hotrod Lincoln belonged to her. "Can we stay on topic?" she asked.

"Isn't Sullivan going to be sliced that you took his car?"

"Noah!"

"What?"

"Chatting about what I'm currently driving is not why I called you."

"Right. You want to tell me how many hours I have to work off." He sighed. "Name your number."

Aidra slowed for another red light. "Forget about that."

"I think your signal is breaking up again. I thought I heard you say to forget about it."

"I did."

"Isn't this the part where you rub my nose in it?"

"I wouldn't do that."

"Sure you would. You should be using words like 'victory lap' and 'in your face.' What did Wilson say to you?"

"Barely anything."

"He must have said *something*."

Aidra modulated her speed so she wouldn't get caught in stop-go traffic again. "It's more like what *I* said to *him*. I asked him about Jean Claude Gascoigne and Mackenzie Fox. He recognized the names."

"Everyone recognizes those names."

"This felt personal. There's some kind of connection there."

"And you want to find it."

"I *need* to find it." She glanced at the back of her hands. They were a mess of tiny cuts from shattered glass. She thought about her crumpled car, shots fired at her. "I think Sullivan's involved, but damned if I can figure out how. You found Wilson."

"I did."

"So let's connect the dots between him and everyone else."

"Give me half an hour," Noah said. "I'll call you back."

* * *

It was more like forty-five minutes before Noah called her back. Aidra changed into a black t-shirt and her most comfortable jeans and got Madeline fed and walked. She was finishing off an order of Chinese dumplings she'd picked up on the way home when Noah buzzed an urgent alarm into her companel. She put the last bite in her mouth and sat on the couch, patting the seat next to her for Madeline to hop up.

"I knew it. I knew there was something there," Noah said without preamble.

"What did you find?"

"Not me, exactly. This is a little above my pay grade."

"I'm sorry Noah. It's past time we increased your hourly rate. How about—"

"That's not what I meant," Noah interrupted. "I mean, a raise! Yay! Nice. But that connection you were looking for? I have no idea how to do that."

"Imagine my surprise."

"So I kicked it upstairs to Morris."

"No, Noah. No. Don't do that. Bad idea."

"Well, this is awkward."

"I'll say. If you could *please*—"

"I mean, I've got Morris looped in on three-way right now."

The screen split to show Morris' face. "Hi, honey. We need to talk."

Aidra closed her eyes and pinched the bridge of her nose. "Um, Noah? I'll call you back." She moved to cut him out of the conversation.

"Darn," Noah said. "I was just going to pop some popcorn." And he was gone.

Aidra hid half her face behind Madeline, and peered at Morris with one eye. He had that look he got when he was about to dazzle her with his brilliance. A playful grin he was trying to downplay, an easy nod before leaning back in his chair and tilting his head to point his nose at her. Smug, but trying to hide it.

"I take it you've found something," she said.

"I've locked down footprints for Zach Wilson for the two months before the incident."

"Two months?"

"The State Investigator's Unit nailed him down for the last five days before Wilson murdered his family, but something Noah said made me want to look further back."

"Noah? But . . . wait. Footprinting?"

"I'm not going to get caught."

"Of course not." Footprinting—documenting an individual's minute-by-minute movements in direct contravention of privacy laws—took a ton of time and effort. Mapping out another person's life required not only computers, but the analytical skills to filter the results. Even with Morris' small army of AIs, he had to put in an enormous amount of work to cull all the data on Zach Wilson. Security recordings, facial recognition, financial signature, vehicle license plate . . .

"There's no way you footprinted Wilson in half an hour. When did Noah contact you?"

Morris waved the question away. "Does it matter?"

"Does to me."

"He called me yesterday morning."

Right after he first told me about Wilson. Noah had blackmailed her into going to see the man, then immediately called Morris for an assist. He was starting to act uncomfortably like a partner, anticipating her needs and trying his best to fill them. Maybe Noah didn't need more guidance. Maybe he needed *less*.

"So, you footprinted Wilson in a day?" she asked Morris.

"I piggybacked on some existing data," Morris admitted.

"What else has Noah told you about this case?"

"All of it. Mostly." Morris played with his t-shirt collar, bunching it up and then smoothing it back. "I figured out some stuff on my own."

"What stuff?"

"Enough to know why you're trying to find answers for a case when you've been fired."

"Morris—"

"I get it. It's personal now. You want answers. I've found you some. The SIU already had Wilson cold on the existing evidence, but they still got a decent amount of useful information about his movements. I used the basic patterns established by their efforts to narrow things down a bit." He tapped a few keys and her screen split into quadrants. One screen showed a map of Southeast Michigan with a yellow dot jiggling about, occasionally winking out and then reappearing. The other three quadrants were multiple images, some from ground-level, others from building top, some from satellites. Each time the glowing dot vanished, the other quadrants froze on the last known image and then resumed coverage when it appeared again. "Do you see it?" Morris sounded indecently satisfied.

He gestured and the yellow light turned blue for a second, streaked and vanished, streaked and vanished, streaked and vanished. Always toward the same place.

"Where is that? Where did he go?"

"There are very few places these days where you can escape coverage. But one of those places happens to be the country homes of the ultra wealthy."

A view of Wilson's company truck—or at least, a blurred shape resembling a DGE van—turned into a long and winding driveway. One Aidra recognized.

"Is that the Fox house?" Wilson told her that his lawyer had raised the Exersleep issue despite protests from the DA. He said the only way he'd been able to afford Exersleep was because it was practically given to him. She'd assumed his employer paid for it, helping out their shift workers. But what if the answer was both simpler and more devastating than that? Was Wilson connected directly to the Foxes?

"I've got a DGE service request for their property about five months before the birthday party of doom."

"Hey!"

"What?"

"Don't be flip," Aidra snapped. "It's a man's life."

"Sorry. But guess who caught the call?" Morris raised an eyebrow. "Wilson. And in the following months he visited the Fox residence multiple times. At least, that's the speculation. I have no plate signature and that picture is an enhanced oblique from a traffic drone that happened to be pointing in the right direction. For all I know, my AIs have gotten a little creative."

There was brief squawk of dismay from off screen and Morris hushed his entourage of computer minions.

"Though they do seem sure of themselves on this one," he said. Another chirp and he shrugged and nodded.

The fact that Morris had hard footprints on all but seventeen and a half hours out of a two-month window was amazing. As he'd no doubt intended. "This isn't a coincidence," she said.

"Nothing is."

"Mackenzie Fox, you right bastard." She remembered the entire wetwork setup in his basement. Fox's Exersleep program was already well-established, and Gascoigne had cornered the market on learning-enhancers, but the field of nanotechnology and brain chemistry was wide open for further developments. Fox had never stopped experimenting. Why wait to do animal testing or get FDA approval? Why not take shortcuts and put n-tech in volunteers? And there was Wilson, walking into his house on a regular basis, ready to try anything to improve his life.

Did Gascoigne know? Or at least suspect? Was that what the lawsuits were about? Did Gascoigne finally kill Fox to stop him?

"I need to call Bryan."

"Why?" Morris asked.

"Because if this is what I think it is, we've just made their case. I'm going to work my channels through Fitz-Cahill, try to confirm—"

"Hasn't double-Y worked your channel enough for one weekend?"

"Excuse me?"

"I suppose it doesn't count as a walk of shame when it's right back up your own stairs."

A chill started on her neck and slid down her spine. Was he footprinting *her?* From right inside her own home?

Her hands shook with a desire to punch something. She wanted to run around her condo, sweep the whole thing clean until she found every one of Morris' spiders. But she was frozen in her seat, staring open-mouthed at him. Her breath came in little gasps. How could he violate her privacy like that?

"I know, I know. I shouldn't say anything. I'm not your . . . your . . ." He thrust his hand forward as if trying to find the word.

"Boyfriend? Significant other? Lover? No, Morris, you aren't. What you are is a complete asshole! A waste of a human." She struggled to find words. "Garbage!"

He flinched and ducked his head, then put hand on his chest as if making a shield. "I just . . . I wanted . . ."

"No, this isn't about you. Who the hell do you think you are?" Her voice was becoming higher and higher pitched, shrill and strangled-sounding.

"I only wanted—"

"Where's the camera? How many of them are there? Do you sit and watch the Aidra show all day? That's sick, Morris. Sick!"

"It's not like that." His eyes darted from one side to another as if looking for an escape. "It's not what you think. Your security system. I was trying to keep you safe! After what happened . . . when your condo . . ." He swallowed. "When we did the security upgrades, I just had a little watchman—a little one!—look at who was coming and going. That's it, I swear."

"Then how did you know I slept with Bryan?" She slammed two fists onto the coffee table, making Madeline yelp and leap off the couch. "Where's the camera?"

"No camera, okay? I wasn't—I wouldn't. I didn't even know you slept with double-Y until just now. You didn't deny it, so . . ."

"His. Name. Is. Bryan. That's Mr. Lynch to you."

"So you're fine with me violating other people's privacy, but when I try to—"

"You're in my *house*, Morris! Gah! I can't believe you."

"If you'd just let me—"

"No, I'm not letting you do a damn thing. Stay away from me. Stay out of my life!" She mashed a finger on the cutoff button, jumped to her feet, and paced a tight line across the room and then back, glaring at the darkened companel. Her chest felt hard, like it was full of rocks. How dare he? How *dare* he? She'd trusted Morris with every aspect of her life, and this is what he did with that trust. He used it to keep tabs on her, to spy on her every move, to judge her.

Her throat felt rigid, as if the muscles were hardening themselves against sobs. She called Madeline to her and buried her face in the soft ruff of the caline's neck. She realized she was taking rapid, shallow breaths and forced herself to slow down. She wouldn't let Morris get to her. She'd done nothing wrong.

The companel signaled that Morris was calling back, but she shunted it aside. She had things to say to him, and they had a lot of issues to work out, but right now, she needed to talk to Bryan. She needed to tell him what she knew.

No answer.

He was probably still in his meetings. She pictured insurance executives in expensive suits sitting at mahogany tables drinking bottled water, trying to figure out how to keep their company profitable in the wake of its worst crisis. And here she sat with important information.

She could only think of one other person to talk to—someone

who knew both the science and the players involved. It had been years since Hannah Wells-Fox had a lab of her own, but she'd worked closely with both Mackenzie Fox and Jean Claude Gascoigne and had kept up with her husband's research.

The companel bloomed to life and Hannah looked out of her greenhouse. "Hello, Aidra. How are you? Is something wrong?"

"I just called to ask you a few questions. To follow up on some things."

"I'm glad you got in touch." Hannah held long-stem roses in one hand, sharp clippers in the other. "We haven't spoken since yesterday."

Aidra paused a moment to wonder what Hannah meant by that, but then rushed ahead. "I have some questions about your husband. About the nanotech he was working on. Were you familiar with it?"

"Of course."

"I know how Learning Systems strengthens the neural connections. And I know how Exersleep changes the chemical balance in your brain. So the two of them . . . together . . ." She shook her head at Hannah's confused look.

"I wanted to ask you about your press conference. You said this technology might be dangerous. Why do you think so? Why now?"

Hannah clipped a few more roses and added them to the bouquet. "Is this about Louisa Samahroo?"

"And Gascoigne," Aidra said. "And Patrick Sullivan. And a man named Zach Wilson."

"Wilson?"

"Did you know him?"

"Of course. He rewired our basement for our studio."

"And then he killed his family."

"Yes. A terrible tragedy." Hannah looked the same way she'd looked after Louisa died. Sad, but distant. As if none of this touched her at all.

"Was your husband experimenting on Wilson?" Aidra asked.

"Did he make Wilson kill his family? Can n-tech even be used that way?" She held her breath, waiting for Hannah's angry denial.

Hannah stripped off her gardening gloves. "The brain is an extremely flexible organ. You'd be amazed at what you can make it do."

"Wait," Aidra said. "You . . ."

It wasn't just that someone could use n-tech this way. It was that someone was *still doing it*. Mackenzie Fox was dead, leaving his widow to carry on his work, but it wasn't Mackenzie's work. It was Hannah's work. She was the one who'd made the breakthrough in the nanotech. What would keep Hannah from using the best of both techniques and adding her own? Making a completely different machine?

Hannah had manufactured custom nano-machines and infected Gascoigne with them. She'd used Gascoigne to kill her husband. And then she kept going, cleaning up loose ends.

Louisa Samahroo had invited Hannah for coffee and started asking uncomfortable questions. She'd gotten too close, suspected too much. But what about Sullivan? He was working for Westrock, but he must have been digging around Exersleep just as Aidra had been poking around Learning Systems.

"So what was Wilson? One of your test subjects? How did you get to Patrick Sullivan?" Those weren't the questions she should be asking. In fact, asking Hannah anything was a bad idea. That was a job for the cops. But it just popped out.

Hannah kept looking at her with cold, distant regard.

"Fine. Don't tell me. I have people who can find out. You tried to kill me twice. Louisa couldn't do it. Sullivan couldn't do it. And here I am, still alive. What do you think my next move is going to be?"

"This is unfortunate," Hannah said. "But I'm afraid we're going to have to end this."

"Damn right we're going to end this. I'm going to the police."

Everything went dark.

CHAPTER TWENTY-THREE

She was shaking her arm. No. Someone else was shaking her arm. No. Someone had seized her arm with fingernails that felt like daggers and was worrying it like a dog with a rat.

"Madeline!" The dozen or so pinpoints on her forearm vanished, but the pain continued, increasing as she became more aware. Why was she on the floor? What happened to her arm? Madeline was making that weird keening noise that Jon called her alarm clock.

Aidra lifted her head and instantly regretted it. The movement sent a rippling bolt of pain down her arm and the sight of her own blood made it worse. She sat up, cradling her wounded right arm, clutching at the punctures she could see through the wash of scarlet. Had Madeline attacked her? Ridiculous.

The Rockston Diamond was on the floor, poking out from under the couch.

What was her gun doing there? She leaned, reaching for it with her left hand and nearly fell on her face when Madeline butted into her. The caline tossed her head sideways and made the breathy "whompf" that seemed to be her idea of no.

Aidra sat against the easy chair. Lifting her left hand, she tilted her head back and felt for lumps. Nothing. But a spot on the ceiling caught her attention. A hole. A very neat, very lethal, very bullet-sized hole. Had her gun gone off? Why had her gun gone off?

Aidra blinked, trying to clear her head. This wasn't like waking up. This was like zoning out in the middle of a conversation and realizing that someone was expecting an answer.

"Sorry," she said, struggling to stand, "I wasn't listening."

Madeline gave another of her soft noises.

"It's okay, girl. I'm just talking to myself." She reached for the last thing she remembered. Hadn't she been on the phone? Yes. On the phone. With Hannah Wells-Fox. Hannah had been apologizing for something.

She stumbled to the companel, which was quiet and dark. Its tell-tales were off, but Morris had set it up to look like that. As a security feature, her companel and the substations were always on watch-and-wipe, even when they appeared to be inactive. She pulled up the menu and keyed in the code to review. A chill settled into her and she began to shake.

Twenty-two minutes she had to go back. She'd lost twenty-two minutes. There she was, hanging up on Morris, her forehead a thundercloud. There she was, unable to reach Bryan and instead calling Hannah. Her hand hovered over the audio control and she left it on silent playback. Something told her she didn't want to hear this.

She didn't much want to see it, either. It was like watching someone else. The shakes worked their way to her neck muscles, a silent denial as this image of her, this other-Aidra, lost all relation to her. Emotion and awareness seemed to drain out of the features, leaving it an idiotic mask. Her eyes were dull, unseeing, like the glass eyes in a piece of taxidermy. It was uncomfortably like looking at the holos of Jean Claude Gascoigne killing Mackenzie Fox.

Aidra felt her numb hands reach to touch her face, horrified by the image on the screen. Was that really her mouth, unhinged and hanging open? The other-Aidra reached for the controls, deleted the call logs, and shut down the panel. From the couch behind her, Madeline watched her alertly.

The not-Aidra lowered herself onto the comfy chair adjacent to the couch. Aidra jerked her gaze to her own chair, still unable to reconcile what she was seeing. *That chair looks just like mine.*

The not-Aidra reached for the purse on the floor. The figure set the purse on her knees. The fitted pocket was opened and the hand that looked so much like her own reached inside.

"No. No. No." She whispered the words into the hands clasped over her mouth. She wanted to turn away, hide this scene from her horror-struck eyes, but she could only stare, her breath coming in sharp gasps as the not-Aidra pulled out the Rockston and contemplated it. Despite the vacuous expression, the hands were deft and sure, ejecting the clip to visually verify the load, reinserting it, chambering a round, thumbing off the safety.

The Aidra on screen socked the muzzle of the Rockston beneath her chin and slid her thumb into the trigger guard.

Madeline struck. She leapt from the couch and her front paws knocked Aidra's head aside and away from the gun just as it went off. They were both out of camera view for a moment.

Then the pickup found them again. Aidra could see herself sprawled in front of the chair on the floor, a marionette with her strings severed. With single-minded determination, the not-Aidra struggled to rise and bring the gun to her head once more.

Aidra held her breath. Bright sparks chased across her field of vision.

On screen, Madeline darted forward again, seized the right forearm in her mouth and wrenched it aside. Aidra hadn't fired a second time. Madeline got to her first, knocking the Rockston out of her hand.

Madeline grabbed Aidra's arm in her teeth and tried to drag her away from the gun. After what seemed like an interminable struggle, the other Aidra stopped trying to reach it and began reacting to the jaws closed on her arm. Aidra watched as the figure on the screen raised its head. It was once again wearing her face.

She cut the playback and sat down on the floor with her back against the wall. She could breathe again. This wasn't at all like the way she felt after Exersleep, but the discontinuity was familiar. This also didn't feel like the sense of purpose and power that came with Learning Systems. It was both and neither and worse than those two things combined could ever be.

It was Hannah. Hannah had triggered something in Aidra's brain and ordered her to kill herself.

Aidra clawed at the back of her neck, trying to feel for the probe. Of course, she couldn't feel it. When had Hannah tagged her? She thought back to seeing Hannah in the hospital, when Hannah had hugged her so incongruously. Had she sent Juniper there just to engineer the scene, or did she simply take advantage of the opportunity she was given?

Hannah had met Louisa for coffee right before Louisa killed herself. She'd been at a party with Gascoigne and had hugged him goodbye right before the shooting. How long did the n-tech last? These weren't ordinary nano-machines with an expiration built in. Exersleep and Learning Systems didn't want their n-tech lasting longer than twenty-four hours. Hannah would. How long would this n-tech stay in Aidra's system?

Aidra was terrified that she already knew the answer to that question.

She got herself up and to the medicine cabinet in the bathroom. The first aid kit she kept there was comprehensive and she didn't settle for half-measures. She slathered her arm in antibacterials and swathed it in absorbent gauze.

She winced as she tightened the bandage. She bent her elbow a few times to make sure everything would stick and then pretended to punch with it, wishing she could punch Hannah Wells-Fox in the face. The woman had tried to kill her three times and if Aidra didn't stop her, she'd try again and again until she succeeded. Aidra looked at herself in the mirror. Her eyebrows came together and she bared her teeth in a grimace. Anger was better than fear, but neither one was going to solve her problem. She needed help.

She stalked back to the companel. "I need to call Sophia Gao."

Discontinuity.

She wasn't on the floor this time. She was sprawled over the arm of the couch. Madeline had grabbed her sleeve, not skin, but her sore arm now felt like it was in danger of being pulled from its socket.

"Madeline! Madeline, sweetie, I'm all right."

The caline released her with a deeply upset snarl. Aidra levered herself upright and regarded the companel two meters away. "Madeline? Watch me."

I need to call police headquarters and tell Sofia about Hannah. Okay.

"I'll just tell the police about—"

Discontinuity.

Wretched, intense pain, this time from her left hand. "Madeline? Mad-dog." It felt funny to use Jon's nickname for her. "I'm okay, baby. I'm back." She disengaged her hand from Madeline's jaws before her thumb could be dislocated.

So she could think of solutions. She could think of them all day long. But she couldn't do anything. She couldn't even say anything out loud.

Hannah had apparently planted more than just a self-destruct command. She also had a trigger to keep her from going to the authorities with what she knew. Just to the police? Maybe she could still call Fitz-Cahill, try to get Bryan to listen to her. She tried it. "Bryan, I need you to call—"

Discontinuity.

And back again. "Madeline! Good girl! Good girl. Let me go. Thanks, darlin'."

She thought about calling Quinn. She tried it out loud. "Hi Quinn, how is Milo? How is Parker doing in preschool?" No problem. She could call her sister and get her sister to call Sofia Gao. "Quinn, I need you to make a call for me—"

Discontinuity.

Oh god. It was like having a spy in her brain. Her mind didn't even belong to her anymore. A dull subspecies of rage at Hannah, and horror at the violation of it, boiled just on the edge of her thoughts and she thrust it away. She had to keep her head. What was left of it anyway. She concentrated on her nephew. On reading him stories and making art projects and playing hide and seek. *I'm just going to ask after Parker. I'm just going to ask after my nephew. Just. Parker.*

Trying to ignore the throbbing of her arm and shoulder, she placed a call to Quinn. She said hello, asked how Quinn's husband was doing, did her best not to sound frantic. She needed a way to hint at her current predicament without saying any of it out loud.

"Have you heard from Mom?" she asked. "Are we getting together for Parker's birthday next week?"

"Parker's birthday is in two months," Quinn said, stonefaced. "Not next week."

Good, Aidra thought. *She knows something is wrong. Come on, Quinn. Call the cops for me. Call the cops.* "How is work?" she asked.

Quinn frowned at the screen. "You never ask about my work."

"Sure I do." Aidra kept her tone light. "Legal work fascinates me. The law." *Yes! I got that word in.*

"Oh, I get it," Quinn said. "You're playing around with a new MASC. Very funny, Morris."

"It's me! It's Aidra."

"Sure."

"I'll prove it. Ask me something only I would know."

"You know everything about her, Morris. You know her whole life."

"But—But—" Aidra bit the inside of her cheek. What could she say? Even admitting she needed help might black her out again.

"I don't have the patience for your games. I'm busy." Quinn hit the cutoff and disappeared.

The dark screen showed her reflection and she saw Madeline behind her, still poised warily. Then it cycled to family photos and Jon's graduation picture was looking back at her.

She was conscious of the sweat trickling down her back, down her sides. She had missed death by a couple of centimeters. She looked at the bullet hole in the ceiling and wondered if it had gone through to her bedroom.

She paced around her condo, trying to think. But she already knew the answer. There was only one person who always saw through her bullshit, always knew what to do, and was always willing to help her. The person she'd just told to stay out of her life. He wasn't the emotionally safe choice, but he was the right choice.

She returned to the companel and tapped the quickdial for Morris.

CHAPTER TWENTY-FOUR

An icy blonde woman with Nordic cheekbones eyed her with crystalline intensity. "May I help you?"

"I doubt it, Sweetheart. Fetch your master like the obedient program you are."

Pouty lips pouted further, but she vanished and a reasonable facsimile of Morris took the screen. It sighed. "We fighting some more today?"

"Nope. I called to apologize."

The MASC twitched and cleared to show a wary-looking Morris, "You did?"

"Absolutely. I thought a lot about it and you are right."

"I am? Since when?"

"Since exactly—" she looked at the timestamp on the video she'd just watched. "Twelve seventeen. I think it would be a fantastic idea to have someone following my footprints. Watching where I walk, so I don't step on something . . ."

"Jesus, Aidra. I said I'm sorry. I swear, I wasn't footprinting you. You can check the security logs—"

"Yes!" Aidra said brightly. "Why don't we check? Together?"

Morris leaned into the pickup. "Are you all right?"

Aidra stared back at him, unblinking, waiting for him to figure it out.

"What happened to your arm? Is someone else there?"

"Just Madeline and me. We're walking around our condo, leaving footprints everywhere."

He was watching her intently. He knew something was wrong. She felt a gust of relief and quashed it. She still wasn't safe. She needed to tread carefully. Relaxing for one moment could be a disaster.

His eyes flicked back and forth. *Please, God, let him be watching the security feed.*

Morris let out a gush of air. "Oh great and mighty fuck . . ."

"So," she said, "I'm walking along here as carefully as I can."

"Trying not to step in it."

"I've got lots of thoughts bubbling in my head."

"But none that you can say out loud."

She nodded.

"But I could call the . . . um . . . people in charge?"

She was grateful he didn't say *the cops*. He didn't want to trigger her. She had to do this carefully. Madeline would hopefully act if she blanked again, but she was betting her life on it.

"But I wouldn't because we can't prove you aren't just another victim of Supremacy."

"I'm not!" Aidra practically shouted. "I don't know what Hannah did, but it's not Exersleep and it's not Learning Systems and it's not a combination."

She thought about Jean Claude Gascoigne, wavering between two explanations for what he'd done, unable to find a third solution, sure it didn't exist. But it *did* exist. It existed in whatever Hannah had cooked up. It existed inside of Aidra at this moment.

Aidra touched her fingertips to her eyelids. "Why did I run my mouth?"

"What?"

"I was gloating. Right to Hannah's face. Feeling smug that I'd figured it out. How could I be so selfish? Louisa is dead because of me. And that chef, Marc Rodriguez. Sullivan is in the hospital. If I hadn't involved them, they'd—"

"Stop right there," Morris said. "There is one guilty person here and her name is Hannah Wells-Fox."

"I yelled at Sullivan," she said miserably. "I stole his car."

"Sullivan! Of course. This is useful."

"How can he be useful?"

"I can't footprint Hannah. She's too layered with protection. But I'll get my AIs to backtrack Sullivan's life for the past week. Tagging him was a desperate move. It might be her downfall."

"Just proving Hannah Wells-Fox and Patrick Sullivan were in the same place at the same time does not mean she's guilty."

"She did it," Morris said. "We'll prove it. But Sullivan isn't in any immediate danger. You are."

"I need two things. I have to disable these nano-machines in my brain and I need to find proof." Aidra waited, but there seemed to be no blackout attached to that concept and the one that followed. "I need Emmy. Dr. Emerald Mathers. She works for LS. Can you call her?"

"Do unidentifiable quantum signatures lead to programming error?"

"I'm gonna hope that's a 'yes' and move on."

He seemed to be working. "Can I tell her it's an emergency?"

"Can you tell me with a straight face this isn't?"

"Heh." The screen showing Morris split and suddenly bloomed with Emmy's alert green eyes.

"Aidra." Emmy's brow was furrowed in apprehension. "Is there a problem?"

Aidra might not be as Supremium as she once was, but she could read Emmy's expression clearly enough. Louisa Samahroo's death had sent ripples of doubt, even through her.

"Hi, Emmy, this is Morris. He saves my life from time to time. We're going to play a little game of show and tell. I'm going to show you something and then Morris is going to tell you something." She swallowed. "Ready Mad-dog?" She returned her attention to Emmy. "You've got to help me. There is illegal n-tech in—"

Discontinuity.

"Madeline! Stop, Mad. I'm okay. It's okay." With blood leaking down her arm and tears prickling her eyes, she smiled at the still-moaning caline, reaching out with her left arm to stroke the side of Madeline's head. The poor baby was shaking and drooling, on the edge of panic. How many more times could Aidra do this before Madeline had a complete nervous breakdown? Aidra wasn't sure how many more blackouts she herself wanted to endure, either. No, actually, she knew how many. The answer was zero.

She stroked Madeline's soft fur and hummed to her, half-listening to what Morris and Emmy were discussing.

"How many times has she—"

"A lot," Morris interrupted. "Too many. What we need is a way to get whatever Hannah put into her head out of it."

"Impossible. I told her this before. You have to understand how tiny these things are. Even if I had equipment—even if anyone had equipment for extraction—by the time we found them all they would probably be degrading anyway."

"I like the sound of that," Morris said. "Any way to tell how long these will last?"

"There's no way of knowing," Emmy said. "Hannah Wells-Fox may be the premier nanotechnologist in the world, but if she's made the leap you're describing here she's using the same platform nano that is the basis for both Exersleep and LS. She's probably using them to increase both suggestibility and fixation on instruction."

"You're supposed to be able to combine these technologies," Morris protested. "People do it every day without harm. How can Hannah be controlling her?"

"Same platform doesn't mean same nano-machines," Emmy said. "Oh, how do I explain? For all anyone knew up to this point, it was all theoretical. The scientific journals are full of this stuff. New research, new directions in n-tech. But there is a lot about brain chemistry that's mysterious, even to us neuroscientists."

"She made Aidra into a zombie!" Morris stretched a hand toward the screen as if trying to reach her.

"Highly suggestible," Emmy confirmed.

"You two are freaking me out," Aidra said. "Once we get the

research, we'll know how Hannah did it. But for right now, I've just got to keep myself safe until these things die off."

"All n-tech is designed to degrade, but there's no telling when."

"Yes, there is," Aidra said, feeling hopeful for the first time since speaking to Hannah. "Gascoigne, you genius!" She held her breath, waiting to black out, but she was still here. Hannah hadn't thought of everything.

"What?" Morris and Emmy asked at the same time.

"Jean Claude Gascoigne. When he was in jail, he had them take fluid samples from him every two hours. They watched the n-tech degrade in realtime. So we know when it left his system." She was already counting on her fingers, trying to do the math. "The last time he saw Hannah was at that art auction and fundraiser on the fourth—Thursday—and the n-tech was gone by five in the morning on Saturday."

"What time did Gascoigne leave the party?"

"Eleven."

"They lasted thirty hours," Morris said. "When did Hannah tag you?"

"It was at the hospital, yesterday. Five? Six? Right around there. Hannah was getting a tissue out of her pocket. Next thing I knew, she was hugging me." Aidra tried not to shiver. "So they should wear off in . . ." she traced numbers on the palm of her hand with her finger. No, that wasn't right. Clocks were base twelve, not base ten. She started over.

"Midnight," Morris said. "That's when they're gone. But I don't know when they start degrading. You've got this fuzzy window where they're dying but still in you."

"Stupid, stupid, stupid," Emmy mumbled.

"I'm trying my best, here."

"Not you. The cops, the consultants, the lawyers. They never analyzed the n-tech that Gascoigne had in him. Now that so much time has passed, the nano-machines have all broken down. There is literally no way to determine what kind they were."

"Don't be too hard on the police," Aidra said. "Everyone just looked for the presence of nano-machines. Nobody cared what kind. They assumed Gascoigne was full of legal n-tech because at the time, that's all the n-tech there was."

Morris sounded hollow. "If these are so similar in form and function to legit nanotech, so that one can be mistaken for the other, how are we going to prove anything?"

"He's right," Aidra said. "How are we supposed to explain experimental nanotech to people who don't even understand how legal n-tech works? By the time the spinners and the lawyers and everyone is done, the public will think they're the same thing."

Emmy Mathers appeared to be thinking. "Only one thing will stand up in court. What we need are the programming files. Whatever instructions she's managed to integrate into these bots, it has to be wildly different from Exersleep or LS. It would certainly be incriminating."

Morris tapped keys. "Your notes said Mackenzie had a lab there at the house, right? Complete with integrated server."

Aidra nodded. "But now I'm pretty sure it wasn't his lab at all. It belongs to Hannah. Could she be making these things right in her basement?"

"Probably not," Emmy said. "It takes a factory and a clean room. But new prototypes are being made and tested all the time. It wouldn't be difficult for Hannah to tweak the specs. She could get the lab to send her anything she designed."

"Checking . . ." Morris' voice sounded like it was fading out. He was partially in VR, using the links in his mind to fight an imaginary battle. "She has a whole-house network to help with her comboviews, but I'm not seeing anything else on her system. She must have an isolated server for her work, because there is nothing but pure vanilla on the one that connects her with the rest of the world. So we tell the cops that—"

"We can't," Aidra said. *We can't call the police. How am I going to explain this without blacking out?*

But Emmy was already there. "It will take hours to get the proper warrant," she said. "By then the n-tech inside Aidra will be gone."

"But Hannah will still have the blueprints on her computer," Morris said.

"So what?" Aidra broke in. "It's not illegal to do hypothetical research."

Emmy shook her head. "Even if we explained everything to the detectives in charge and they got an expedited search warrant, the cops will barrel into Hannah's house, box up everything they can find, and send it all to a lab. In the meantime, Aidra's body will break down the nano-machines, and there will be no way to prove that Hannah's experimental research was used on her—or on anyone."

"She committed the perfect crime," Aidra said. "The evidence destroys itself."

They sat in miserable silence for a moment. "Unless . . ." Aidra said.

"No!" Morris said. While Emmy said, "Out of the question." They both knew what was coming—Emmy because she was Supremium and could think several steps ahead, Morris because he knew her so well.

It was impossible, of course. Aidra needed to break into Hannah's house and get the evidence from her computer server, and she needed to do it while there was still n-tech inside of her. Just having the blueprints wasn't enough, and just having the n-tech in her body wasn't enough.

She needed them both at the same time. She needed to show the authorities that not only did Hannah make the nano-machines, but that she infected Aidra with them. But to do that, she had to risk being under Hannah's control.

"There is no way you're going to the Fox's house," Morris said.

"We don't have time to do anything else," Aidra said. "I have to go there and open a link for you to get into her system. If Hannah figures out I'm alive all she has to do is wipe her files and we've got nothing. I'm the one who knows where her computer system is. I'm the one who can get you into it."

"You'll run your car into a tree!"

She shook her head so hard it began throbbing again. "This is the only way. I'll find someone to drive me out there who will promise not to ask any questions that might make me black out."

"Hannah thinks you're dead," Morris said. "She's not going to come after you now. Sit tight, wait for the n-tech to leave your body, then act."

Aidra realized that Morris didn't care about Hannah's guilt or innocence. He only cared about Aidra's safety.

But until Hannah was behind bars, no one was safe.

"She thinks I . . ." Aidra swallowed, unwilling to say *killed myself* for fear of triggering herself into doing just that. "She thinks I already did it. That's my advantage. It's the only one I've got."

"Some of the n-tech in you is already degrading," Emmy said. "Hang onto them as long as you can. Don't eat anything. Don't drink anything. Don't use the bathroom. And try not to bleed."

"I like that last one the best."

"We've got a very short window to work in," Emmy said. "You need to do this while the n-tech is still in you but no longer active."

"This isn't a window," Morris protested. "This is a rabbit hole. Emmy, tell her. Everyone metabolizes these things differently. Our estimates could be off by hours."

"Then I'd better move fast." For the first time, Aidra was grateful she'd missed Exersleep for the last two days. All the n-tech she was carrying came from Hannah.

"I'm already halfway to the monorail station," Emmy said. "I'll be in Detroit in an hour. Which hospital did you say Patrick Sullivan was in?"

"Detroit Medical Center on MLK."

"Sullivan should still have some n-tech in him. I'll pull it and freeze it."

"I'll meet you there as soon as I've gotten what I need from Hannah's computer."

Emmy nodded and winked out of the call. Morris' face filled the screen, watching her gather her things.

"If you show up at her house, she'll kill you," Morris said. "Or she'll tell you to kill yourself. Either way, you'll be dead."

"She won't even see me," Aidra said.

"How can you—oh shit."

"What?"

"There's a cop approaching the door. What do you want to bet they got an 'anonymous' tip about a dead body in your condo?"

Aidra snapped the leash on Madeline and hefted her purse over her shoulder. "Hey, Morris, you know that security system I said I hated?"

"What about it?"

"I don't hate it anymore."

"You know I live to hear things like that."

The WelcoMat announced a visitor. One person. That meant the cops were only checking. But if she didn't answer the door, there would be more. She nudged her gun farther under the couch and headed out the back.

"Lock up behind me," she told Morris. "I'll call you from the car."

CHAPTER TWENTY-FIVE

"You left your gun behind," Morris said.

"Yes." Aidra felt ridiculously vulnerable without the Rockston Diamond—especially after Louisa Samahroo—but she was more afraid of what she might do to herself. Or Gilly.

"You're in the back seat aren't you?" Morris asked. "I don't want your face on any traffic cameras and I certainly don't want you on a spin. If Hannah knows you're alive, she'll start destroying evidence."

"Of course I'm in the back seat." Aidra ducked down further.

"What?" Gilly asked. "I know where you are."

Aidra pointed to her ear. "I'm talking to someone else. Just drive."

She'd left Madeline with Gilly's husband and hustled Gilly into the parking garage before she could ask too many awkward questions. Once there, Aidra had raided the trunk of Sullivan's car. He kept the contents of a well-stocked hunting store in there, but she only needed a few items. She was hoping to find a jacket, since she didn't have time to grab one on the way out of her condo, but all he had was a plaid shirt with multiple pockets. She slipped it on and rolled the sleeves to her elbows. She'd also taken zipcuffs, a length of paracord, and the oversized ear protectors Sullivan wore when he shot his loud antique weapons at the range.

She was tempted by the bottled water, but remembered what Emmy had told her and put it back. She'd go hungry and thirsty for a few hours if that's what it took to stop Hannah.

Now, she fiddled with the ear protectors in the back seat of Gilly's '39 Ford. She tried them on to see if they'd fit over the tiny earbuds she used to communicate with Morris. Immediately, the road noise and the music from the dashboard disappeared. "You there?" she asked Morris. "I need a mike test." She could see Gilly's lips move, probably answering the question, but couldn't hear her.

Morris' voice purred in her ear. "I'm here, baby. Twilight Radio spinning all your favorite tunes from dusk to dawn, from classic rock to today's top hits. Call me up, make a request."

"Can you hear me okay?"

"Five by five."

"Good." The triggers Hannah had buried in her mind were auditory. Simply looking at Hannah hadn't made her black out. So as long as she couldn't hear, she'd be fine.

The nano-machines should be inert by the time she got there, but *should* wasn't a word she wanted to rely on. She planned to sneak in and out of the house without getting caught, but in case she didn't succeed, she couldn't risk being under Hannah's control. She slipped off the ear protectors.

"—and that's why I decided to drive you, even if you were acting like a flighty bird." Gilly had apparently been talking the entire time Aidra's ears were covered. "Where are we even going?"

"I gave your car the address."

"I know where," Gilly said. "But why?"

"Work."

"Drive yourself."

"Can't."

Gilly gave her a measured look in the rearview. "You know I want to help you, right? Mitsu loves Madeline and is happy to dog-sit, but that never happens. I looked across the condo courtyard and saw a police car. Don't you think you owe me an explanation?"

"Don't tell her," Morris said in her ear.

"Wasn't planning on it," Aidra said to Morris and Gilly both.

"Huh," Gilly grumped.

"Gilly, sweetie, thank you for driving me, but it's safer if you don't know the details."

"I don't buy that. If I'm in danger, I need to know what I'm getting into. Who should I trust? Should I stay or run? Run where? I think not knowing things is more dangerous than knowing them."

"You're not in danger. I just needed a ride."

"I could turn this car around."

"Not a bad idea," Morris said. "I still say you should—"

"Shut up!" Aidra snapped. She tapped the back of the driver's seat. "Look, I saved your marriage. Your career. I got that jerk PI off your neck and gave you your life back. So could you please be quiet? That goes for you, too, Morris. I need to think."

Aidra looked out the window. The sun was low in the sky and would be below the horizon by the time they reached the Fox farm. She wished there was a way to get there faster, but with only the two of them in the car, they were only allowed on thoroughfares and smaller trunklines like M-50. Aidra cursed the carpool laws and huddled in her seat.

She mentally walked through Hannah's house, planning her best route in and out. The house had a central brain. Morris could control the house's alarm system and lighting, but it was still up to her to make it in the door, down to the basement, and out again without being seen.

Stereotypes aside, she'd never known a PI who enjoyed breaking and entering, especially when people were home. And with one of her senses cut off, she'd have only sight to warn her of danger. She trusted Morris to be her ears, but it would be so much nicer to be able to use her own.

She was still revising her plan an hour later when they neared Hannah's house. They had to drive ten kilometers out of their way to avoid the spinners. Morris directed Gilly's car to a dirt service road at the edge of several wooded acres behind the Fox property.

"Okay. Stop here."

Gilly pulled to the shoulder of the road. They were between widely spaced houses and the street was deserted. She remembered the first time she was here, how jealous she was that Hannah could keep such a large spinner-free perimeter. Now, she was grateful. A spinner—anyone—following her could ruin everything.

"Just wait here," she told Gilly. "I'll be back soon. If something goes wrong, you'll get a call from a friend of mine who will tell you where to go."

"But don't you want me to—"

"Please," she held up a hand. "Just listen to him. Thanks, Gilly."

She got out of the car and patted her pockets. It would be nice if she were wearing all black instead of her jeans and Sullivan's plaid shirt, but it wouldn't matter much in the dark. She checked her datapad and then stowed it with the rest of her equipment.

The evening light was fading, but Aidra could still make out a bar gate as thick as her forearm across the service road, It was meant to prevent vehicles, not people. Aidra ducked under it.

"All right," she told Morris. "I'm on the move."

"Follow that path through a little patch of woods three hundred meters and then bear left."

The path wasn't much more than a tramped-down area, and she nearly tripped over a tree root in the dim light. She slowed her pace. She had a job to do and spraining her ankle was not in the plan.

"Why do you suppose she did it?" Morris asked.

"Hannah?" Aidra had been going over it in her own mind. Even through her fear about sneaking into Hannah's house, part of her was still trying to reconcile the perfect mother and comboview star with a murderer.

"I can't figure her out," Morris said. "I watched that press conference she gave after Louisa Samahroo died."

"After *she killed* Louisa," Aidra corrected. She stepped over a fallen tree limb that was blocking part of the path and kept walking.

"Right. Hannah didn't take any questions from the press. She came out, made a statement, and went back inside."

"I can't stop thinking about that. You know what? It was the only time Hannah Wells-Fox spoke the truth."

Hannah wanted her technology used for the social good. She

wanted more therapeutic and medical uses. Aidra ran a hand through her hair, touching the scar on her head. She thought of the promising medical breakthroughs that were always just around the corner. Instead of helping people, Mackenzie Fox and Jean Claude Gascoigne had used Hannah's brilliant research to give more time and resources to people who already had it all. No wonder she was angry.

People were saying that Jean Claude Gascoigne snapped when he grabbed a gun and killed his former friend. And that's certainly what it looked like. But nobody had snapped. Hannah had been planning this for a long, long time.

She'd been experimenting for years. Wilson was her most obvious subject, but there must have been more. And when she knew it worked, she'd waited for the opportunity to remove both the cold-hearted bastard who'd married her and the arrogant asshole who'd corrupted her most promising research. And do it all in a way that would turn public opinion against the misuse of nanotechnology.

"I should have seen it," Aidra told Morris. "As soon as she gave that press conference, it was obvious what she was doing."

"It's only obvious in hindsight. You couldn't know at the time."

"Hannah tried to play it off as tech gone wrong, but it was really tech misused. She did this deliberately."

The trees were thinning now and Aidra glimpsed the edge of the large, manicured lawn surrounding the farmhouse.

"Once your technology is out in the world, you don't own it," Morris said. "You can't control how it's used."

"That's just it. She wanted to." Aidra could sympathize with Hannah up to a point. That point was when she started hurting people. Killing people. Because no matter Hannah's motives, the means to that end were horrific. She'd killed people, and if they didn't stop her, she'd kill many more.

Aidra stepped in a mushy area at the edge of the treeline. She moved closer to the nearest trunk, trying not to think about leaving muddy footprints in Hannah's immaculate house.

"I'm here," Aidra breathed.

"I'm ready," Morris said.

"Shall we?"

"The motion sensors and locks belong to me. Walk straight through the back yard. I'll keep it dark and open for you. Are you heading for the deck or the screened-in porch?"

"Porch." It would be one more door to get through, but it would also lead her directly to the kitchen, and from there, to the basement.

"Got it," Morris said. "Go."

The open lawn between the greenhouse and the house seemed much too empty, even in the dark. Anyone could look out the window and see her. Aidra covered it at a run and hunched beside the door. She slipped the oversized protectors over her earbuds.

Morris had disabled all the door locks for her and she unlatched the back door with no difficulty. She eased through, closing it gently behind her.

She stood among rustic porch furniture staring at the oversized fireplace she remembered from her first visit. It was open on three sides, and if she squatted down and looked through it at the correct angle, she could see into both the great room and the front parlor.

Both rooms were bright, although the glow from the great room was the flickering light of a hologame. Looking through the smaller firebox into the front parlor, she could barely make out two sets of legs—Hannah and Juniper sitting together at the piano. Since she knew where Hannah was, Aidra risked lifting the protector away from her ear for a moment. She heard a classical tune and Hannah giving Juniper instructions. Perfect.

She covered her ear again, giving herself only her own vision and Morris' hearing.

"You'll have to watch for them," Morris said. "I've got the

internal cameras and I can see most of the house—the parts they have wired to record their comboviews. But some areas aren't covered."

Aidra nodded instead of answering. Being unable to hear the outside world, she had no way to judge how loud she sounded in relation to the ambient noise, and didn't dare speak. But Morris knew this and wouldn't expect an answer. She pointed to the kitchen door.

"Unlocked in five, four, three . . ."

Her hand was on the knob and she felt, rather than heard, the soft snick of the lock. Inside, she shut it gently behind her. The kitchen was warm and fragrant with fruit. Fresh jars of homemade strawberry jam sat on the counter.

"Move slow," Morris said. "I have to override the motion detectors so a room doesn't light up when you go in it."

Aidra nodded again. It was surreal to be able to hear him and only him, to be dependent on his direction. But she also trusted that voice—she trusted *Morris*—no matter what.

She wanted to promise him that when this was over they would . . . what? Talk more? Spend more time together? She realized she was just reacting to the adrenaline in her body, the intimate sound of Morris' voice in her ear, and the comfort of having a partner at her back. Still, the urge was almost overwhelming and she pressed her lips together to keep from blurting out her feelings.

Instead, she crept to the hallway door and put a palm against it, waiting for Morris' instructions.

"The piano stopped," he said.

She looked with quick guilt at the other door, the one leading to the parlor, wondering what she would do if one of the kids came through it.

On the countertop was the stegosaurus knife block, reminding her—with a pang—of Sullivan. *Don't underestimate the dinosaur*, she thought as she pulled a few handles speculatively, settling on the boning knife. It was lean and sharp, and she hoped it looked intimidating.

"I've got Juniper thudding up the stairs," Morris said. "Quick, slip through the door to the hallway before Hannah sees you. Wait—oh, shit. She's coming your way!"

Aidra didn't give herself time to think. Knife held low and away from her, she burst straight ahead, through the door to the parlor, on her toes, nearly running. There were way too many potential weapons in the kitchen. She had to take the fight to the other room.

Hannah had barely stood from the piano bench. When she caught sight of Aidra, her expression went from surprised to calculating in an instant and she mouthed words Aidra couldn't hear.

Aidra was in front of her in a flash. She brought the wicked curve of the knife up and held it so Hannah could see it. Hannah's eyes went wide and her lips drew back from her teeth. Aidra used her other hand to grip Hannah and back her into the wall. She pressed the knife under Hannah's chin. Aidra hoped it was cold.

She was sickened in a way by the depths of her own hatred. She wasn't even shaking with rage at this woman. Her anger had made her rigid and precise. It would be so easy to draw a grin across that bare white throat. So very easy.

Hannah was still trying to say something. She was shouting up the stairs, probably to Juniper.

"Shut up." Aidra lifted the knife so that Hannah was on tiptoe, jaws clenched, frozen. Aidra, her pulse hammering behind her earplugs, chanced a quick look up the stairs, back into the dining room and the kitchen. No sign of Juniper or Jovan.

"Walk to the staircase with your hands in front of you. No, arms stiff and straight out. Bend them and I will open you. I will open you up! Morris?"

"Here. I take it you have her."

Aidra let Hannah feel her arm strength by gripping tighter. "I've got her. Hear anything?"

"I heard her shouting some numbers at you. Must be the trigger. Nothing out of her now."

"Tell me if Hannah says another goddamned word. Listen hard."

She maneuvered Hannah to the stairway and ordered her to put her arms through the balusters. Pressing up again with the knife in her right hand, Aidra used her left to snag the plastic loop protruding from her hip pocket. Moving slowly, she reached over the banister to put the zipcuffs into Hannah's fingers.

"Slip the loops over your hands right now. I don't want to have to kill you."

The instant they were on, Aidra reached over, pulling the cuffs above Hannah's elbows, pulling the zips tight to bring the elbows together, the strips sinking into the meat of her arms. Painful for Hannah, no doubt, but secure. Best of all, painful.

She wanted to finish the job with paracord. She wasn't sure how solid the antique balusters were. Could Hannah pull them apart? But she didn't have to secure Hannah forever, just long enough to upload the data to Morris and leave. She'd probably bought all the time she needed. She turned toward the basement.

"Get out!" Morris yelled in her ear. "Now, now, now, get out of there."

"What?" Aidra whirled, looking at Hannah, who was still firmly tied. Juniper hadn't returned and Jovan was still immersed in his hologame. But if Morris said go, she'd go. She moved to the kitchen door.

"Not that way!"

Aidra spun in place and headed for the front door while Morris said something about popping all the locks.

She saw movement at the periphery of her vision and chanced a look behind her. She froze in place.

Bart Klaver stood in the kitchen doorway with a gun pointed at her face.

CHAPTER TWENTY-SIX

"Aw, shit." Aidra raised her hands in surrender.

Morris was still talking, but Aidra couldn't make sense of the words. All she could do was stare at Klaver and remember his threats. She had no doubt he'd meant every one of them.

Klaver was fast for such a big man. The gun in his hand was nothing but a blur as he leapt forward. Pain exploded on the side of Aidra's head and she was suddenly on the floor with Klaver looming over her. She knew the kick she should be aiming at his lower half, but nothing seemed to work. Darkness swirled around the edges of her sight and she realized over the ringing in her ears that she could hear Hannah screaming. Klaver's blow with the pistol had jarred her ear protection loose.

"Three-three-three! Kill him! Three-three-threeeee—"

A sharp slap cut Hannah off. Aidra got her hands under her, her knees to bend, started to turn her head, but Klaver's booted foot came down in the center of her back, driving her chest into the floor and the breath from her. She'd landed painfully on her datapad and she shifted aside.

The numbers Hannah had shouted must be her triggers, but Aidra was still herself. At least the n-tech was no longer active. She just hoped she still had enough of the nasty little bugs inside her to prove Hannah's guilt.

Klaver's voice came from farther away, out of reach. "Get up, bitch."

"If you wanted me on my feet, why'd you kick me down?" Moving more slowly than she had to—but not much—she struggled to her feet, leaving the heavy ear protectors on the floor. She saw no sign of the knife anywhere, had no idea where it had gone when he struck her.

She became aware that Morris was still speaking in her other ear, keeping his voice calm.

"I've already called the cops. Keep him talking. Tell me his name."

"Wh—" She stopped, swallowed and tasted blood, tried again. Her mouth had completely dried up and she couldn't seem to get a deep enough breath. "What the hell do you want, Bart J. Klaver?" She couldn't remember in the moment what the J. stood for, but it would be enough for Morris.

"You know what I want," Klaver said.

"How did you even find me?" But as soon as the words were out, she knew the answer. Gilly. There was no way Klaver could have found Aidra, but he knew everything he needed to know about Gilly. He must have followed them both all the way from the condo complex. Aidra had been so worried about staying out of sight, she'd never thought about a tail.

She'd left Gilly parked on an empty road, right there in the open, a target. What had Klaver done to her?

Gilly, she mouthed, hoping that whatever camera Morris was looking at would pick it up.

"I've got Noah on it," Morris said. "He's taking care of your friend. I'm staying right here with you."

Aidra shook her head.

"She's going to be okay. Focus, Aidra. Figure out how I can help you."

Klaver had his gun trained on her. "Don't play stupid. You're going to put that money back into my accounts. Or I'm going to take you to a doc I know and we'll sell your organs. You're a little banged up right now, but I bet some of your stuff is still warm and wet. I'm getting that money back one way or another."

"What should I do?" Morris asked. "Lights?"

That wouldn't help. There was nothing Morris could do. He was a genius with the computer, but right now she needed a weapon or a way out, and he couldn't give her either of those things.

Klaver was appraising her, taking in the arm swathed in bandages, the blood she could feel trickling from her scalp. He smiled. "You don't look like such hot shit now. What'cha been doing?" He made a little motion toward Hannah with the barrel of his gun. "I don't know what you have going on here—"

"Please," Hannah whined. "She attacked—"

"Shut it, rich bitch." His hand came up again and Hannah flinched. He turned back to Aidra. "We'll be leaving now."

No. No, no, no. Every bit of self-defense training made Aidra plant her feet. She couldn't go with Klaver. He could take her anywhere. Do anything. She was no longer in control of the situation inside the Fox house, but it was better than whatever Klaver had planned.

"Your money," Aidra said. "I can get it back."

"Good," Morris said in her ear. "Stall. Cops are still ten minutes away. This house is at the ass end of nowhere."

Ten minutes. I could be dead by then. "I lied when I said I returned the money to its owners. I kept it all." Aidra looked at Klaver to see if he was buying it. "How do you want it? Bank transfer? Tempcash?"

"You know, I'm warming up to the organ idea."

"Listen to me. Klaver, you'll get your money."

"I know it. Now move."

"Don't leave me like this," Hannah whined. "You have no idea what she did to me. You've got to cut me loose."

"I don't got to do nothing," Klaver waved the gun at Aidra. "Now move. What the hell?"

Aidra followed his gaze to the landing at the top of the stairs.

There, elfin features blank in a way that had become frighteningly familiar, stood six year old Juniper Fox. She held one of the newer, lightweight 9mm automatics. In her tiny hands, it looked huge.

Juniper took a tentative step down and Aidra felt a twisting, draining horror. She wasn't even like an automaton. There was nothing mechanical in her. It was much more like something, some *thing*, pretending to be human.

Aidra opened her mouth to call to her, to try to reach past the terrible blankness, but the sound wouldn't come, only a whisper that no one could hear or heed. "Juniper. Honey, no." She tried to raise her voice but it came out a cracked warble. "Klaver, watch out! She—"

The muzzle flash was a stabbing tongue of flame, and the tiny pop-crack of the shot sounded too loud in the still house. Aidra reeled away as Klaver vanished from the nose up, a fountain of blood fanning onto the wall beside the dining room. *Christ! Hannah keeps a gun loaded with starpoints?* Klaver's body, absurdly stiff and upright, swayed, teetered and crashed. His dying hands spasmed and a shot burst from his weapon and went wild into the dining room.

Aidra caught herself on the piano, stumbling against it so hard that the lid fell with a discordant crash. Her wounded arm throbbed with pain like a tolling bell.

"Shoot!" Hannah yelled. "Juniper, shoot!"

The little girl on the stairs raised the gun again. It still looked ludicrously large in her hands.

Aidra scrambled backwards around the freestanding bookcase. She turned and sprinted into the darkened great room. The lights came on as she entered, and she saw Jovan standing next to one of the enormous sofas, struggling out of a gaming harness.

"Aidra, can you hear me?"

"Morris! Lights off in the great room."

The room plunged into darkness, with only the holoprojector glowing a soft blue at one end of the room.

"I've got no cameras in here," he said. "I'm blind."

Aidra pitched herself toward the sofa, almost colliding with Jovan. He looked terrified and wide-eyed as he called "Mom!" into the next room. "Juniper?"

Aidra turned to see Juniper standing in the doorway. She held the gun with both hands, arms bent, her stance wide. Aidra scooped up Jovan and dived over the back of the sofa, twisting to shield him. What felt like a hammer punched her in the upper arm as she tucked and rolled. She heard herself gasp as if from far away. It must have been nothing but a minor graze, or her arm would be gone. She could still move it well enough, but dammit, now both her arms hurt.

Two more shots from the parlor into the room, thumping into the walls above their heads.

"Hannah!" Aidra yelled. "Call her off! Your son is in here."

"Aidra, what's g—"

"Shut up, Morris!"

"Shoot!" Hannah yelled.

A spray of bullets zinged above them. Aidra covered Jovan with her body as they huddled behind the sofas. Did Hannah not believe her, or was she monster enough to sacrifice her own son to get to Aidra?

It didn't much matter if Juniper was going to keep shooting. How many rounds did that gun hold?

Light bloomed on the far side of the room. "Juniper?" Jovan called, facing away from her, toward the light. Dancing robots filled the holo-stage. He'd started a program to distract his sister, maybe confuse her. Smart.

Aidra pulled him back, rolling over to get him behind her again. "Jovan, honey?" she clenched her teeth against the pain. "We're going to run. When I count to three, get in the fireplace. Crawl through and keep going."

"But what about—"

"Count with me, baby. One, two, three."

Then Jovan was out of her weakening grasp and running for the huge hearth, the one sized for a medieval castle. Aidra scrambled after him. She could feel blood sheeting down her arm, flowing but not spurting. There was another pop from the gun, but Juniper seemed to have lost track of them. Another report and the light from the holo-stage died.

Jovan vanished into the dark mouth of the cavernous fireplace and Aidra followed. But instead of turning toward the back porch and freedom, he slid through the small opening leading to the parlor and his mother.

She wanted to tell him to stop, but was afraid to let Juniper know where they were. She had no choice but to follow.

She wondered what she would do if she couldn't fit through the opening on the other side. She couldn't. She was stuck. She moaned as her aching arms touched the rough brick of the firebox. With a little sob, she twisted, feeling the skin tear with fresh agony as she drove herself through.

On the other side, Jovan had already made it to his feet and was heading toward the entrance hall. Aidra scrambled after him.

"Jovan," Hannah said. "Dear heart, bring Mommy the gun. Bring me the gun, right there. From the man's hand. Don't look at him, darling, I just need that gun."

Aidra skidded to a stop as she saw Jovan lifting Klaver's bloodstained automatic. This was it. Either Hannah would shoot her or Juniper would.

But Jovan turned his back on his mother and held the gun out to Aidra, ignoring Hannah's squawk of anger and dismay. She took it and steered him to the kitchen, bending to whisper, "Go out the back door. Hide in the woods. Come out when the police show up."

"Behind you!" Morris said.

Aidra pulled Jovan sideways to shield him as another gunshot snapped and echoed. Wood exploded from the kitchen doorframe and Aidra felt her screaming arms peppered with splinters. When was a little shock going to kick in? She could use it right about now.

She and Jovan hunkered down behind the kitchen island. Juniper stood in the doorway, her empty expression unchanged.

Aidra raised Klaver's gun, knowing it was useless in her hands. She couldn't shoot Juniper, not even to wound her. Juniper was a child. An innocent. She had no idea what she was doing. Aidra had to find another way. But how could she stop Juniper without hurting her?

She turned to Jovan. "I don't suppose you're a black belt in karate? No? Damn."

Juniper was circling the island, getting between them and the back door, cutting off their escape. Jovan scooted past her and through the door to the hallway. Aidra shot once, far above Juniper's head, just to make her flinch and duck. She took off after Jovan.

They moved to the staircase, taking a wide path around the spreading pool of blood under Klaver's body. Aidra stood behind Hannah. She scooped Jovan into her arms and pressed him to his mother's back, sandwiching him there. She lifted Klaver's gun and pressed it to Hannah's temple.

Aidra couldn't shoot Juniper, but she couldn't shoot Hannah, either. Not with Jovan standing right there. She wouldn't gun down a mother in front of her child, no matter how horrible that mother was. Besides, stopping Hannah wouldn't stop the killing. Juniper still had her instructions.

The moment hung suspended. She stared at Juniper. Juniper stared back. The little girl was shifting position, ready to shoot through her own mother to do as she'd been told. Aidra looked down the dark and empty eye in the end of the gun. She could feel Jovan's sweaty back, hear him heaving barely contained sobs.

"Wait!"

It was as if the room held its breath. Hannah's voice seemed to echo on the word and her body strained against the zipcuffs. She stared at her daughter.

Over. It was all over. Aidra realized she didn't have to kill Hannah. It was enough that Hannah believed she would. Hannah believed it because that's what *she* would do.

Aidra felt more winded than she did after a 10k run. "Call her off, Hannah."

"You'll never prove anything. All you have is speculation."

"No one else has to die," Aidra said. "Tell Juniper to put the safety on and put the gun down. Do not tell her to drop it. Set it down carefully."

"Juniper. Put the safety on and set the gun on the floor."

Aidra breathed another sigh of relief when Juniper followed her orders.

"Tell her to push it over here with her foot."

When Juniper had done so. Aidra swallowed, tasting her own blood in her mouth, her own fear and self-loathing at what she had so nearly done. She gently moved Jovan away from his mother. The boy was leaking silent tears that ran in clear channels down his sooty cheeks.

"Aidra." Morris' voice was still urgent. "You need to get me near that system before the cops get there."

"On my way."

Aidra put both the gun Juniper had used and Klaver's Smith on top of the piano. She took Jovan and the unresisting Juniper by the hands and went swiftly down the basement stairs. Leaving her datapad resting on top of one of the computer servers, and Morris chuckling happily to himself, she walked the children back up to the kitchen to wait for help to arrive.

CHAPTER TWENTY-SEVEN

Getting ready for bed didn't feel natural. It was as if she was going through the motions of some long-forgotten dance. When was the last time she'd done this? She'd had more sleep than usual this week, but none of it on purpose and none for more than a few hours. Intentionally settling in for a solid block of uninterrupted slumber made her feel vaguely guilty. Like she could be working now and was lounging about instead. She squashed that thought. Sleep was necessary, sleep was normal, and sleep was something she needed to get better at.

She'd brushed her teeth and put on comfortable pajamas and settled Madeline in Jon's room. She'd curled up in bed and turned off the light. Now what? How was she supposed to do this?

She turned her pillow over for the cool side. Jon was coming home tomorrow, and his first tuition bill for next year would follow along in a few weeks. She had to visit Gilly and call Quinn and she had to return Sullivan's car and arrange for her own car to be fixed. Sullivan himself was out on bail. Aidra had fronted the money, feeling it was the least she could do, and Sullivan was back to his grouchy old self. The police were expecting depositions, so she would have to lawyer up. Louisa Samahroo's funeral was in two days. How could she doze off when she had so much on her mind?

She turned on the light and commanded the companel to call Morris.

"Hey, you," Morris said. "Thanks for calling. I know you didn't need to."

"Yeah, I kind of did."

"No video?"

"I just wanted to hear your voice." She cocked her head at the dark screen. "You're thinking about hacking into my video right now, aren't you?"

"Thinking about it, but not doing it. Don't I earn points for that?"

"A point. Singular."

"I'm also not going to ask you about the job in D.C. So another point for me."

"I know I owe you an answer, Morris. They're not going to hold the job open forever. But I'm not quite ready to move."

"Is Fitz-Cahill going to take you back?"

"I'm not sure if I want to go back," Aidra said. "Insurance companies don't seem like such safe, steady work anymore."

"See? So maybe you are ready to move."

"I don't know. I'm just taking it day by day. First thing tomorrow, I've got to visit Gilly."

"How is she doing?"

"She has a concussion. Her husband is playing nursemaid." Aidra touched her own head in sympathy. Klaver had hit her *hard*. The bastard. "I couldn't believe it when I got to her car and saw Ugly Ben directing the ambulance."

"And I couldn't believe Noah called a spinner for help." Morris paused. "Not the move I would have made."

Aidra smiled. "No, definitely not. Noah's got his own style."

"I knew he'd grow on you."

"Like mold on leftovers."

Morris laughed at that, and she remembered how much she liked that sound. Maybe she could get down to Washington next week. Or the week after. There were so many details chasing after her, so many things to worry about.

At least Hannah Wells-Fox's conviction seemed a sure thing, especially after her loud justifications acting as a confession. A life sentence for murder would probably keep her out of the lab long enough for her expertise to become obsolete. It would be extremely unlikely for another scientist to follow in her footsteps. Hannah was a toxic combination of rage, brilliance, and just enough instability to justify her actions. Even if someone else tried, regulatory agencies were on notice now.

Aidra had been right all along. It wasn't the n-tech at fault. Not legal n-tech anyway. Even though Hannah Wells-Fox had ruined her life's work making it seem so. Her *entire* life's work.

"You okay?"

"I was just thinking about Jovan and Juniper. It's not like they weren't the most bizarre children in the world before this. I'm sure living with their aunt will be better than living with their mother, but it's not going to be easy."

Juniper wouldn't remember what she did, and Aidra hoped her aunt shielded her from finding out. But little Jovan had seen both his mother and sister try to kill him. How did a kid ever recover from that?

"Good thing they can afford therapy," Morris said.

"Years and years of therapy." Interspersed with prison visits to whatever facility Hannah Wells-Fox ended up in. The n-tech in Aidra and Sullivan, coupled with the uploaded data, meant that Hannah was going away for a long time. This new evidence also meant that Zach Wilson would get a new trial and Gascoigne would never face one.

Aidra adjusted the covers. They were smothering her feet. She punched her pillow, trying to flatten it into a more comfortable shape. She'd thought that talking to Morris would calm her down and help her nod off, but it was just giving her more wheels for the hamster.

"I should probably let you go," she said. "I just called to say good night."

"Thanks. I'm not going to bed, though."

"I am. Look." Aidra turned on the video to show Morris that she was already in her pajamas, makeup off, under the covers.

"Oh, wow," he said. "Like, actual, real sleep."

"If I remember how."

"Well." He blew her a kiss through the screen. "Sweet dreams."

"I doubt it." She adjusted the blankets. "Morris?"

"Yeah?"

"Will you call me in the morning?"

"Sure. I'll keep the line open all night if you want me to."

"No, I'll be fine. Madeline is here and Jon will be home tomorrow. I'll call you later."

"Hold on a sec." Morris looked away from the comscreen and then back at her. "I'm sending you something."

She sat up in bed. "What?"

"A new coffee maker. You said your old one broke. This one will be on your porch when you wake up. It makes the different hues. Blue and green and orange and—"

"Coffee should only come in one color. Black."

"You don't want to try something new?"

"No." Aidra hugged her pillow and smiled at Morris through the screen. "It's time for me to get reacquainted with the old things I love."

M.H. Mead is the pen name of Alex Kourvo and Harry R. Campion.

Alex is a blogger, reader, and writer who lives in Ann Arbor, Michigan. She loves key lime pie, hates waiting in lines, and adores anything cute and pink. She is saving up for a flying car.

Harry is a teacher, parent, and writer who lives in Harper Woods, Michigan. He loves the Detroit Tigers, can deep fry anything, and has more books than shelves to put them on. His favorite things in the world are camping and canoeing with his family.

Alex and Harry have been friends and co-authors for many years. To read more of their stories, including free short fiction, be sure to visit their website.

www.MHMead.com

Made in the USA
Charleston, SC
18 March 2016